BAD
LOKI

REBEL GODS BOOK 1

REBEL GODS BOOK ONE

When the gods turn bad…

…reapers come out to play.

My name's Autumn, and I was raised by a fanatical witch cult. I made a deal to be possessed by a god. I was tempted by forbidden whispers of eternal pleasure. Then a lethal but sexy-as-hell god broke me, stealing my magic.

Loki, God of Mischief.

Now, I'm the Infernal: a witch who reaps both gods and demons. I guard the World Tree in the shadows of an ancient forest, which is stalked by scorching-hot but dangerous monsters.

When a curse binds my greatest enemy, Loki, to me as mate by his shifter soul, it's *my* turn to break a god. I'm seduced, however, by his beautiful mayhem. Then he spins a wild tale, and it turns out that everything I've known could be a lie.

Can I trust Loki and my other gorgeous rebel gods and demons?

Hades — My brooding Hellhound God of the Underworld who's a giant of muscles, midnight black hair, and shadows

Ra — My Phoenix Sun God who's tall, blond, and my loyal friend and lover

Kit — My Kitsune Fox Spirit with powerful magic and mesmerizing eyes, which I could lose myself in forever

Oni — My roguishly handsome Demon with a lady-killing smile who's my first love and Soulmate

They're the enemy, royalty, friend, virgin, and second chance. They're also my obsession...and secret protectors.

When the gods are rebels, the demons are wicked, and the shifters are savage, it's lucky that I love bad boys...

CONTENTS

BOOKS IN THE REBEL VERSE

RECOMMENDED READING ORDER

ALL BOOKS ARE STANDALONE SERIES

REBEL WEREWOLVES - COMPLETE SERIES
COMPLETE BOX SET COLLECTION
ONLY PERFECT OMEGAS
ONLY PRETTY BETAS
ONLY PROTECTOR ALPHAS

REBEL: HOUSE OF FAE - COMPLETE

HOUSE OF FAE

REBEL ACADEMY - WICKEDLY CHARMED
COMPLETE SERIES

CRAVE

CRUSH

CURSE

REBEL ANGELS - COMPLETE SERIES

COMPLETE SERIES BOX SET: BOOKS 1-5

VAMPIRE HUNTRESS

VAMPIRE PRINCESS

VAMPIRE DEVIL

VAMPIRE MAGE

VAMPIRE GOD

REBEL GODS

BAD LOKI

BAD HADES

BAD RA

REBEL VAMPIRES - COMPLETE SERIES

COMPLETE SERIES BOX SET BOOKS 1-3

BLOOD DRAGONS

BLOOD SHACKLES

BLOOD RENEGADES

STANDALONE: BLOOD GODS

AUDIO BOOKS

LISTEN HERE...

BOOKS IN THE OXFORD SERIES

RECOMMENDED READING ORDER

OXFORD MAGIC KITTEN MYSTERIES

A FAMILIAR MURDER
A FAMILIAR CURSE
A FAMILIAR HEX

OXFORD PARANORMAL BOOK CLUB
BITING MR. DARCY

CHAPTER ONE

Night of the Bacchanalia, House of Ecstasy, 1,000 YEARS AGO

G ods either break you or possess you.

But I don't break easily, and possession is an honor.

Especially, when it's by my god, Bacchus, the God of Ecstasy, with his honey curls and those amber eyes of his that have haunted my dreams for years.

Every witch in my fanatical cult, the Bacchants, wishes that they were chosen. Bacchus whispers temptations of the sweetest pleasures. If I only give myself to him, heart, body, and Soul, then I'll be granted eternal pleasure. Lonely nights locked in my room, I've sat waiting for the day that I'll finally meet him.

He's mine, as much as I'm his.

Bacchus belongs to our whole cult, my sister says, but I don't believe it. He chose *me* to become his vessel.

Sweet Hecate, his statues don't do him justice. They're marble beauties of naked muscles and sweet curls. When I catch the Bacchants, sneaking them into their own rooms, I doubt that it's to pray to him.

My hands clench, as jealousy streaks through me. Outside on this special night of the Bacchanalia, I tip my head up to stare at the stars. The night skies swirl into raging storms; the wind catches at my hair. I revel in the raging tempest.

Let it all be torn apart.

I've been denied love or marriage and kept apart from the rest of the world because I belong to Bacchus.

Is possession my birthright or my curse?

I take a deep breath, resting against a tree in the glade and spreading my own magic into the calming well of nature's. Then I quest further, into the night. Werewolves howl, and demons snarl outside the grove.

I close my eyes.

Music — dancing — ancient magic.

I thrill with it. *I am the wild.*

I'm Bacchus' official Favored Vessel for the ceremony tonight. This is my first ceremony at the sacred rite of Bacchanalia. Only women are allowed to worship Bacchus, but we can't attend until we turn twenty-five. My sister who heads the cult, Ecstasy, has still trained me to be worthy of this night my entire life. I love her with a fierceness that's only equaled by her love for me because we're all that the other truly has.

If she says that this is the deal us Bacchants must make for our god, then I'd make it for her alone. I just want her to be happy.

Although, I've heard wild gossip about the orgies, drinking, and frenzy.

The Bacchants always try to scare you like their warnings not to walk alone in the woods because werewolves will savage you or not to swim alone in the ocean because mermen will drag you away into their underworld.

For witches who thrive on our gods' pleasure, we also live on the fear of so many *nots*.

When I'm possessed by Bacchus, will I become unleashed and free for the first time in my life?

The tale in the House of Ecstasy goes that my parents named me Autumn because even when I was born, my curling hair was the color of dying, autumn leaves, and my eyes burned the same fiery umber.

Did Bacchus choose me as his vessel because I walk the line between life and death like him?

Am I death?

When my parents were torn apart by Shadow Demons, as they protected me from them, my sister raised me amongst her Bacchant witch followers and claimed that I was called *Autumn* because my mischief was like a tempest.

How flattering.

Perhaps, I can bribe the younger witches to nickname me *Chaos*?

My lips twitch, and I twirl my long hair between my fingers. After all, my sister enjoys her orgies enough to be named after our coven, the House of Ecstasy.

I've been kept a virgin for Bacchus, but my sister is secretly known amongst the Bacchants as the *Cock Charmer*. It was amusing to bring that up over breakfast and watch her spray her eggs all over the table in shock.

I grin, sharp and feral.

I may be the youngest but I'm *not* the weakest in the coven.

The ash grove on the top of the hill is wreathed in dancing shadows from the vast bonfire that burns in its center. Its smoke stings my eyes, and I wrinkle my nose at its scent that still can't hide the tangy copper of the blood offerings in the urns that circle it. I study the slick blood, which bubbles like its alive.

Did they kill the sheep before I arrived or…*something else?*

I lazily wave my hand, the silver and amber bracelets at my wrists *clink*, and vines grow up the trunks of the trees, whose roots tangle in knots across the glade. I pluck a fat grape and moan at the sweet burst of flavor as I bite through its skin.

Where's my sister? Why's she left me alone here tonight?

I swagger further into the glade, and my bare feet *crunch* and *snap* over the leaves and twigs.

In the dark, I can make out the weaving and dancing shapes of my fellow Bacchants; their eyes blaze like cats'. The fever of our god is starting to overtake them.

I gasp.

Possession.

I've never seen it before. It's thrilling and dangerous. Mine will be special, but the taste of wildness is intoxicating.

I want more.

The Bacchants' eyes swirl to amber. They beat on drums and shake rattles, bells, and tambourines in a wild, terrifying rhythm as they *whoop* and dart between the trees.

I snatch up a wooden goblet from the floor and down the warm wine like life; it licks down my throat. I groan because it's *Bacchus* in the wine, the music, and the heady scents.

He's inside me, and I'm inside him.

I rub at the skin on the back of my hands, *scratching, and scratching, and scratching...* My long nails are painted bloody. I crave to rip myself or someone else apart.

The sensations are too much.

The veils between the realms of the gods and the mortal world are thinning; they're sticky spiderwebs across my cheeks. The trees groan, their branches wave along with the music, and the trunks split open.

I can feel Bacchus...*moving*...like the blood beneath my own skin.

My eyelids flutter, and I run my hand down my white toga, which is slit, like the wings of a moth, down the sides. I dash the goblet to the floor and raise my arms to the side, giving in to the call of the drums, dance, and Bacchus.

I twirl around, laughing. The sides of my toga spin out, and I *am* the white moth in the night — *freed.*

I'm Bacchus' bride, and my bridesmaids are the Bacchants in their golden togas.

My magic surges in a powerful wave. It's a fearsome, thrilling thing within me and soon, I'll use it in the service of a god. Now, however, it has its own plans.

Mischievous ones.

It's Ecstasy's own fault for leaving me here alone. She knows what happens when I get bored (which is most of the time because there's never been a way to turn off my smart mind or tongue).

She brought me up with the Bacchants in the manor at the bottom of this hill, which is freezing in the winters and sweltering in the summer. I'm rarely allowed outside the walled gardens, but trouble still finds me (or I find it).

I'm known as a Chaos Witch. *Why does the coven expect me to have perfect manners?*

Chaos means more than the void or disorder. To me, it's glinting bright moments of *change* that can fracture everything and let a new world slither through.

My magic quests through me, searching magpie like for such precious moments, hoping to discover them.

It's why I'm feared.

It's also why I'm dangerous if I'm not kept busy. The last time that I was bored, I invented a bronze, mechanical bear cub (like the shifter who I'd once seen on the edge of the woods), imbuing him with my magic, who chased the other Bacchants around the manor.

I told them that it was their own fault he could sense their fear. *Why do the other witches hate shifters?*

Caesar doesn't growl or chase me though. He asks for hugs.

I pleaded to bring Caesar tonight because he's part of me, but Ecstasy looked like she wanted to spit something at me that was far nastier than eggs, before announcing that males were only allowed at the Bacchanalia by special invite, and the only invite that she'd offer Caesar was to become a bearskin rug.

Yet I didn't create Caesar anatomically accurate enough to be a *male* bear. If Ecstasy thinks that denying him access will keep out magical creatures, then she's wrong.

When flaming moths burst from me, flaring into the sky, the Bacchants stumble in their dance in shock. The moths flare into the sharp black like golden stars. Then they fall on the heads of the watching witches: embers of the fire.

The Bacchants squawk and pat at my moths in outrage, hopping around in true chaos. I laugh, before tumbling over onto my behind.

The world spins. I blink, woozy, before collapsing onto my back. I stare up at the night sky.

Is this possession?

Perhaps, I shouldn't have drunk that strong wine. *What was in it?*

I startle at the unexpected *clapping*.

"I'm impressed. A witch with power and a mischievous sense of humor," a man's amused voice, low and threaded with a danger that makes my own magic reach out to his. I struggle up onto my elbows.

"I hadn't imagined that a Bacchant would create a potential chaos moment at her own holy rite. Clearly, I stand corrected."

I stare up at the most beautiful man who I've ever seen...including Bacchus.

He's naked like all men who attend the ceremony by *special invite*. His skin is moon-pale, and he's lean but with a warrior's muscles. I can't help the glance down at his prick, which is as pretty as the rest of him. It jumps at my scrutiny, and my cheeks flush.

When I catch his gaze, his lips quirk.

I shall not apologize for appreciating beauty.

He's young for a god. Is he the same age as me? Although, age moves differently for gods like they're trapped in amber. How many centuries will he be trapped in youth?

My skin tingles, and warmth curls through me. My magic flutters across his: *shifter*, it whispers.

Shifter God with chaos magic.

I suck in a desperate breath. I've never met anyone with the same magic as me before. A thousand questions tumble through my mind.

Do chaos moments look like shattered shards of glass to him? Can he hear the threads of Fate sing? Does he catch his own family eying him with fear like he's about to transform them into beetles (and I only performed the If You Bug Me, Then I'll Bug You Hex the one time...)?

Yet no male, by special invite or otherwise, starts up a conversation like this is a *marriage matching* at the Bacchanalia.

Hecate above, he's in for a shock.

The smile slips from my face.

A surge of protectiveness washes through me for the Shifter God, who's now watching me with intense but twinkling emerald eyes — his brunette curls, which burn a deeper red, as the light catches them, tumbling across them — because if he's been tricked here and knows less than I do about the ceremony, then he'll be *broken* by Bacchus.

Is that what happens to all the men who attend?

I study him more closely, and my heart aches. With his muscles and curls, he's like Bacchus' statue sprung to life but a fire version with his brunette hair to match my own magic.

He's perfect and he's not a statue, which is a bonus.

I'm surprised by the possessive way that Ecstasy rests her hand on his arm almost like she's restraining him. Has she already claimed him?

Ecstasy glows with fervor.

She's tall and at official ceremonies, her air of predatory danger even makes me tremble. She's every supernatural's nightmare, the leader of our cult, but also the witch who saved me from the nightmares that snatched away our parents. She's the sister who spent hours braiding my hair, answered all my questions about magic no matter how tired she was, and created a giant magical chess set in our garden for me.

Our chess championship is still waging a decade later. *Who's winning?* Ecstasy and I are drawing. No other Bacchant can compete with the sisters of the House of Ecstasy. Together, we're light and dark but lethal.

Why do I get the sense that this Shifter God is equally lethal?

Ecstasy's floor-length, purple toga, which is pinned at the shoulder with a moth brooch, shimmers. Her amber necklace glints in the light from the fire. Her midnight black hair falls to her waist, and her eyes are large and hazel.

To my surprise, the Shifter God shakes Ecstasy off and holds out his hand to me.

I stare at it in surprise for a moment, before being unable to stop myself shooting my sister a smug smile, as I allow the Shifter God to pull me to my feet. His hand is surprisingly cool but not unpleasant. I startle and pink, when his thumb circles the back of my hand in a single caress. It's so light that I barely feel it; like a moth's wings, it's there and then gone.

I want his touch back again.

His cold scent cocoons me like sweet strawberries over crushed snow.

Does he taste of frozen strawberries as well? In the

heat of this early autumn evening, as the wine still burns my insides in a way that I'm unused to, can I be blamed for desiring to lick him and see?

My tongue edges out of the corner of my mouth.

One lick? Just a tiny one? He won't notice if it's somewhere discrete like…

His gaze meets mine and then darts away, across the woods to the caves beyond.

I narrow my eyes.

The men are taken to the caves for an initiation, before the ceremony. I don't know what happens there but crack my broomstick, I don't imagine that it's anything good. If it was, the Bacchants would boast about it, rather than whisper darkly at night about the *secrets of the caves…*

For a brief, mad, moment, I consider warning him. But then, I remember the honey curls and amber eyes of *my* god, Bacchus, and I snatch away my hand from this new Shifter God.

There shall be no licking, no matter how strawberry sweet. After all, I don't worship *him*.

His eyes widen with surprise.

"*Clearly*, you've never met a Chaos Witch before." I turn my back on him because I've waited all my life for this ceremony and no Shifter God wrecking *eternal pleasure* for me. But it's too hard to keep looking at him, when I'm desperate to wrap him in clothes and safety in a way that breaks all the rules

12

of the House of Ecstasy. "Can't you take him away and have your orgy somewhere else, Cock Charmer?"

Come on, just a little blush…

Instead, Ecstasy sweeps a bow. "I can have an orgy anywhere. You should know that by now."

The Shifter God stiffens. "Huh, I hadn't realized that I'd magicked myself invisible. I guess that my balls and dick have a magical Ignore Me Now Spell cast on them."

"Let me introduce *your* offering for tonight. Charming, isn't he?" Ecstasy's voice is cultured and sultry; her aroma of mulled wine winds around me, until my head aches. "Don't you feel the way that his darkness and chaos calls to your own, darling?"

"Loki of lies," Loki counts off on his elegant fingers, "fire, the sky, nets, and mischief at your service."

I stare at him: *Loki*.

Men can be specially invited to Bacchanalias but they're never *introduced* to witches. Ecstasy calls them nothing but *sacrifices to Bacchus and pleasure* (whatever in the witching heavens *that* means).

Why would she risk bringing a god as dangerous as Loki to my first possession by Bacchus?

Everybody knows that Loki is a *bad* god.

The Bacchants whisper about the other gods, and tempting…*forbidden*…as Loki is, none of the stories about him are good.

He's a rebel god.

I mean, everybody also knows that I'm a Chaos Witch. But let's not make this all about me.

I narrow my eyes at Loki. "Why's he still talking?"

Loki snorts. "Why are you still rude?"

"This one is as yet untamed and a half-breed," Ecstasy drawls, and Loki flinches. *I hate that.* "But Bacchus was keen for you to have him. After all, little leaf, you need something special on your first ceremony as vessel. A *god* to worship *you*."

"Little leaf?" Loki mouths.

"Half-breed," I snarl.

Hexes and curses, can't you just feel the worship already?

Loki gestures at the bonfire, dancing witches, and sparking magic in the glade like we're simply at a feast. "Your first time?"

I draw myself up to my full height to look him in the eye, which sparks my magic through me in a way that makes me shiver. "I'm Bacchus' new Favored Vessel."

Is that a flash of pity?

I jolt. Why are Loki's expressive eyes glinting with concern, even as his lips thin?

"And how do you feel about your possession into a puppet?" He asks, tilting his head.

My eyes blaze. "How do you feel about your initiation in the caves?"

I wince at the same time as him. When Loki's expression hardens, I regret it.

The whispers about the secrets of the caves make me shudder. The young nobles, the sons of witch families in our cult, must go through an initiation. They say some never come out and those who do, then belong to the frenzy of the Bacchants.

How has Ecstasy managed to catch a god for me?

"Witches," Loki's smile is sharper than mine, "you're all the same. By the Norns, why did I hope that you'd be different?"

I am.

I've always hated that label: *Different.*

I've caused trouble all my life because I don't fit in. Why now do I *hate* that Loki believes me the *same* as any other witch?

"Then why are you here?" I demand.

"Why are you?" He studies me with a sudden flash of shyness, as his mask slips.

He steeples his long fingers, and his eyes blaze with curiosity. Then he sniffs, scenting the air like his own magic can weave out and *taste* mine…*my truth.*

Witches above, he truly wishes to know…? Why would he care?

Unexpectedly, I wish that this bad god would run from the glade, down the hill, and as far from the House of Ecstasy as he can. My heart beats too fast, thudding painfully in my chest. My breath becomes ragged.

He shouldn't be here.

No god with chaos magic should be at the Bacchanalia, even if *my* magic winds through me like the vines around the trees, desperate to entwine with his.

Ecstasy strokes her amber necklace, and the bonfire flares higher, reaching up to the sky like hundreds of flaming horses. Loki jumps.

Ecstasy laughs. "Bacchus is the power of the carnival: music, dance, and fucking. You're both here because it's your Fate. There's pleasure in losing yourself. Bacchus appeals not to the reasoning mind but beneath it to the darkness of our chaotic emotions. He destroys the old and brings forth the new. He lowers the boundaries between the magical and the real. Do you think that he can't entrap a god?"

Loki swaggers to lean against a tree (and I'm in no way checking out his ass). "I owed him a debt, and I pay mine. Sorry, that's not as dramatic or as fun as the *carnival of fucking* sounded." Ecstasy makes a choking sound, and I smother my laugh. Yet is any debt worth turning up naked at a ceremony amongst your enemies? *This is why I don't gamble.* "Anyway, who could give up the chance to experience a good frenzy?"

Sweet Hecate, his sarcasm is better than mine.

I can't look away from Loki. I've heard the stories

of this deceiver, mischief god but none of them told of how he burned like one of the stars fallen to earth.

I've spent most of my life loving Bacchus and preparing for his possession. It's confusing to be tempted by another god now.

The protective, possessive urge shakes me again. How can I let him be taken to those caves?

Let him run…

I rush to Loki, gripping his arm.

He straightens, shaking his hair out of his eyes. His gaze is questioning.

I rest my cheek against his.

"That's the spirit," Ecstasy says with the same pride as when I mastered my first hex, "allow the dark pleasure to flow through you."

"No debt is worth… Sweet Hecate, you have a choice. You're not a prisoner." I press closer to Loki as an excuse to whisper to him, and he wraps his arms around my waist to keep up the ruse. His chest is hard, but his skin is as soft as silk; his breathing is faster than mine. He moves with me, understanding what I need instinctively. *No one else ever has.* "You'll be hurt; I can sense it. Escape now."

"On the World Tree, *you* have a choice too." His lips are cold against my fevered cheek. Is that the first time anyone has ever said that being a vessel is a *choice*, rather than a *duty*? "Are you caged? Why don't you escape or stop this travesty?"

My chest aches. How can he suggest that? Where would I go? This is all I know, and I love Bacchus, don't I?

"I can't. Everybody here is relying on me. Possession is an honor. This is what I've been trained since birth to do."

He rests his forehead against mine. "And that's what makes us all prisoners."

Loki's glass-green eyes gleam, but the look in them is fragile like I could shatter them with a word.

"You won't run?" I demand.

"Valhalla! I'm many things but I'm not the god of running away."

I huff. "Then after the ceremony, oh god of taking stupid risks, stay close to me. You're my…"

I bite my lip. *What is he?*

Would saying *mine* be too forward?

"Your reward?" He demands, haughtily.

"My *responsibility*. On Hecate's tit, I'll keep you safe."

Loki's expression gentles for the first time. I glance at his strong shoulders and the beautiful dip of his collarbones.

What would this be like if I was wearing white for Loki and not Bacchus?

Isn't that sacrilege?

His lips twitch. "An oath on a goddess' tit *is* a

powerful one." I shake, as Loki pulls back, raising my hand gently to his lips. "May I?"

I nod.

I've never been kissed before, but this is my first Bacchanalia and Loki is my offering. It's just that I'd always imagined that Bacchus would become my first lover.

Loki gently kisses the back of my hand. "Who knew that I'd be happy to be proved wrong? You *are* different. But omens and runes, I have responsibilities too."

"What…?"

Bacchus' firm grip on my arm drags me away from Loki. When I look back at him, his mouth is set in a grim line like he knows better than me what comes next and is preparing for it.

My guts churn.

This should be the happiest day of my life. This is the everything that I've excitedly waited for and dreamed about. It's my purpose. The Bacchants teach that *a vessel is nothing without a god to fill her up.*

My hands clench. *I'm not nothing.* I'm the wild, dark, chaos…

It's too late.

The swirl of the dancers close around us. The beat of the drums and shake of the tambourines increases in ferocious waves.

Bacchus is coming…

ROSEMARY A JOHNS

His golden magic already weaves like ivy through the air; it prickles my skin.

The Bacchants howl and shake.

I wrench free from Ecstasy, whose eyes are swirling with Bacchus' amber.

He's here…

"It's the most glorious time of our god's death and rebirth. I need to prepare your special *offering*," Ecstasy announces.

Ecstasy prowls towards Loki, before yanking him away through the Bacchants, who howl their delight. Loki's muscles bunch; he's *allowing* himself to be manhandled. What will happen if he decides to fight back? His eyes hold the same predatory danger as my sister's.

They'll tear each other apart.

The hairs on the back of my neck rise. I swallow, struggling to push my way after them.

"Wait," I holler. "He's a *god*. How can we worship Bacchus, but take Loki as an offering? Just…don't do this…*please…*"

Why am I quivering…*sick*…with terror?

I trip over an urn. Congealing blood spills over my bare feet in a crimson wave. I scrunch up my nose at the coppery stench, shaking my feet in disgust. Each step leaves bloody footprints across the glade: I'm the blood-soaked sacrifice.

Is Loki a blood offering too?

Ecstasy drags Loki towards the gaping mouth of the ancient caves. The crash of the ocean behind, where the merman live in their underworld, throws up a salty tang.

What secrets are inside those caves?

I shove through the fevered throng of the Bacchants, burning a path with my magic, and snatch hold of Ecstasy's sleeve before she can disappear inside.

"Why is Loki special?" I demand.

Ecstasy sighs. "He may only be a half-breed…"

"My cock is well and truly *charmed*," Loki mutters, balling his hands into fists. "I'll have to remember the *insult* seduction technique."

Ecstasy ignores him, brushing my hand off her sleeve. "But he has a communion with both the living and the dead. He can walk the veils."

My eyes light up. "Like Bacchus. He died — *was torn apart* — and then was reborn. That's why I need to let him into my body, so that he can continue to live."

"Generous of you." *Why are Loki's eyes so sad?* "Of course, it *would be* if the re-enactment didn't need an extra added ingredient."

Ecstasy snatches Loki by his fiery curls and wrenches back his head. He yelps and then shoots her a look that should've burned her to ash.

Ecstasy only laughs, low and dark.

"I shall hunt and kill you," Loki snarls with such

certainty that I shiver. "I'm not your caged creature."

"But you are," Ecstasy murmurs against his neck, pulling back his head further. "And I hunted you first. Shall we see who dies?"

"*Enough.*" My magic slams them both against the cave wall. "No one dies for me."

Ecstasy scrutinizes me like she always has when my chaos side shows through. Then she lets go of Loki and raises her arm. A short iron spear appears in her hand, which is covered in ivy and topped with a pine cone. A sharp tip at the end slides out, which is coated in poison: her bacchal thyrsus.

I bite my lip, taking a step back. The power of our cult rests in the thyrsus.

"Excellent," Loki sneers, "your Stabby Pine Cone Orgy Wand."

Ecstasy's eyebrow arches. "This bacchal thyrsus incites frenzy and madness. I can lead whole villages into—"

"Orgies?" I offer.

Loki chuckles.

Ecstasy's eyes narrow. "Your place is kneeling before Bacchus. The power of the House of Ecstasy rests in our dark chaos. Why do you hesitate now, little leaf, over a god who all revile as a cunning trickster? Your true lover shall be here any moment, and he loves us all. We must worship him with our very Souls. Can't you taste him?" *And I can*: Bacchus' warm, honey presence scents the air and coats my tongue. *He's almost here.* My knees buckle. Loki's gaze is intent and serious. Why do I desire emerald eyes over amber? "Bacchus already has your Soul. Give him your body, and you'll be filled with his pleasure for eternity. *Let him possess you.*"

"Or don't," Loki grits out.

Ecstasy snorts. "This half god is only jealous of what he can never be." Loki's eyes flash with hurt, before shuttering to blankness. His shoulders hunch. "What does a disgraced God, who no-one worships, think when he looks on a golden god who's even earned the worship of witches? What does he do?"

"Wouldn't you like to know." Loki glares at her from underneath his thick, butterfly eyelashes. "Why would I want to be worshiped? Without it, I'm free."

"Free of family, home, and love." Ecstasy's smile is sly. *Why is she saying this?* "You're alone, and soon you'll belong to the frenzy of the Bacchants. At least you'll be unique: the first god on his knees."

Loki bares his teeth. "Too late. I'm a generous lover; I have no problem being the one on my knees."

When he waggles his eyebrows at me, I smother my laugh.

Ecstasy hisses, pointing her thyrsus at Loki; its sharp point hovers over his chest. "The god of lies can become the god of madness. Your mind doesn't need to be intact for the initiation to work."

Loki clenches his jaw. "Reassuring."

My sister has always broken my toys.

I tilt my chin and take a step forward.

To my shock, Ecstasy swings the thyrsus over her head and towards me. I dodge, but the press of the Bacchants behind me, push me back towards her. Loki snatches at Ecstasy's arm to pull her away from me.

Why is he helping me?

Yet Ecstasy wrenches free, and before I can dodge again, her thyrsus pierces my chest.

I can't think anymore…can't see…*can't breathe…*

The frenzy curls through me like roots unfurling. I shake and drop to the floor. My head bangs against a rock, but the pain is dulled beneath the *beat — beat — beat* of my heart and the rasping of my own breath.

Wailing…whoops…drumming…

My sight is blurred and hazy.

Where am I? What's happening? Who am I?

Hot. Tingling. Wet.

My head lolls back, and my eyes dilate.

I yank at my toga — *tug, tug, tug* — desperate to pull it off. If I could just cool down the heat, which rages through me…

I hike up my toga and slide my fingers beneath my slip. I gasp, as I circle my fingers over my clit and tap it gently in the way that I learned to satisfy myself alone in my room, dreaming about Bacchus.

I can feel him.

His golden presence encircles…*traps me*. Amber eyes meet mine, and a pink bow mouth smiles.

I pant, moaning. My eyes flutter shut. I'm lost in the madness of frenzy.

Yet fear flutters through the pleasure. Just for a moment, I think I see green eyes, instead of amber. An ashen face studies me in concern.

Help…help…help…

I thrash from side to side.

Then hands pick me up and carry me into the darkness of the caves. Waves of Bacchants pass me between them: *I'm the offering*.

How didn't I know? I'm coated in blood. Ready to be served up to our god. I try to struggle, but pleasure crashes through me like an attack; it weakens me.

An eternity of this…? *It'll break me*.

Dying-and-rising god! The chant echoes through the cave. They're calling Bacchus, welcoming him in.

I open my eyes, but I can't see or focus. There's nothing but fragments in the ocean of frenzy.

A pale god on his knees at Ecstasy's feet…a white werewolf in a silver cage…and my god in golden glory, shimmering to life in front of me.

Dying-and-rising god! The chant grows louder and wilder.

"I'm here, Favored one," Bacchus whispers in a voice as soft as honey. His golden curls are beautiful but somehow, now look the wrong shade. His amber eyes don't blaze with the danger that I desire. I can't help the glance to the *other* god, who's beside the cage. *Wait, why's there a cage in here?* Why a were-wolf? Bacchus brushes his soft fingers along my cheek. This should be the moment that I've waited all my life for but it's shadowed in secrets. "Let me in."

I've been taught this part. *Over, and over and...*

Even in the midst of the frenzy, I know what to say.

I simply choose not to say it.

Bacchus' brow furrows at my hesitation.

"*Let me in*," he repeats more powerfully like I'm an actor who's merely forgotten my line.

Dying-and-rising god! The Bacchants' chant rises to a wail; my temples throb.

I battle a moment longer, but Bacchus is intoxicating, and I'm already under the influence of the thyrsus.

"Possess me," I whisper.

Bacchus' eyes light up, before he touches my forehead.

And he possesses me.

My back arches. My eyes are blinded. I'm being hollowed out and filled up again. I don't know how long it takes; it could be seconds or hours, but I'm lost in the closest connection in all the realms. Bacchus' golden essence flows into mine.

I'm birthing a god, and the pangs are agonizing,

but I finally understand why this is an honor. Who doesn't crave to feel chosen?

All of a sudden, there are screams, the furious blaze of fire, hot against my skin. Caught in the web of my possession, I can't move.

Then in a shock that drags a scream from me, Bacchus is wrenched out of me.

Too soon…the ceremony isn't over…the possession isn't complete.

Bacchus isn't reborn yet. He'll die because of me.

I gasp, and my eyes can see again.

Everywhere is chaos but not one that I can revel in. Bacchus looks like a faded ghost; he's transparent, as if he's caught between the veils. He's vulnerable like this and deadly creatures live where he's trapped.

Have I murdered our god? *How did this happen?*

I stare at the cage that lies ripped open, the terrified Bacchants, and Loki who stands savage by the side of the freed werewolf. His expression is fierce and triumphant.

Ecstasy huddles by the wall; she's trapped by a blazing ball of fire.

My eyes widen in shocked understanding.

Loki was never here to pay his debt. He allowed himself to be caught. He played us in his own game of chess, and he just won.

He killed Bacchus.

I push myself to my knees and snarl, "*I'll* hunt you."

Just for a moment, Loki's expression softens. "I look forward to it. I warned you that I had responsibilities."

To my shock, he transforms into a black stallion, which is just as beautiful as he is in his godly form. His mane and tail flickers with emerald magic, and his eyes that are rimmed by long black lashes are emerald as well. His black coat shines obsidian.

Even in my devastation, I'm desperate to stroke him. What would it feel like to ride a shifter as wild as him?

Loki raises his head and snorts, pawing the ground. Green magic flares from his mane. He walks out of the cave with the wolf prowling at his side like the God of Stallions.

Perhaps, he is.

I hear the thunder of his hooves, as he gallops away. He's escaping, just like I begged him to do.

But it's different now. *He broke my god.*

I stare at Bacchus. Can my chaos magic save him? I have to try.

Tears burn my eyes. How could I've been distracted…tricked…and risked the life of the god who I serve? How can I fail in the one thing that I've been trained for?

In desperation, I search again for the golden connection.

"Possess me," I whisper. "Possess me...*possess me*."

Honeyed gold blasts back into me, hurling me against the cave wall. The air is knocked out of me with an *oomph*.

Please, in the name of chaos, let me make this right.

I'm burning up, gasping...*dying* with the effort of wrapping my magic around Bacchus' weak light.

Let him take what he needs and live through me.

I howl, however, as my magic is wrenched out of me with a *snap* and into Bacchus. He's reborn, and I'm hollowed out. Yet this time, there's nothing to fill me up again.

My magic is gone.

I collapse, as Bacchus rises in a golden glow. He bends over and cradles me.

Bacchus' fingers are warm, as he strokes my hair. "Thank you, Favored One. Your sacrifice will be rewarded; no one has ever risked so much on my behalf. Do you understand what that means to me? Well, how could you? I'll keep you safe. I have ways of giving strength, even without magic. How would you like to become a Guardian in the Eternal Forest?"

He's going to separate me from my family and the Bacchants...?

Yet I nod. After all, I'm no longer able to practice magic. What use am I to them here?

Bacchus' expression darkens. "Loki *shall* be hunted for his crimes."

"He shall be *hurt* for them." Ecstasy scratches her long nails along the cave floor like it's Loki's face. "Nobody attacks the House of Ecstasy."

My sister loves me. Loki has made a mistake tonight. My sister will dedicate everything to hunting and hurting him now.

Bacchus expression is no longer soft but terrifyingly hard. "Every Bacchant will be filled with my spirit, and in my name given immortality. Loki and his descendants will never find rest again for this outrage."

The sudden silence in the cave sounds like a promise and an oath, which binds us all here tonight.

Yet I'm numb. My magic is like one of my senses, and now I've lost it.

Why are my cheeks wet?

Is this a chaos moment? To be shattered and remade?

Tonight, I should have been possessed. Instead, I'm broken because Loki is a bad, bad god.

What will happen when we hunt and catch him? Will he also be shattered into sharp but beautiful shards and broken?

CHAPTER TWO

Eternal Forest, PRESENT DAY

T he destruction of the godly realms begins with a demon's kiss.

I lean through the silver bars of the cage and accept the kiss of the demon who's my best friend and first lover.

Loki doesn't count.

Plus, I allow myself to forget in the desperation of the moment that this is my *ex*-lover.

It's complicated.

His lips are soft, but they spark with a dark magic. Its aroma winds through me: a warm cinnamon that makes me desire to taste it.

Sweet Hecate, my soul aches.

I'm empty. The place inside me, which was hollowed out of my own chaos magic, tries to reach out in response. But there's nothing there...*never anything there.*

I sacrificed it to save the god who I worship, Bacchus. Now I can only taste magic second-hand in my sorcerer lover's...*ex*-lover's...power.

Merlin's prick, why is it so hard to remember that?

My demon's magic is delicious.

Oni's gorgeous skin gleams like crushed sapphires, the same as his sweep of hair and curved horns. I wish that I could reach through the bars and stroke them to reassure him because he loves that.

Horns have many...*creative*...uses.

The muscles of his large shoulders are tight with the stress that he's trying to hide from me. He's naked (*does he have an allergy to clothes?*), and he's been forced to his knees. He's far too tall for the cage.

He hates to be trapped.

Reluctantly, I pull back from the kiss.

Just for a moment, I flash back to the night a thousand years ago, when I lost my magic, to a white wolf in a silver cage just like this, before it stands freed next to a black stallion with flaring green magic...

I shake my head, grimacing as I snap the thin band around my wrist, as Ecstasy has taught me to do if I spiral about *that* night.

Bacchus gave all us Bacchants immortality. I've now lived for a thousand years. Yet sometimes, it feels like no time has passed at all.

Bubbling cauldrons, that scares me.

The Bacchants have gained power and influence around the entire world, while I've been trapped *for my own safety* because I don't have magic in the Eternal Forest (just like once I was kept in the House of Ecstasy). Of course, as a teenager, there was the time that I attracted the Shadow Demons crawling around the walls by accidentally blotting out the sun (an eclipse, Ecstasy called it), or *accidentally* transported the entire West Wing into an alternate universe.

I rather enjoyed that universe: *they* didn't scream at me for the *accidental* mistakes of my magic but planned to crown me Queen of Chaos. Plus, they told me about the gods. Loki was imprisoned in a jail in Asgard for badmouthing the other gods. I believe they said something about him being *tied to a rock, while a snake dripped venom on him for all eternity.*

Win-win.

Ecstasy brought me back, however, for *my own safety.* She was fiercely protective of me, just like I was fiercely protective of her. Yet I think it was more that the Bacchants feared that *I* wasn't safe.

I'm not.

What's wrong with an inquiring mind or the way that wild magic spills out…?

Yet after giving my cult immortality and placing me like a delicate toy that's already broken in the Tree of Life at the center of the Eternal Forest, Bacchus disappeared.

In a thousand years, why's he only visited me once? Does Bacchus love me or has he forgotten me?

Bacchus' golden curls and amber eyes still haunt *my* dreams. I crave my god, who possessed me and then was reborn through me…*for whom I gave up my magic.*

Ecstasy has spent the long years hunting and hurting Loki. Yet I no longer hope that Loki will be caught. I definitely don't wish to break him.

Loki cared about responsibilities, and I have mine like the one who's trying to give me the *demon puppy eyes*, even though he's got himself into trouble again.

Oni attracts trouble in the same way that my sister attracts cocks.

My lips twitch, but I ruthlessly smother my grin.

The cage is bound in ropes and swings from the high yew tree. I glance up at the thick branches. Oni's lucky that I came across him on my patrol before the Shadow Demons, who are massing in greater numbers every day.

Shadow Demons don't have loyalty to other demons. They're beings of destruction and death. Just like they tore apart my parents, they'd have killed Oni.

My stomach roils.

The Eternal Forest is on the edges of Oxford, in England. Yet it's also a meeting place of the godly realms, where the veils meet the Other Worlds, the underworlds, and portals to places that are beyond even my imagination. It's dangerous and the spirits, demons, and gods are equally deadly.

They're as vicious and wild as I am.

This has been my playground for a millennium, and I'll protect it with my last breath.

The gloomy grove is a ring of dying yew trees. Vines hang between them like shrouds. The thick canopy of branches blocks out the late afternoon sun. My boots sink into the bed of curling, fiery leaves that crackle like paper. I wrinkle my nose at the scent of damp moss.

The Eternal Forest doesn't change with the natural seasons but adapts to those who dwell inside it. Plants from across the realms grow next to each other, preying on the weak.

Yet there's beauty in the ancient forest. Luckily for me, I find that the deadliest are usually the most beautiful. Oni, for example, is a psycho but he's also a *beautiful* psycho.

I love him, until my Soul bleeds. I just can't give him as much of me as he needs.

Once, our love was the only thing that held me together. Oni stopped me from breaking apart, when I was first brought to the forest. Demons are immortal.

He became my best friend, tearing through the shadows at night with me, swimming in the river that gushes through the heart of the forest, and climbing trees to battle spirits, rather than treating me like I was weaker than any another witch. Like he could make me strong through his love and as if I was just another demon at his side in the dangerous black of the night. We were two creatures of the forest and we fucked with the same savagery.

We simply can't be together now like we once were. *And it tears me apart as well.*

Oni's black eyes study me intently, as he wraps his clawed hands around the bars. "Come on, love, help a bloke out."

The cage swings in the breeze.

I raise my eyebrow. "You stole a kiss. What more do you want?"

He shoots me a lady-killing smile. "*Stole?* I offered, and you accepted. That's called a deal in the demon underworld."

"You're a rogue."

He grins. "I never pretended that I wasn't. Don't we know each other well enough for a little familiarity?"

"Over familiarity."

What am I saying? I'll kiss him a thousand times if it calms his ragged breathing.

Who's hunting him?

I eye his glorious nakedness (and his dick hardens but then, he's always been an exhibitionist; demons mostly are). "It's freezing in the forest right now. The breeze is like needles under my skin. Where's your striped pelt or at least a thong…?"

"*Thong…?*" He tilts his head, and his horn hits the bar with a *clang* that makes me wince; his horns are sensitive. He does a good job of concealing his own wince, but I know him too well. "Of course, you're wearing such a lot yourself."

I mock gasp.

What's wrong with these leather pants and top, which are laced down the side? They're comfortable.

Forest creatures don't wear much. Perhaps, Oni has a point on the nakedness, apart from the twigs, rocks, and beetles sticking in uncomfortable places.

I lean closer. "Sass is dangerous when you're inside a trap, asking for help."

"Sorry." Oni's eyes sparkle in the way that I love. "Even my spinster aunt would approve of your outfit."

I narrow my eyes. "You don't have a spinster aunt."

"Good thing too or demon or not, she'd have a heart attack over what you're wearing," he mutters.

I slam my hand against the bars. "And this imaginary aunt loves naked asses?"

Oni wiggles *his* naked ass. "Aren't you enjoying the view?"

He sounds sincerely disappointed.

I roll my eyes. "What did you do this time?"

Oni's expression becomes serious.

"Nothing," he says, affronted.

Liar, liar, demon ass without pants on fire…

"Then what's the Demon Emperor punishing you for?" I demand.

My heart clenches, and I scuff my foot through the leaves. I've never been able to save Oni from the other demons, and he's never asked me to.

I can't leave the forest to kick some Emperor ass. Who knows what dark plots go on in the kingdoms of the demon underworld? Yet I'd give anything to be able to hex their Emperor with a Hot Ginger Root Horn Hex.

For a demon that's worse than shoving the ginger root somewhere far more intimate.

Oni puffs up his chest. "By my claws, there were twelve gods, and they attacked me from behind, or I'd have crushed them with a single blow from my hammer…"

"It *was* the Emperor, wasn't it?"

Oni deflates, pushing a strand of blue hair behind his ear. "Work with me here. Allow a demon some pride."

"You could easily crush twelve gods in one go with your hammer," I reassure him.

He brightens. "Really?"

"Of course not."

He rattles the bars of the cage. "Just a *minor* disagreement over *minor* infractions of the rules. How about you let me out, before I'm eaten by something in a *major* way?"

My rebel demon...

"You'll go too far one day," I mutter.

"I already have."

I look at him sharply.

Oni is an outcast, and he's one because of *me*.

When he waves his hand, cinnamon scented dark magic shimmers in the air between us, and my breath catches. I weave my fingers through it, catching at the threads. It sings to me, but I no longer can sing back.

I burn inside at the loss.

Out of the magic, bursts a song that burns the same as me about an ex's loss and jealous love. The moody hip-hop *anti-love* anthem rips through me. It's not exactly the rock love song that Oni usually serenades me with.

My possessive guy who I love.

I tap my foot. "The Prince of Fire has spent too much time in the human world. He's totally wrecked you with all this modern *human* strangeness, which he brings back from his travels."

Is Oni making a point with his choice of song?

Oni blinks at me with pretend innocence. "You're

no better. You're always peering at the advancements of the non-magical. And Sol, my flame baby…"

I snort. "Disrespectful."

Oni waves his hand dismissively. "The prince loves it. Anyway, love, my flame baby's obsessed with music."

"*Uh-huh.*" I glance at the ropes, working out whether I can untangle them and let the cage down gently. "Do we need to talk about anything?"

"What do you suggest? Our favorite sexual position? Who should play me in a movie of my life? How am I so devilishly handsome?" He waggles his eyebrows.

"What about why you're blasting the glade with a song that makes it sound like I ripped your heart from your chest and then ate it?"

He pats at his chest. "Didn't you?"

My own chest aches like he's thrust his claws through *my* heart. "*Ha-ha.* Have fun playing with the Shadow Demons."

I spin on my heel away from him.

"*Wait,*" he calls, and the pain that threads his voice with anguish makes me screw shut my eyes, "you say you love me but then we can't be together. That's not how it should be. Your blood beats through mine. Even when we're apart, I feel you…*I need you.* By demon tradition, we're Soul Bonded…"

"It doesn't matter." My eyes snap open, and I turn

back to him, stalking closer. All I want to do is kiss him again, and it hurts that I can't. It wasn't fair to accept his first kiss. "On the Tree of Life, I won't bind us, when my sister has already forced it on you."

"My love is real," Oni hisses.

His fangs elongate from his sharp white canines. I shiver with desire to lick over each one, as I once used to, lying on his chest high in the branches of the trees. His gentle bites in our Soul Bond were a claiming.

But that was the illusion because my sister was the one to claim him.

When our love was fresh, and Oni and I were first exploring the forest together like wild things, I didn't realize that he was breaking the rules of his own Emperor, Anwealda, by venturing into the forest.

By loving a witch.

When he disappeared, I was frightened to begin with because there were many terrifying creatures in the forest that could have hurt or killed Oni. Desperate, I searched for him for weeks…months…*years.*

I never gave up hope.

I never gave up on him.

I never gave up…

I begged Ecstasy to help me, despite her hatred for demons. Our sisterly love for each other has never dimmed; I've forgiven her for her role in the Bacchanalia. After all, she was only following Bacchus' will. And she's my only family.

I was still shocked, when she finally agreed. I was even more shocked, when she dragged Oni to me in chains from the Emperor's dungeons.

She made a deal with the Emperor that bound Oni to me by a Personal Guard spell. He was now an outcast to the underworld, the bodyguard servant to witches, and mine by Bacchant magics.

How could I hold him to his Soul Bond and as my lover, when he was held to me by a *spell*?

When he wasn't free?

"How about we chat about this, when you've got me out of this cage? That's unless you've suddenly developed a kink I don't know about...?" Oni winks. "If that's the case, love, you know I have almost no limits, at least with you. Shall we test it out?"

Why is he always so dangerously tempting? He loves playing with fire, as much as I do.

I reach for my scythe, which leans against the tree next to the cage; I only placed it down earlier to examine the cage. The scythe shakes and glows, welcoming my touch.

It craves me, as much as I need it: *The Infernal Scythe.*

I shudder, as its ancient magic creeps around my fingers, drawing them around its shaft. Like an addict, I shudder at the taste of its magic.

That's right... Join with me... Live and seek savage death...

My leaf brown eyes fade to milky white, as I snatch the scythe.

Bacchus didn't leave me without a job in the Tree of Life. Instead, I was granted the role of Guardian to the forest. My sister's magic connected me to the ancient Infernal Scythe, transforming me into an Infernal: a reaper with the power to kill both demons and gods.

I thought that I was feared as a Chaos Witch but that was child's play. Now, I can reap the Souls of the most powerful beings in this forest. And by reap, I mean *kill*.

Blotting out the sun and traveling to alternate universes doesn't sound so bad now.

Yet I only devour with the scythe the wickedest Souls: *killers*. They're those who escape the deepest dungeons of the underworlds and flee to the forest to stir up the spirits here. I maintain the peace for all the worlds. I'm the balance, rather than the chaos.

Or are they the same thing…?

Hollow as I am, the scythe's borrowed magic fills me up with dark whispers. Hewn from the Tree of Life, it gleams with malicious magic, tipped at the bottom with a sharp steel point. The huge curving blade, which is fastened to the shaft by chains, is sharpened on both sides (all the better to fight with). The blade glints with silver and is deformed with gaping mouths like the souls that it's devoured.

It's shaking, desperate to devour more.

This morning, the Infernal Scythe called me to it. I've been on the hunt ever since.

Two demon souls, a bonded couple, escaped from the demon underworld. They were traitors, who were executed for the murder of the Emperor's own son.

It's no wonder Anwealda is a cold prick, when his kid was assassinated.

They'll be hell to pay if I don't catch these Souls.

In fact, worse than hell. Demons and gods hate each other. It's a war that's rumbled on for millennia. Yet the Demon Emperor allows Bacchus' cult to live in the heart of the forest's shadows, as long as I reap for the demons as well.

On Hecate's tit, why was I distracted from my patrol...?

My eyes narrow on Oni, before I swing my scythe and slash through the ropes. Oni yelps, as the cage smashes to the glade floor with a *clang*.

"A little rougher next time," Oni peers up at me, "my balls aren't totally crushed. I won't be able to reach the high notes of a castrato."

"Now don't you wish that you weren't naked?" I smirk.

He makes the universal sign with his hand for *fifty-fifty*.

"Shuffle back," I say.

He edges to the back of the cage, and I swing the

44

scythe again. The sharpened edge of the blade sparks against the cage's door, breaking the enchantment.

The door swings open.

I rest the scythe over my shoulder because I allow myself a certain quotient of smug a day, and this is mine.

Oni crawls out of the cage, before pushing himself to his feet and rolling his broad shoulders with a hiss of satisfaction.

He's so tall.

I raise my chin, and the familiarity of needing to look up at him, tugs a smile to my lips. "Do you want to talk about our love life or do you want to hunt?"

He flashes a hint of fang, before darting closer and wrapping his strong arms around my waist. His breath is hot against my cheek, and my skin prickles at his tightly coiled danger that always somehow also means *safety*.

"Thank you," Oni breathes. His fingers dance lightly across my lower back; his claws draw light circles. Then he pulls back, and his dark gaze is serious. "I'll forever protect you. Who are we hunting?"

My breath hitches.

I protect the Eternal Forest, and Oni protects me. It's like the rainbow after the rain. I know it's true. Yet I wish that I could be sure it's because of the Soul Bond and not because he's my Personal Guard.

"Two fire demons," I reply. "The ones who killed the Emperor's son."

Oni's expression darkens, and he stalks to the other side of the grove, lowering his horns aggressively. "We couldn't be reaping a worthier pair of criminals. Those bastards conspired to let the Shadow Demons into the underworld. They became known as the Shadow Traitors. They planned to do it on the day of the funeral, when the kingdoms were distracted by grief. Who uses someone's kid like a chess piece?"

"A demon." I tap my fingers on the scythe's shaft.

Oni snorts. "Gods are just the same. You don't even know half the screwed-up..." He peers at me. "What's the consequence if we don't catch them?"

I love that he never hesitates over the *we*.

"Does it matter? We have three days and nights as normal to make the reap." I struggle to meet his gaze. Anwealda was too *graphic* on this point. Oni merely continues to look at me steadily. "He always hurts me through you."

Oni stiffens but then shrugs. "Good, then it means he's not hurting *you*."

"He'll take your horns," I whisper.

A demons' horns are their weapon, pride, and manhood. For them to be broken or taken is the ultimate shame.

If you wish to hurt a demon, hurt their horns. If

you wish to break them, break their horns. And if you wish to *destroy* them, then *take* their horns.

Oni's expression is solemn. "Then we better hunt those bastards, right?" All of a sudden, his eyes light up. "Summer! Baby, did they hurt you?" Oni crouches beside a giant iron hammer, which glistens with runes. He cradles it to his chest like a lover. Then he kisses along its ash handle. "Naughty men taking you away from me."

Witching heavens, is he about to hump it...?

I refuse to daydream about Oni fucking the hammer.

Stop it, I said *refuse, refuse, refuse...*

Oh, all right then.

Too late.

When I laugh, Oni shoots me a too knowing sideways glance. Then he attempts to stand and swing the hammer in his hand in as *demonly* a fashion as possible.

"Look at my terrified face," I deadpan. "The horror of the demon and his mighty hammer."

Oni points at me with Summer (his magical hammer...and broomsticks, how he did sulk, when I nicknamed him *Thor*), "Don't be jealous. Summer may come before Autumn, but I always make sure that my lovers are equally satisfied."

I groan. "That's truly bad, even for you."

He prowls closer. "I promise that it wouldn't be."

47

"And I promise—"

"Down," he hisses.

Instinct bred of centuries fighting together kick in, and I duck.

Oni swings the hammer over my head, and something *screeches*.

It's a hideous wail. The hairs along the back of my neck rise, and my fingers tighten, until my knuckles are white around the shaft of the scythe.

Devour...devour...devour...

I am Infernal.

The scythe calls to me, thirsting.

The Shadow Traitors are here.

They hunted *us*. No Soul has ever sought out the Infernal before.

For the first time, it shudders through me that these truly are the demons who in life, tried to topple their own underworld. They're not the average killer that I reap. *What do they want now?*

Flames flicker across my skin; I close my eyes against the intense heat. Oni hollers. I twirl around him, and my eyes snap open.

The souls of the Shadow Traitors are ghastly orbs, which blaze like flickering suns. Unlike less dangerous spirits, which are hunted by normal reapers, these are misshapen. Arms and legs bulge in and out. Horns stick from the top of the orbs and malevolent black eyes watch me from their centers.

Why did they escape to the forest? Are they planning to conspire with the Shadow Demons here?

I bite my lip. *I won't let them.*

My scythe howls in fury at the presence of the Souls who were once lovers in a murderous pact. Are they still?

The scythe heats in my palms. I swing it over my head in a practiced rhythm, and it *swooshes* through the air. One of the orbs flares brighter; the face of the male demon pushes itself free from the orb for one horrifying moment.

The light blinds me.

Don't let me miss.

This is what I'm trained to do. I've fought and reaped escaped Souls for centuries. I've never failed a mission.

Why does it feel different this time?

Oni's claws and horns elongate, glowing. He growls, and his savagery rumbles through me.

I hook the scythe, catching the male fire demon before he can escape, and then pull down, slicing him in two.

It's the *female* fire demon who screams.

Devour...devour...devour.

I howl to the skies, as the gaping mouths of the scythe open and *devour* the orb. The shaft vibrates with a stinging dark magic, but I don't let go because if I do, I feel like the world will shake to pieces.

Perhaps, it will.

My eyes narrow, and my shoulders straighten.

Now, to reap the female demon…

All of a sudden, the season of the forest changes, however, and a blizzard sweeps through the glade. I stumble backward, as a snowstorm gusts, driving snow into my eyes in a white shroud. The ghostly wail of the mourning Shadow Traitor echoes through the snow.

Why are the seasons changing so violently? Even for these unpredictable woods, it's unusual. What's triggered it?

"*Now* I wish that I wasn't naked." Oni braces me with an arm around my waist.

Unexpectedly, something soft…the softest fur in all the realms…whirls out of the white, sinuously flying on the wind, before winding around my neck.

I breathe in deeply; the aroma of sweet apple blossoms coils through me.

Oni senses the new magical — *trickster* — presence and growls, but I sooth my hand down his arm.

"It's my Kit," I whisper because I'd know my kitsune fox-spirit blindfolded, after centuries with him living at my side. "Now isn't the time for cuddling, nine-tails, I'm on an Infernal mission, and I can't fail."

Kit clings tighter around me like a scarf, draping his nine golden tails down between my tits. He's a gorgeous fox shifter, who's mischievous but heart-breakingly loyal.

He'd never follow me, *unless...*

My gaze darts out into the blanket of white. Where's the second She-Soul? Has she escaped deeper into the forest?

Kit's golden eyes swirl, mesmerizing through the storm. "Has Kit broken the rules? Is Kit in trouble?"

Sweet Hecate, I wish that I could kick the ass of the witch who captured Kit as a cub, Hestia. She restrained his magic and raised him to make the fox-spirit believe that he had no more freedom than a pet.

Now as a gorgeous man and shifter, at times of panic, he slips back into that thinking. I refuse to bind either Oni or him like that.

I stroke over Kit's silky head, and he huffs. "No rules with me, remember? You're wild. But it's dangerous out here."

Horns sticking out of deformed orbs...ghastly wailing...blazing fire...

Then I think of Kit and the way that his soft tails brush against my skin. I pale, before glancing back at Oni.

Oni nods. "I'll check out if the She-Soul is still in the glade. Nice day for it."

He draws back from me, and is swallowed by the white.

My hands are sweaty on the scythe.

Why does it feel like Oni will disappear on me again? That I'll lose him for good this time.

My heart would shatter.

Kit rubs his ear against me. "Kit eats danger for breakfast: *munch, munch.* All eaten. No more danger." I stifle a laugh. "But it's safer out here than in TOF. That's what this intrepid kitsune came to tell you."

I stiffen.

TOF is our name for the Tree of Life. It's my home, shelter, *everything*. I'm the tree's Guardian. No one threatens it and survives.

I shake, and the Infernal Scythe glows with dark, dangerous magic. "Who dares to bring danger to *my* forest...*my* tree?"

Kit's eyes blaze. "*Loki.*"

CHAPTER THREE

Tree of Life, Sun Workshop

I burst through the golden doors into the Sun Workshop, shaking with rage and distress because the bad god of both my dreams and nightmares — *Loki* — is inside my tree.

I flush. That's not a euphemism. I don't *want* it to be a euphemism.

Kit snickers into my ear.

He's not inside my mind again, right? The wily fox-spirit winds in and out of my thoughts like mist.

Kit can't help it (he always promises innocently), it's because his magic's tied to mine. *And not at all because he's searching for tasty treats or where I've hidden the special coffee.*

After I discovered about Loki, I stormed through

53

the forest back to my Tree of Life (a thousand years of guarding the tree, which holds up all the godly realms, creates possessiveness), with Kit clinging around my neck.

What if Loki was laying siege to TOF? If the tree ever fell, it'd mean End of Times…*Ragnarok*.

My breath caught.

Was Loki here to bring destruction again but this time to the entire world?

My heart pounded hard against my ribcage. It was my duty to protect TOF. When Loki's actions had taken my magic, he hadn't left me with much. But Bacchus had given me the role of the forest's protector, and then I'd sought out my own destiny and lovers.

And one of those was inside the tree…

Was he at Loki's mercy right now…?

Please, Hecate, no…

I forced my aching legs on faster. If Loki touched one hair on my lover's head, then he'd wish that it was Ecstasy who punished him and not me. And *no one* ever wished to be punished by Ecstasy.

The Bacchants would ground themselves in their own rooms or write magical apology letters that appeared in the air above the heads of those who they'd wronged to avoid trouble from Ecstasy.

It was usually only me who created the trouble.

Bubbling cauldrons, what if Loki had finally

decided to turn on the witches who'd hunted him for centuries and take even more from me…?

I *snap* the band around my wrist, forcing myself back into the present.

"Where's Loki?" I hiss.

What I truly want to demand is: *where's Ra?*

Atum-Ra is my Egyptian Sun God. For centuries, he's been *my* god in a way that Bacchus isn't and never was.

I was an innocent when I thought that I loved Bacchus with every part of myself. Yet I know now that Bacchus was never anything but a dream. He was no more real than the beautiful statues that the other Bacchants crushed over in their cells. I was told that I should desire him and so I did. He whispered temptations of eternal pleasure into my virginal ear, until I craved his touch.

But now, I'm no virgin.

I know what I want, and I want Ra.

Ra is warmth, love, and life. He's softness wrapped in golden strength. He's both creator and destroyer. He's my protector inside the tree, as much as Oni is outside in the wilds of the forest.

He's also my obsession.

I spin like Loki is hiding in a corner of Ra's workshop, ready to spring out. My scythe glows and pulses with dark magic; the mouths on the blades gape, hungry.

They want to devour Loki. I can feel it in the way that the shaft quivers.

He's close.

"Loki," I whisper, "it's scythe feeding time."

The huge cogs and wheels of the workshop *clank*, and I jump, as a chain falls with a sudden rattle.

The Sun Workshop is Ra's domain. An obsidian obelisk, which is carved with hieroglyphics, rises through the center of the workshop, which has no roof but follows the curve of the inside of the giant tree. A spiral staircase, which is decorated with lapis lazuli scarab beetles, rises to a gallery level.

The light is so bright that I squint.

Counters bubble and spit with potions and experiments. I wrinkle my nose at the spicy scents of sage, incense, and myrrh. I don't risk touching anything because the last time that I did, it took Ra three days to transform me back from a donkey.

At least, he said that he couldn't do it any faster than that.

Where's Ra?

I peer up at the second level, which is hidden in streaming light. TOF allows sunlight through her branches up there because she knows that Ra needs the sun to thrive. Ra bathes in the light like water.

All of a sudden, electric viola breaks into an intoxicating, delicious version of The Velvet Underground & Nico's *Venus in Furs*.

I grin: my Ra adores music as much as light. Sometimes, I have to pry his favorite violin out of his hands to force a fork in simply to get him to take a break and eat.

Decadent waves of viola drift from the gallery, along with Ra's sexy, growl of a voice that makes my stomach flip, as he sings a song that sends a shiver down my spine, psychedelically transforming the workshop into an opium den, where the drug is *me*.

In every stroke of the strings and aching note sung, he promises his service and love that burns me with its intensity. I can't breathe. Even after so long together, Ra shocks me with his devotion.

My Ra is safe.

The Infernal Scythe quietens in my hands.

But where is the other god...*the bad one*?

Kit pushes his silky head against my neck; his eyes are bright. "Kit has Loki under control." He smiles smugly. "Bad god is our prisoner. No problem." Then his tails unwind and lift, tapping on my head to force my gaze away from the gallery, until I'm facing him. "You don't need Ra. You have Kit."

Save me from possessive, competitive kitsune.

"But Ra..."

In retaliation, Kit nibbles lightly on my ear, before his tails whirl and he flies away from me, landing on the obsidian floor.

In a golden spray, he transforms into a cute man

with high cheekbones and dazzling hazel eyes that sparkle with gold flecks. His silky white hair tumbles to his waist; a pair of fox ears poke out from it, twitching. He's pale and long-limbed.

He's impeccably dressed in a tawny suit and waistcoat. Kit is a vain fox-spirit. He wraps his nine-tails that poke out of a hole in his pants (a clever design) around his middle like he's hugging himself.

Telling him that he looks adorable right now would further dent his warrior image and possibly lead to him playing Hide and Seek for weeks…with emphasis on the *Hide*.

Never play that game with a kitsune. Since they can go invisible, they'll always win.

"Kit will solve this." Kit strolls to TOF's trunk, which is the wall of the workshop, still stroking his own tail. My fingers itch to stroke it for him. "TOF likes me. Of course. Loki's trapped in the Moderation Room on the other side." At his words, the Moderation Room's door forms in the trunk; TOF is constantly changing and magically adapting. "He broke the rules."

Kit rests his hand on the trunk.

I freeze.

Loki's just on the other side…? If I lay my hand where Kit's is, then I'll almost be touching Loki.

I *ping* the band around my wrist again. I bet there'll be a bruise there now.

Kit's brow furrows in worry. "Kit hates that *rabbit about to be eaten* look on you. You're the fox...like me...not the rabbit. Why don't we just throw him out?"

So tempting...

I shake my head.

Kit twirls his tail. "One little boot. Out he goes into the forest, *bye bye*, no more Loki."

"Enough." *Why am I shaking?* "However he came here..." *Don't say it.* "... He's my responsibility."

Traitorous tongue.

Kit's eyes twinkle with a mischief, which unfortunately, is a look that I recognize too well.

Kit's nails extend into claws, and his fingers press into the soft wood. "Bad Lokis are not welcome in our home. TOF will eject him now into the forest to protect us. Then *say hello to the demons*. They go *munch munch* and no more Loki."

"Stop it." I drop my scythe (I won't risk injuring my kitsune), and it *clangs* to the floor, snarling in outrage. I dive to Kit, snatching his claws out of the wood because TOF has a crush on Kit, and witching heavens, it'd be just like the tree to listen to his wish. "He's here now and that makes him my beautiful problem."

"Silly hair problem," Kit sniffs.

I arch my brow. "He has silly hair?"

Even for Kit that's weak.

Kit's breath is uneven, and he's trembling.

I grip his chin. "I'm safe. You're safe. Our home won't fall. Whatever's happened, we'll face it together. You won't be alone again, I promise."

Kit's breaths steady; he calms. Finally, he nods.

I let go and turn back to the gallery. I glance up the spiral staircase, caught in the spell of the music. Then I steel myself to break it.

"Ra!" I holler. "I need you, my Sun-bird."

Instantly, the music falters and breaks off.

Silence.

A *whoosh*, the prickling static of ancient magic that pulls at my insides like the winding of a rubber band, and then a phoenix swoops from the gallery and across the workshop towards us.

Ra: my Sun-bird.

The Sun-bird flares with flame along its golden feathers and tail. Its body is dark with ash. I lose myself in the swirling suns of its eyes.

It's majestic and from a time when the gods wielded the power to overturn all of creation. I taste it fizzing on my tongue.

Yet Ra is bound to me; he's my Soul Bonded.

I love him now as fiercely as the suns that blaze inside him, but once, I'd taken him in to save his life.

I do that: take in the unwanted and rejected and fix them because once, I was broken too.

Ra's consort was Mut, queen of the goddesses and

Lady of the Heavens. I'd watch them in the forest together, like I often watch the gods, traveling between realms or the Other World.

I desired Ra. Who wouldn't? Yet I also worried for him because Mut was a violent goddess.

Then one day, Mut brought Ra to me in the Tree of Life...*broken*.

I dropped to my knees beside him.

"Sweet Hecate, what have you done?" I gasped.

Ra lay, unmoving. His body was covered in a film of ash.

Was he even breathing?

I ran my hand carefully through his hair. It was filthy and matted.

Was he going to die?

Please, please, let me be able to save him.

"He needed to be broken." Mut's dark eyes blazed. "No one god should be as dangerous as him, especially when he's a Sun-bird."

"I don't understand," I whispered.

She waved her hand dismissively. "A Sun-bird is a special type of phoenix. They can only survive if they're Soul Bonded to another. The god or immortal who holds the Soul Bond, also holds the reins of their power."

"If you're Soul Bonded," my eyes narrowed, "then how dare you hurt him?"

Her lips quirked. "How righteous you are, Infernal. By the Book of Thoth, I hurt him because I can and because he deserves it. It was decreed that I be his owner. He needs one."

"You mean consort?"

Her smile was sly and sharp. "I mean *both*. And it shall for you, if you wish it."

My hand froze in Ra's hair.

She couldn't mean…?

I shuffled back from Ra.

Don't offer me this temptation, just as Bacchus did.

"He's too wicked for me to wish to own him any longer. Yet you're immortal with powerful protectors *and* the power to contain him inside the World Tree. I see how you look at him, like you wish to devour him. Take him; he's yours."

"I'm not like that." I pushed myself shakily up; my knees almost buckled. "Love isn't… I won't force him into a Soul Bond."

Mut barked with dangerous laughter. "You believe that *you're* the only one who steals looks or that this is about love?" *Ra noticed me too?* Did he secretly desire me like I did him? "But it's your choice. This isn't about forcing anything, Infernal. If you don't take him, he'll sicken and die." My guts roiled. How could I let him die? "Your scythe cries out *devour gods*, doesn't it? Even now, you shiver with the need for death. If you don't crave him as your Sun-bird, then reap him."

Who would've reaped him?

Instead, I held him close and I Soul Bonded. I gave him a new life, freedom, and a chance. In turn, our love burned each day over the centuries, until it was as bright as the sun.

My Sun-bird dives towards me in a blaze of radiant flames. I shiver every time at the sight.

Before my Sun-bird lands, he transforms back into the hot man who Mut was right — I'd always desired to devour.

Ra looks regal as always in his falcon helmet, which is crowned with a sun disc; the golden coils of a cobra hang down like a fluttering cape. He's encased in feathered gold armor, which peels away like his helmet, as he stalks towards me, revealing the neat waves of his golden hair and his rich caramel skin, which skitters with magic.

He's dressed in a lily-white linen suit that's lined with glittering thread. It's so light that it's almost transparent; I can make out his muscles and his heavy dick outlined through the material.

He unfurls his vast wings and stretches them out. The light catches on his feathers, and they glint in the light like the colored glass around his neck on his wide collar necklace of phoenixes that rests from breast to collarbone: his symbol of being a Sun-bird.

He once wore his collar in fear but now he wears it with pride.

Kit huffs like he's not impressed by Ra's display, but I know that he is…and Ra knows that he is…and *secretly* Kit knows that we all know that he is.

It's complicated.

Ra sweeps closer, wrapping his wings around me. I allow myself a moment to luxuriate in their softness and his powerful scent of Frankincense, which cocoons me.

This touch…*his touch*…is how I know that I'm home. The aroma of Frankincense means protection, loyalty, and love.

Passion.

I gaze into his sky-blue eyes, which are rimmed by Kohl and gleam with shimmering gold eyeshadow. He glows like sunshine.

Beautiful, light, and soft, he draws his finger down my cheek. "The fox wasn't meant to go barking to you about our problem. Did he ruin your patrol?"

"The *fox* can bite viola strings with his sharp teeth *snap snap*." Kit bares his teeth at Ra.

When Ra raises an unimpressed eyebrow at him, Kit shelters behind me.

"Only half," I reply.

Yet I wince at the thought of shattered horns.

Ra's intense gaze meets mine again, and my skin tingles. He slides his hand down my jaw to my neck, while his wings rub up and down my back. The sensation is as familiar as the sun on my face and it heats me just the same.

The Leaf Tattoo on my shoulder warms. TOF gave it to me, when I bonded to Ra, but only because TOF sensed that the bond was willing on both sides. TOF connects to winding Fates but doesn't allow forced bonds.

Kit's pranks on Ra come from the fact that there's only one leaf on my arm: Kit's bound to me by a spell, just like Oni, but he isn't Soul Bonded. I love them with equal fierceness, but I won't cross that line.

I was given a choice between two bad options once before by Mut, and it'd break me to do it again.

When Ra drags me even closer with his wings, I'm safe.

I nibble at his lower lip. He pushes back, nipping at *my* lip. When I gasp, he thrusts in his tongue with the same force that he usually fucks me with, entwining our tongues and taking me, in the way that he knows I love because no one will ever know us as well as we know each other.

The thought makes my eyelashes flutter with desperate yearning for my Sun-bird.

My fingers find out his dick through the thin linen of his pants. It's hard against his hip. He can never hide from me when he's aroused. I love that. Just like I adore how his skin glows with light in his excitement; he's the sun come down to earth for me.

I work the heel of my hand up and down the length of his dick, before teasing its outline. I drag a gasp from him and smile against his lips in victory.

In retaliation, his fingers slip between my thighs, rubbing backward and forward, and I moan.

Hecate above, damn him...

"Excuse me," Kit murmurs into my ear, slapping all nine of his tails against my ass, "Loki's not down there."

I squeak, pulling back my hand.

Whoops.

Sometimes, in the radiant connection with Ra, I forget everything around me, even Kit, and fox-spirits are prideful.

Still, Ra dazzles me. I can barely remember my name or concentrate enough not to bite off my own tongue.

Ra smiles, and Hecate's tit, now is *not* the time to notice his dimples.

Yet my blood cools at the name *Loki.*

I draw back from Ra, immediately missing the feel of his warm feathers.

Don't let me be cold and alone again.

Kit narrows his eyes at Ra; his delicate fingers tangle together. "I got here first; she's *my* Infernal."

Kit is pretty but *so* dangerous.

"Remember the agreement we had about sharing and how we all love each other?" I say. "We talked about it a lot."

Why do I have the feeling that I'm being ignored?

Ra casually leans against a counter, far too close to a spitting potion for my comfort.

"I've got you beat by several centuries," Ra drawls in a way that sounds both relaxed and agitated at the same time. Then he turns his attention back to me. "Loki's caught. There's no danger to the tree." *He knows me so well.* "He arrived gift wrapped for you."

Toads and frogs, it isn't my birthday or Christmas. Who'd send me a joke gift anyway?

I blink. "Who...?"

Ra smooths down his suit; it doesn't hide that his dick still tents his pants. "Two guesses...three, I'm feeling generous."

Of course, it's obvious.

"Ecstasy," I growl.

"What a waste of my generosity. You only needed one."

I can't breathe. My chest is too tight.

"She caught him?" I force out.

Ra nods, watching me closely.

For a thousand years, the Bacchants have hunted Loki. Except, he's a god of boundaries, who walks between the veils and hides in the non-magical human

67

world. If any god can keep himself hidden, then it's Loki.

I mean, I haven't been keeping track of where he's spent all those centuries by sneaking Ecstasy's reports on him or making a secret magical folder with pictures and data.

Not at all.

And if I have...it's for practical, scientific, *non-romantic* reasons and in the interests of my god, Bacchus.

Yet even then, there are huge gaps in that knowledge. Does he have lovers? Kids? *A family?*

I never believed that they'd catch Loki. He's too clever. The best prey that I've ever tracked.

"Why send him here like this?" I ask.

Ecstasy always enjoys dishing out punishment herself. She has a thing about teaching lessons by making the punishment fit the crime. When a Bacchant (who bullied me for an entire hot summer), stole my favorite spell book, she didn't ground her or ban her from classes. She merely magicked all *her* spell books to refuse to open, until she admitted her theft and apologized to me on her knees.

Happy childhood memories.

Ra shrugs his strong shoulders. "Now, why would your sister deliver Loki to you wrapped in chains? Tefnut's tit, you *are* a nightmare to buy for. Remember how last Christmas, I spelled all those robins to sing carols on the branch outside our bedroom and you just whacked me over the head with a pillow? You were totally ungrateful."

I furrowed my brow. "That's not—"

"Ungrateful," Kit agreed. "What happened to Kit's tail fluff? That was a perfect present. Why's it not hanging on your wall or knitted into a hat? Where's your fluff hat?"

Merlin's prick, that'd been one interesting present to open: *for the witch who has everything...*

"I've hidden it somewhere special to keep it safe," I promise.

"*Called the bin*," Ra mutters.

"I meant," I say, as Kit puts his hands on his hips, miming *fluff hat* by placing his own tails on his head, "why's she gifted me Loki?"

My guts churn.

I know about the tormenting. After all, Loki wrecked our Bacchanalia and attempted to murder our god. He deserved the curse from Bacchus. *But I don't want him here.*

I didn't ask for personal revenge a thousand years ago, and I don't want it now.

Ra tilts his head. "I don't know. Could it have anything to do with the fact that he's the god who destroyed your cult, wrecked your possession with Bacchus, broke your magic and ended up with a crazy 1,000-year vengeance pact on his head?"

"Oh, that." My shoulders slump.

"Your sister must've cast a spell on him or he was trapped by it." Ra pushes himself off the counter and prowls towards me.

"You've analyzed it already?"

Ra pushes up my chin with his wing, as his fingers play with my hair. "Just call me the Sorcerer Sun God Extraordinaire." He takes a deep breath like he needs me to live...*and he does*. That thought does funny things to my insides. He whispers against my cheek, "My mouth is just aching for your tongue."

I nudge him with my shoulder, and we both laugh. "Then it'll have to ache. Tell me your analysis."

His expression becomes serious. "A dark hex covers Loki like tar. It's the hex of Enemy You've Hurt the Most. It's an arcane one that was used on prisoners of war or more precisely, spoils of war. It magically transports them to whomever they've wronged in the war. It was considered *honorable*. The magic ties you to the enemy, to whom you most deserve to make reparations. Pharaohs and pyramids, I bet that worked out: servant in the household of your greatest, most wounded enemy. See," his lips turn down, "totally fair."

Enemy You've Hurt the Most.

The hex chose me.

In the millennium long war between the Bacchants

and Loki, the hex must've decided that Loki wronged me the most.

And that means we're the greatest enemies, and I deserve reparations: *war spoils.*

I cross my arms, hugging myself.

Ra turns away, swooping to the counter and adjusting a complex system of bronze cogs and pulleys. I admire Ra's quick intelligence, but he's also the strongest man that I know because he survived Mut and offered me his love and trust. I'll never forget that it's a gift.

"What do you advise?" I study Ra.

Ra has been my adviser for years. He's my Soul Bonded and equal. His instinct is better than anyone's. Yet the way that his face lights with joy at having his opinion sought out and respected would mean that I'd do it anyway.

"The hex knew what it was doing. It can only be broken if Loki heals the hurt that he made. Well, good luck with that. Your magic was given to save Bacchus. That means that Loki will eternally be tied by the hex to you. The outcome of that...?" Ra rattles a chain. "It's already thrown out the entire rhythm and structure of my day. Two experiments are ruined and the third..." He shoots me a quick look and then away. "It's too important for me not to save it. We were doing fine without this..."

"Chaos?" I venture.

His lips thin. "Exactly. At least the hex will have its own way of keeping this unexpected god who's crashed into our lives in check. It won't let him leave TOF without you."

Kit bites his lips, and his hands tangle more tightly together.

Is it wrong that excitement thrums through me? That the wildness inside me sings to the chaos magic in Loki? Hungers for another taste of it?

I am the wild. I am the chaos.

I was.

A hollowness inside me almost drives me to my knees.

Loki took it from me. The hex knows that. It's why it brought Loki to me.

Ra rubs his hands along the chain. His experiments are his babies. I don't envy Loki for disrupting them.

Ra glances at Kit. "Oh joy, another trickster to unsettle my routines and make certain that my experiments blow up in my face. Precisely what I wished for."

Kit preens.

Should I speak to Ecstasy? Yet I vibrate with rage and uncertainty. Did Bacchus know that this would happen? *Is this meant as a reward?*

Ra, who always knows me better than I know myself, asks, "Should I portal call your sister?"

Humans have their technology, and us witches have magic. I've come to think they're pretty much the same. I have no problem with using both when I need them. *Portal calling* is the use of portal magic to connect across space to see and talk to another witch.

Don't humans call it Skype...?

I shake my head. "The hex chose me. I should face this alone."

Ra frowns. "Wait, that doesn't mean without your Sorcerer Sun God Extraordinaire?"

"Or your nine-tails?" Kit rests his chin on my shoulder.

"Alone," I whisper, striding towards the Moderation Room.

Loki is my greatest enemy: the god who's hurt me the most. But he's here, and everything has changed.

The Tree of Life is my refuge. Yet now Loki is inside it.

I must face him. But why if he's the prisoner, do I feel like the one in danger?

CHAPTER FOUR

Tree of Life, Moderation Room

I edge into the darkness of the Moderation Room.

It's pitch-black. Freezing. Silent.

I shiver, wrapping my arms around myself.

How long has Loki been kept like this, shrouded in such cold dark?

Sweet Hecate, *too long.*

I've been on patrol for most of the day in pursuit of the Shadow Traitors (and it burns that the She-Soul escaped, risking Oni).

So, five hours, six, *or longer...*?

TOF must be even more furious with Loki than I am. I never keep light or warmth from my lovers.

I'll never keep it from Loki.

There's no meaning in the void. Loss of sight —

darkness — breaks you faster than any nightmare because your mind conjures your own.

What's Loki's?

When you're in the dark, you'll beg even for your enemy, so that you won't be alone.

The hairs on my neck stand up, however, with the chaos magic that sparks through the room. I shudder, wishing that I could draw it inside me.

Sweet Hecate, if only it could be mine.

It's been too long, since I tasted this chaos and I burn for it...*what's been taken from me.* Can Loki still grasp the glistening shards of chaos moments and hear the sweet notes of Fate?

Should I have brought my scythe in here with me, rather than leaving it behind in the Sun Workshop? Ra begged me to, but Loki is already tied by the hex. I'm not here to reap him and I won't hold that threat over him.

I don't need the borrowed magic of the Infernal to *be* someone. For decades, I believed that was true. But not anymore.

Now, I rush forward, desperate to know *everything.*

I don't care that Loki's meant to be my prisoner and war spoils. He's a Chaos Mage, just like once I was a Chaos Witch. And Merlin's breath, I've missed someone who'll understand.

Yet I shift from foot to foot because I feel

uncomfortably like I did, when Ecstasy delivered Loki to me as an offering. He was supposed to be a god to worship me. Yet he tricked me and the entire cult.

I crave him now, but he broke me then. *Don't let this be another mistake.*

Is he *still* tricking me?

Yet I'm lost in this void with Loki, and he doesn't even know that I'm here. Can't I at least save him from this?

"TOF, light," I command.

A pulsing purple light floods the tiny room, which blinks into existence. The Moderation Room is the traditional room for prisoners. It's nothing but gnarled roots that twist together over the floor and up the walls to the low roof.

There's a pained gasp: Loki is hanging from the back wall like a sacrifice. His arms are dragged above his head by roots that tangle out, encasing his hands up to his wrists. His toes dangle above the ground, and I wince at the ache that must run through his shoulders.

At least he's not naked.

Toads and frogs, I'm not disappointed at the loss of all that moon-pale skin...

Not disappointed.

His ruby cashmere jumper appears so soft that I have the sudden urge to run my fingers along it. I'm prowling towards him with my hand outreached, before I know what I'm doing.

He's beautiful but glaring.

Fiery curls tumble over Loki's emerald eyes. His breathing is too rapid. For a moment, I remember the black stallion and wish that I could see him galloping through the Eternal Forest. He'd be glorious amongst the shadows and savagery.

Loki's magic is restrained; it's held inside him. I can only feel the whisper of it. Is the Enemy You've Hurt the Most hex responsible for that?

This close, I can trace the sparking crimson chains that bind him. They're invisible to anyone but me because I'm the one who he hurt, and I hold the other end of the chain. They bind him to me. To a magic user, they must feel as heavy as lead.

Yet Loki lifts his chin like they're lighter than silk.

I respect that.

I pull my fingers back to stop myself from stroking his jumper, and rest my hand on the roots beside his head instead. This close, Loki's scent is sweet and cool. My tongue darts out, licking my lips, as I glance at his.

Are his lips strawberry scented too?

He watches me warily.

"Your first time tying a guy up?" He drawls.

"Not even close." My hands clench at his deliberate echo of our first meeting. I move to snap the band on my wrist but then, I stop myself. Hecate above, I'm stronger than him. He *didn't* break me. I stroke over the band, instead. *I can do this.* "Your first time being tied up?"

He bares his sharp, white teeth. "Not even close."

His accent is soft and American. So, that's where he's been hiding for the last, few centuries, while Ecstasy refused to tell me about the hunt. He's been making his home in the New World, during the time that my magical folder — dossier — all right, *spying* to keep tabs on him, lay empty.

Why did he stop traveling the realms and in the dark spaces in between, where creatures that I don't even have words for dwell? It would've been safer for him.

Perhaps then, he wouldn't have been caught. He wouldn't now hang like a pretty bauble from my wall.

I smirk. "Good to know."

He tries to hide his smile, but his eyes crinkle with mischief. He doesn't look as young as he did in small ways, but it suits him like a skin that he was always meant to slip into.

"You've aged well," I say.

He smirks. "You mean I look fuckable?"

I flush. "You look *older*."

Crack my broomstick, am I under a Stating the Obvious Spell?

This isn't a date. *Why does it feel like a date?*

78

He's my enemy. I should hate him. *I do.*

Would someone please tell the butterflies cascading through my belly?

Loki arches his eyebrow. "And you don't. Bacchus sure knows how to spread the immortality around."

I study Loki, letting my gaze drop lower. "You're wearing *jeans*?"

When I raise my gaze, laughter dances in his eyes.

"Seriously, are you checking me out or ripping apart my choice of clothes? On Odin's beard, I apologize for failing your dress code. What *is* the dress code for being held prisoner by a fanatical cult?"

I gape at him. Now I remember why he's my enemy. He's a haughty prick who just happens to look delicious in those tight jeans. I open my mouth to answer something, when he cuts me off.

"Oh, I forgot, witches prefer me naked."

"Anyone would prefer you naked," I blurt.

Black cats, did I just say that out loud? *Lips, you're on punishment duty.*

My gaze drops to his crotch in those jeans that leave nothing to the imagination. To be fair, Oni's birthday suit leaves even less.

Eyes are you joining in the treachery now as well?

Why does he have to be so beautiful and so deadly?

Loki's eyes widen. "I know that I'm irresistible,

but how about you fight to keep your witchy hands off me?"

Arrogant...cocky...*infuriating* god...

"I''ll also fight the crushing disappointment," I grit out.

"Although, hate sex can be hot," Loki muses. "Bad boys do have the most fun." *Curse my attraction to bad boys.* He shakes his head. "I take it back. No touching the godly goods."

I only just manage to hold back the growl. Why does knowing that I *can't* have him, even if I want to, make me want to slam him against the wall and discover just how hot *hate sex* truly is?

Of course, I won't.

I take a careful step back, and Loki smiles like it's a victory.

Then I notice that Loki's shivering. Even though I've made sure that it's light, it's still freezing in the Moderation Room.

"Are you warm enough?" I demand. "Have you eaten anything since you've been here? I mean, that'd be tough because...no hands..."

Why am I babbling? The Infernal doesn't babble.

And why am I acting like this is a date still? *Bad, bad god*, remember? But it's hard to think that, when Loki looks at me with those wide, emerald eyes, and flashes me a smile with just a hint of shyness lurking beneath it, which is suddenly so different to his earlier one of triumph.

Was that simply a defensive act or is this new *nicer* version the act? He's like water, slipping through my fingers.

"Last time, it was as if I was invisible, simply because I was a male initiate and a *half-breed*," he says. "You've changed."

I tilt my head. "So have you."

It's true.

The wildness is still there, the chaos, but there's something else too. I don't understand what yet. Unwillingly, I sense that I need to; it's a burning in my chest. Until I work out a way to break the hex, Loki will be part of my world in the Eternal Forest. If I don't protect that world, then all the realms fall. Not that there's any pressure at all to figure out the deceiver of gods then...

Fire flashes through Loki's eyes, and I gasp. "By the runes, a lot happens in a thousand years."

"True. I am the Infernal now."

Curiosity creeps through his expression. "Since I am the *infamous*, we'll get on then."

I snort. "Doubtful."

He narrows his eyes. "Perhaps, you'd be kind enough to tell me where I am? It's always double the fun to know where you're being held captive. It's just much more cozy, even with dislocated shoulders."

"Your shoulders are really...?" I rush to massage his right shoulder, and he hisses in pain. "You're inside the Tree of Life."

"*Yggdrasil*," Loki whispers with a reverence that makes me shiver. He turns his head, swinging away from me to rub his body like an undulating snake against the wall. I wince; that must hurt his wrists and shoulders. Yet it's like he needs to be in contact with the wood and to let his magic connect. "My sacred World Tree with many names, whose branches and roots extend so much further than the Nine Realms but to every godly realm and to the void in between. I suspect, that it reaches to more worlds than there are grains of sand...*an infinity*. Each one has a Guardian." He scrutinizes me with a new interest like this is the first time that he's seen me. "*Like you*. Well, that's a surprise. By the Norns, I never dreamed that I'd be granted such a gift as to step inside Yggdrasil."

"It must be your lucky day. Although to be fair," I point out, "you're *hanging* from TOF (Tree of Fun) — which is my cheeky little name for the Tree of Life—"

"*Cheeky little name*?" He stares at me like I've just announced that I sprinkle the Tree of Life in glitter, blast the baroque rock of Florence + the Machine through the sacred branches, and use it to host orgiastic parties.

Which, of course, I do.

I grin. "She loves it." I glance up at the roof. "Don't you TOF?"

The room pulses.

Loki swallows. "Lady TOF, I retract my earlier curses." *Why does TOF become a Lady and I don't?* "I didn't know where I was. How about we ignore that I called you a *dickish asshole of a tree*?"

The purple light pulses again with a *harrumph*.

Kit has called TOF worse, when he's played chess with her. TOF will forgive Loki. Probably.

"Why don't you let Loki go?" I say.

Instantly, the roots slither back into the wall, freeing Loki's hands and wrists. He yelps in surprise and tumbles onto his ass. I flinch at the way that he cradles his wrists, hunching over. His breathing is ragged.

"Are you in pain?" I ask. "I can't do the spell myself because..." I bite my lip. *Not going there.* "But my lover could heal..."

Loki pushes himself to his feet, ignoring me. His curls hang over his face.

When he straightens with an effort, I pretend not to notice his grimace.

"Well, I've used up any dignity that I had left, so...bye then. I'd say it's been a pleasure, but even as the god of lies, I can't make that believable." He tips his imaginary hat to me.

83

Except, just like that, he *is* wearing a hat that looks like it's woven out of webbed fire.

He winks.

Hecate save me from Shifter Gods.

His relaxed (so human that it makes me uncomfortable) clothes transform seamlessly into a fiery red suit with black silk shirt and knot-like rope buttons.

Once more, he's a glowing star fallen to earth. He'll burn me. No star should be bound.

Yet Ra's the sun and isn't he bound?

Loki smooths down his shirt. "*Now* do I pass the dress code?"

I cough. "Better."

Loki strolls past me. I hate that he doesn't even glance back at me over his shoulder.

"Don't leave, Loki," I say, testing the hex.

Every spell has its own rules. The crimson chains jerk and tighten.

I spin on my heel and cross my arms, watching as Loki snarls and pulls against it, as the chains become heavier.

He's stubborn just like me. Can I help it that I like that? I bet that my sister loathes it.

"What have you done to me?" Loki demands, struggling. At least he's not ignoring the magic that we can both feel connecting us. "I'm seriously not loving your boyfriend hooking techniques. There's possessive and then there's psycho."

I bristle. "I don't... This isn't... Boyfriend?" I take a deep breath. "I haven't done anything. My sister must've cast a hex on you."

When Loki turns to face me, his expression is hard. "What hex?"

He's giving me the kind of look that Ecstasy used to give me, when Caesar terrorized the Bacchants. Perhaps, Ecstasy and Loki have more in common than they realize. They both bubble with darkness and chaos. And they've both mastered the *stern* expression, which means *explain yourself now, before you're tipped over my knee.*

Except, imagining that with Loki makes my neck and cheeks pink. As long as it's all in role play fun, I can't help the way that I squirm at the thought of being held down and...

"Excuse me?" Loki says. "Did your brain just go somewhere that my wank bank would be begging me to follow?"

I choke on my own tongue.

Then I wag my finger at him. "You're a bad god."

He blinks at me. "I'm not the one having naughty daydreams, when I'm meant to be explaining hexes."

Right...*that.*

"Enemy You've Hurt the Most, which means that you hurt me..." I break off, as Loki twirls away from me, slamming his open palm against the wall.

His breathing is uneven.

Silence.

Awkward and uncomfortable. My perfect combination.

"I never meant to hurt you," Loki says so softly that I almost miss it; I have to strain to hear him. "I didn't know that you'd be caught in the middle."

I notice *sorry* is missing from that sentence.

I clench my jaw. "I was just an innocent casualty caught in the crossfire between Bacchus and you...?"

Loki stiffens. "I warned you; I tried to stop you becoming a vessel. But you were one of the Bacchants. Omens and runes, you're not an innocent, right?"

Why do I expect anything different from the god of lies? But my chest still aches because there's enough truth in it for me to wish that he'd take it back.

I've imagined this moment many times. Loki on his knees; his fevered apologies. Tears. *Grief* at what he's done to me.

I never expected...*this*.

Why does he have to look so handsome still with his lean body stretched out: haughty and arrogant?

My eyes burn, but I steel myself to press closer.

"I lost my magic," I grit out.

His searching gaze meets mine. "And I regret that. But I don't regret what I did. You think that I'm the bad guy, but do you want to know a secret?" His breath is hot against my ear, as he leans in and whispers, *"Everybody's the bad guy."*

I draw back, and white-hot fury blinds me.

Why's he making me doubt everything?

He's the one bound in heavy chains. I'm the one holding their gossamer light end.

"You're lying."

"Am I?" He turns to lean his back against the roots. "Everybody lives a shadow version of themselves. The mask protects them. Valhalla! What do you think would happen if people went around living *truth* every moment of every day? Would things be better? And for whom?"

I stare at him. His intense, *geeky* sincerity like my own quirky ideas, which the other Bacchants never understand, reminds me of the side to him that I catch glimpses of underneath his own mask.

Also, I can feel with shuddering certainty that he's *not* lying.

What does that mean?

Fear flutters in my guts.

Everybody's the bad guy…

I rest against the wall next to him. "Hecate above, you're one of those pricks who say *whom…?*"

"That's what you got from that?"

"Uh-huh."

Loki's brow furrows. "I'm wasting my breath."

"Then don't." I entangle his fingers between mine. "Kneel."

His lips pinch. "Hey, don't get me wrong, you're hot. But this relationship is moving too fast for me."

"I'd heard that you were a legendary lover."

He preens. "Legendary but not with witches."

I wince, before shoving him to his knees harder than I mean to. "Don't flatter yourself. I already have lovers, and we worship each other in ways that would make your exploits look like innocent fumblings."

"Doubtful." He still looks at me with interest. "I'm listening."

"I'm not giving you a free session of dirty talk."

I can't help a glance at his tight pants; his dick is hard. I drop to my knees next to him.

He arches his brow. "Why? How much will it cost me?"

I will not set Caesar on our new guest... I will not set Cesar on our new guest... I will not...

I nod at the thickest root in the room, which runs like an arching pillar from floor to roof. "To be accepted here if you're not of my blood, you need to carve your name in the root. TOF will protect you then."

Loki becomes serious. He examines the names carved into the violet root:

ONI
RA
KIT
BARD

PETAL

Loki rubs his finger over them, and I hold myself still. His touch is intimate like he's touching those who I love in turn, and it's hard to allow it.

They're safe. I'm safe.

Am I crazy to allow Loki in?

I remember vividly every time that I knelt here, as my lovers in turn carved their names. Each time, my heart soared with joy. This is different. Loki doesn't know what it means.

Can I go through with it?

Yet Loki's touch is light and respectful like he's memorizing the feel of each carved name as intimately as he would the curve of their bodies.

He avoids my gaze. "These are your other prisoners?"

I jolt in shock. "Merlin's prick, no. You're more of a *servant* in my household than a prisoner now, and they're those who I love."

He glances at me dubiously. "You'd want to add me to this list?"

"I don't want you."

"Thank you for the bracing honesty."

"I mean, you need to carve your name to live in the tree."

He continues to trace over Ra's name. Does he know him? "Huh, so they obey you?"

"Great Hecate, of course not. This is like signing a

contract to obey the Tree of Life. Why'd I expect anyone to obey me?"

His expression gentles. He touches his forehead to the root, as if in blessing. "I'll always obey Yggdrasil."

"You say that now but you don't know her crazy sense of humor."

His lips curl up. "I have come across it before." His thumb finds out Ra's name again, and he circles it. "I take it that Ra is the glowing, golden god...the Sunbird shifter...who belonged to that bitch Mut?"

"He's also the pissed off god, whose experiments you ruined by turning up today."

"Being kidnapped has screwed-up my busy calendar as well." Loki shoots me a sideways glance. "Have you freed Ra or is he still singing mournfully behind the bars of a gilded cage?"

What does he know about Ra? He's *my* lover.

"Just sign," I insist.

Loki turns back to the root and with a steady hand, uses his magic to carve his magic fizzing underneath the other names:

LOPTER

When I look at him, Loki flushes. All of a sudden, he looks younger again.

"It's my real name," he says defensively. "True names have power."

He's right, and he's just granted me more power

over him than he needed to. It's a show of trust in both the Tree of Life and me.

I won't break it.

Ra's hidden name is so powerful that anyone who discovers it can control him. It's why I asked him not to carve it into the tree. It was too dangerous. If anyone takes control of him, he'll be a weapon that can destroy realms or bring about Ragnarok.

Relieved, I sigh. "Now you're utterly TOF's to command."

Loki scrambles around onto his hands and knees comically fast. "Sorry...*what*?"

I give a bright smile. "And punish."

Loki sits back, hunching against the wall. He pulls his knees up and encircles them with his arms. He's shivering.

"The only two things that were certain in my life were the tricks that I'd play and the punishments that I'd pay for them." He darts a glance at me, as if weighing me up. "Then I had my sons, and everything changed. Nothing mattered but protecting them."

My heart stops, and my eyes widen.

He has sons...?

I splutter out a breath, as my lungs remember how to draw in oxygen. I wildly stare around the tiny Moderation Room like Loki's sons (and his lover... wife or husband...*hex me now, I haven't truly consid-*

91

ered that he could have a partner), are stashed somewhere.

"What are you doing just sitting there?" I snap, crouching. How can he be so calm? If they're not here, then that means they were left somewhere alone, while he was magically dragged here. *Why are my guts squirming with something uncomfortably like guilt?* "Tell me where your kids and wife are, and we'll go save them."

Loki rolls his eyes. "I don't have a wife."

"Husband?"

"Neither. Lucky you, I'm free and single." He pulls his knees closer to his chest. "Weird how I'm not in the sharing mood about why that is." Yet he peers at me. "You didn't know about my sons?"

I shake my head.

Bacchus cursed Loki and his descendants. I simply hadn't thought about him having kids. Stuck in amber here in the Eternal Forest— never aging — time stretches forever and yet it also passes in the blink of an eye, never changing.

Is that the difference in Loki: *fatherhood*?

"You truly didn't know about my sons?" Loki repeats. Then he looks as if he comes to a decision, holding out his hand like he wishes to take mine. "May I?"

When I place my hand in his, he strokes across my knuckles with his thumb; his touch is moth-light.

I sink back onto my knees and lean into his touch.

"My sons were already kidnapped by your cult and kept hostage." Loki's intense gaze searches out mine. "Your sister has them in Rebel Academy."

I freeze.

Lies, lies, lies...

Yet my sister's been living in America for the last few centuries. She's been teaching there and making her name as the foremost witch. Then she took up a professorship at Rebel Academy, which is the academy in Oxford for the bad boys of the supernatural world. It's the deadliest of the academies; Ra told me that all paranormals fear being rejected by their kingdoms, both Princes and immortals, and sent there.

I begged Ecstasy not to teach in a place like that, but she laughed and said that as *Professor Bacchus,* she needed to build her reputation in Oxford's secret college.

Is my sister the one who's lying? Is she only working there because she's keeping Loki's sons as hostages?

Sweet Hecate, that doesn't make me feel good.

"Why would she do that?" I demand.

"You're sister's good at chess, right?" Loki shrugs. "I'm also a kickass player, but I tend to be reckless when my kids are in check. I'll always be the knight who sacrifices myself for them. They were the bait, and of course, I bit. When I tried to rescue them, this dickish Enemy You've Hurt the Most hex must've been triggered and *voila*," he gestures at himself, "here I am."

"She won't harm them," I promise him.

"Like she doesn't harm other shifters?"

I look away. What can I say?

Urgently, Loki grips my hand tighter. "Look."

His suit jacket and shirt melt away, and I'm once more staring at the pale-moon perfection of his skin. Unlike the first time, however, tattoos coil up his arms.

I gasp because these tattoos move: *alive*. The glimmering coils of a serpent wind up one arm and on the other, growls a cinnamon red werewolf with bristling fur that prowls around an aquamarine, *eight-legged* horse, whose mane and tail glitter like crushed gems, as if he's protecting him.

These are Loki's sons?

They're *monsters*...in the eyes of witches, Bacchants, and my sister. Yet I love a demon, kitsune, and a Sun-bird. I was a Chaos Witch, who transformed into an Infernal.

I'm attracted to the different.

Loki's gaze is fragile, hopeful, and defiant all at once like he expects me to reject both him and his sons and yet is just *daring* me to, all at the same time.

"Your sons are savage and beautiful," I say.

Loki's eyes widen in shocked awe like no one's ever said that to him before. *Perhaps, they haven't.*

I reach out to touch the shimmering snake, but Loki snatches his hand away from mine to stop me.

Instantly, I miss his touch.

"Sorry," I mutter.

"The tattoos are magical." Loki strokes over the werewolf, who's snarling at me, and he calms. "I can feel my sons' emotions and distress through them but I can't protect..." He ducks his head, and his hair covers his face like a bronze waterfall. His emerald eyes glint at me through his curls. "I can still feel them. They were my chaos moment."

"Kids are chaos...?"

"So says the woman without kids."

A flash of hurt lances through me, and he gently reaches out to touch my knee.

"I didn't mean..." He withdraws his hand and traces over the tattoos like he's truly able to reach through to Rebel Academy. "My sons are my world. I swear, they're the only truly good...*pure*...thing that I've ever done. My kids are everything. And now...?" At last, he looks up. When his gaze meets mine, it's anguished but determined. His chaos magic seethes beneath the binding of the hex. Its power takes away my breath. "Don't let them be hurt. *Please.* I'll do anything to stop that."

Why am I desperate to help Loki's descendants?

And why does it bother me so much that I may not be able to? Ecstasy runs the Bacchus cult, not me. It's always been that way. Since I lost my magic, however, I've also lost my status within the Bacchants. They were prepared to let me behave like a wild thing because I *was*: their powerful Chaos Witch.

Now I belong to the Eternal Forest as the Infernal. I hold no magic of my own without the scythe.

I square my shoulders. "I always find a way."

He relaxes, and his lips twitch. "I imagine you do."

Why is Loki's trust and belief in me such a twisting, *living* thing, coiling between us, when I've done nothing so far to deserve it?

Shouldn't he still be at the insult stage? I'd better be the sensible one and get us back onto stable ground. "Of course. I'd never let an innocent be harmed." I can't help the sharp grin. "But *you're* not an innocent."

To my surprise, the grin that he flashes back is just as sharp as my own. "Touché." Then he tells me in a rush like he can't keep the words inside, "My sons are fierce, smart, talented, and a total nightmare, I mean, they're like a whirlwind of rage, pranks, and chaos, which is karma, of course — *they're perfect*."

He lights up with each word, *burns*. Is that what pride looks like? I can't look away from him; he's magnetizing about his kids. He cradles one arm around his stomach, flushing.

I try to say something but discover that my throat is too dry.

Then Loki's glow fades, and I'm desperate to bring it back.

"You'd hate them," he murmurs.

"I wouldn't."

He considers me, carefully. "Everybody hates a monster."

"Does everybody hate you?"

He hisses in a sharp breath. "Why don't you just punch me in the dick or balls while you're at it?"

"What are they called?"

"My dick or my…?"

I raise an unimpressed eyebrow, and he grins.

"I told you," he says, "names have power. You may have mine but not my sons'."

I look at him closely. "So, if we're talking about family, will I have your parents crashing the party to rescue you? You know, some giant Loki?"

His glow fades entirely, and his expression crumples. *What did I say?*

With a twist of his wrist, his shirt reappears, and he fusses with the buttons. "Would that be my *dead* dad or my Aesir mom, whose life I ruined?" He clasps his hands together, as if to keep them still. "At least, she told me that almost every day."

I stare at him in shock. *What in the witching heavens did he do to his own mum?*

He appears to read my thought, and his gaze shutters.

"How did you...?"

"Ruin her life?" Loki gives a bitter bark of laughter. "Honestly, I should've said *ruin her.* Having a son like me was the worst thing to happen to her. Yet she still protected me when I was a baby and when I was a kid, found me somewhere to live, as well as work." *Weren't those things that a mum should do automatically without you feeling grateful? And why was a kid working?* "She warned me that if I ever had my own kid, then she'd disown me utterly. Funny thing is that having my sons was the *best* thing that ever happened to me." His voice lowers to a whisper, "It was worth it."

How could a mum say such things to her own son? Deny him the right to his own kids?

"You're saying that no one's coming to save you because your mum disowned you?"

He nods. "On fear of Ragnarok, it's the truth. On the birth of my sons, I lost my mom but I gained *everything* and much more than I deserve." He stares at a point on the far wall fixedly like he's being interrogated. *Did he think that this was an interrogation all along?* "So yeah, you can stop shaking in your witchy boots. There's no Loki Mama Bear about to burst in here to free me."

"I'm sorry." I flush with satisfaction when he breaks from his fixed gaze at the wall to look at me in shock. His expression is vulnerable and open; I hope to surprise him more often. "I lost my mum too. The Shadow Demons murdered both Dad and her."

"Then you can grieve them. It's harder when your parent is still alive, but you're the one who's dead to them. To know that they love others but can never love you." His expression becomes dangerous. "When you've never known family or love and then suddenly get the chance through children to experience it, your love for them is like a blazing star. You burn with it. I love my sons more than worlds or death. Know that I'd suffer anything for them. Nothing — *no one* — threatens my sons."

Is that a warning?

I snatch Loki by his curls and wrench back his head. "And I love those whose names are carved into the tree just the same."

When Loki swallows, I can't look away from the milky white of his long neck; the temptation to bite, as I would with Ra, is almost overwhelming. "Then we have an understanding."

All of a sudden, an explosion rocks TOF, which rumbles and groans.

My pulse pounds, and my mouth dries.

Please, no…

It sounds like Ra's workshop is at the center of the explosion.

Ra and Kit are in there…

My hand tightens in Loki's hair.

Can Loki have been tricking me? Was he distracting me in here, softening me up with stories about his sons, so that he could attack my lovers out there? I know that Loki's power transcends realms.

Are Ra and Kit dead?

CHAPTER FIVE

Tree of Life, Moderation Room

"What have you done?" I hiss at Loki.

"Huh, you'd be surprised how often I'm asked that." Loki's neck arches back further, as I tighten my hand in his curls. "Or perhaps, you wouldn't."

The Moderation Room's door slams shut, which is the protocol if any part of the tree is damaged or attacked.

Yet I need to get out of here.

"Open the door," I holler. "Tof, for me... I n-need to... *P-please...*"

Blinding fear and rage howls through me. No one attacks my tree and lovers. It's my role to protect them, as they protect me.

Why have I let this snake into our home?

"If they're dead, then so are you." It's not a threat; it's hard truth.

Loki's eyes become steely. He knows truth when he hears it.

He gives a curt nod. "Painfully fair."

Why did I leave my scythe behind? I can feel Loki's chaos magic whipping out in agitated waves, but I'm hollow.

Vulnerable.

I haven't felt like this since… I resist the urge to *snap* the band on my wrist.

The Moderation Room feels unbearably small. The gnarled walls are closing in. Its earthy scent battles with Loki's sweetness. The light flickers purple — *pulse, pulse, pulse.*

The tree groans and trembles.

My temples throb, and I wish that Ra was here to rub them. Every night, Ra gives me a massage, even if it's only a foot rub, as if I'm the most precious thing in the world and every touch is a reward that he can never deserve, which leaves me melted into a puddle of goo beneath him on our bed.

Are Ra and Kit…? I can't think it. *Won't.*

Loki pushes himself up. He's not attempting to escape my hold, rather testing it.

"I take it that you know less about how this dickish hex works than I do," he says. "There's this crazy thing called *control*. You witches are usually pretty into it. So, if you want to let go of me and lighten the chains of the spell, then click your fingers or call out to the spirit of Christian Grey three times and..."

He looks at me expectantly.

I study the crimson chains. Is it as easy as that?

"Why would I?" I snarl. "Why should I trust you?"

Hurt skitters across Loki's face like a wounded thing. "Yeah, why?" His gaze searches out mine. His bottle-green eyes gleam. "It's easy to forget who I am; what I've done. Release me, and I'll prove why."

Toxic dread and indecision churns in my guts. I'm trapped, *helpless*.

Do I lessen the bands of the hex and let Loki release us from this room or risk freeing the bad guy who planned the attack on the tree? Was this Loki's scheme all along? The way that he plotted to get me to free him?

His face is inscrutable.

I clench my hands, before I concentrate on the chains. Slowly, they wind back into me. The chains that bind Loki reduce in thickness to as thin as the gossamer thread, which leads to me. He lets out a shuddering breath, and the slight tremors that have been wracking him all along, slowly stop.

Has he been in pain and hiding it?

I let go of his hair, and he pulls away from me. His back becomes ramrod straight, and he reaches up to smooth down his hair. Instantly, he looks far more like a god and a thousandfold more powerful. His chaos magic that had been restrained inside now bleeds from him, just like it had at the Bacchanalia. I gasp, drawn towards it with a thirst that takes me by surprise.

Chaos magic. *I crave it.*

He winks. "You can't keep a good god down...or a bad one."

Then he vanishes.

"Hex his prick to eternal impotency," I howl.

I'm a witching fool. Why do I trust the wrong men?

To my shock, however, the door crashes open. Confused, I leap to my feet. I sprint out of the Moderation Room and into the Sun Workshop.

I choke on billowing smoke, which curls through the workshop. The room's thick with ash, smoke, and *magic*.

What's happened?

The counters are broken, and twisted pieces of cogs, pulleys, and cauldrons lie in charred disarray.

Ra's experiments...

He's going to be seriously pissed off.

Except, my breath hitches, when I realize that he may not be *anything* because Ra's lying unmoving underneath a pile of shattered glass. His lily-white suit is smothered by it. The light catches on his wide Song-bird collar, which isn't shattered. Even in my terror, I register my relief. Like this, he looks like he's entirely made out of glass.

I freeze. *Am I even breathing?*

Weirdly, I notice that the Kohl underneath Ra's eyes is smudged and that he'd hate that; he's always so careful that it looks perfect and immaculate. I'm the only one that he allows to mess him up. It's the sexiest thing about him. There's a purpling bruise along his cheekbone, and his golden wings are covered in ash. It's too close to how Mut delivered him to me.

I quiver, and my chest aches.

It took centuries to let Ra fix himself; I refused to see him as something broken that I could remake as I wanted. Instead, I gave him the space to remake himself, after Mut crushed him. I didn't know who he'd been before Mut or if he'd have been someone different without our love.

But I can't lose who he is now.

Ra's eyes are closed.

Yet I force myself to tear my gaze away from Ra because Loki is standing over him — *directly over him* — and his magic is swirling above his head. Bubbling black toxins leak from the shattered glass that coat Ra like diamonds, and Loki is drawing it away from his body and into his own magic, absorbing it.

Is he stealing it? Taking its power?

My Infernal Scythe hums darkly — *devour, devour, devour* — calling to me. I snatch it from where I left it leaning against the wall, and it's warm against my hand. Its familiar in my grip; it belongs there.

It wants to reap Loki for what he's done. He caused this explosion, right?

Yet I hesitate because all this debris — cauldrons, pulleys, and vials — belong to the workshop. Plus, Ra's experiments are often risky.

I take a step towards Loki. "Stop whatever in the witching heavens you're doing and step away from Ra."

I pull on the hex, adding just a touch of weight, and Loki winces. He tilts his chin in defiance, however, not moving. Instead, he raises his hands, and the deadly black cloud is dragged into him. He hisses, as he bends over in pain, before it disappears like it's been sucked out of the air.

I gape at him. "What did you do?"

"You see how often I get asked that?" Loki's lips twitch. "I sent your misguided sorcerer's failed experiment far away."

I glance at Ra, who twitches, as he surfaces back to consciousness.

Thank Hecate.

Except, if this is a failed experiment, then my Song-bird will soon have a lot of singing to do.

"I'm smart, you can use long words." I lower my scythe, marching closer.

Loki rolls his eyes. "I sent the magical equivalent of high explosives that would've ripped a hole in our reality into the void. Would you rather that I hadn't?"

"*Ehm*, thank you?" I bite my lip.

Loki cups his ear. "Did I just hear gratitude from a Bacchant?" *The haughty, cruelly handsome, son of a toad...* "Hey, it took serious skills to pull off that move. It's a tragedy that bad men make the greatest sorcerers and lovers."

Two can play at this game.

"Lucky that you're my type of bad then," I say, casually.

Loki's confidence falters, and he stares at me.

Ra's chest is rising and falling steadily now. He shifts and glass *tinkles* to the ground. He's awake and playing Sleeping Beauty. I don't blame him. He learned an excellent survival instinct from living with Mut. It sickens me that he can think of me like that but it doesn't make me less angry. He knows not to push his powers like this and the risk to himself if he does.

I kneel down. "I know you're awake."

Ra opens one eye. "Sphinx! Look at that, I am." He smiles, and I ache to press my lips to his. But mine are still trembling with the fear at nearly losing him. *It was too close.* "Hello there, you."

I wish that I could fall into our easy familiarity. The calm of his sky-blue eyes. The way that his words fit with mine like the press of his palm, or the way that he knows how to make me laugh, my favorite place in the world (our garden under the stars), and how he always washes the dishes, while I dry them, as he asks me about my day like it's the highlight of his.

Yet I can't because he just almost killed himself.

"I told you not to work on such dangerous spells by yourself." Why are my hands shaking? I clutch them together. My warming Leaf Tattoo only reminds me that it was cold a moment before. "Didn't we have this conversation like a hundred times?"

"By my count it's hundred and three," Ra replies.

Loki tenses, watching me warily. He looks like he's desperate to say something but is holding himself back.

Ra pushes himself up onto his elbows, wincing; the glass falls away from him in a sparkling wave. I'm relieved that it's only ripped his suit and not cut him.

"But I'm so close to finding a way to return your magic..." Ra snaps shut his mouth. He shoots me a sheepish glance. "Well, there goes the surprise."

The hollow feeling inside me becomes a cold ball. He risked this for me...*again*?

"Ever living witch, how many times do I need to

BAD LOKI

tell you this before you'll believe me, I don't need you casting such deadly spells just to try and restore my magic. When will you let it go and realize that it's *impossible*?"

"Never I guess because it's *not*." Ra's eyes blaze.

"I said..." I hiss but then I break off at Loki's expression.

He's ashen, but the glare that he's directing at me is icy. He's never looked at me like that before. He steps in front of Ra like he's protecting *him* from *me*.

I freeze.

I'd never hurt Ra. We banter and we argue because we've been together for centuries and that's what you do when you know each other so well that you're each other's heartbeat. Yet he was hurt for millennia by Mut and rejected.

I'll never do either to him.

Why does Loki think...?

Of course, over a thousand years of being hunted by witches.

It's strange that until I witness Loki's paleness, balled fists, but cool courage in the face of his certainty that I'm a danger to *both* gods in this room that the truth of his life under Bacchus' curse becomes real to me. It's only now that I begin to understand what it must've been like for him.

I'm a hunter. Yet Loki's been the prey for longer than cliffs take to crumble and crash into the oceans

109

and new countries die and are reborn. Even a rabbit will turn around and fight the fox, however, when it's cornered or to protect its young.

For the first time in longer than I can remember, I don't thrill with the sensation of knowing that I'm the hunter.

I gaze at Loki, and the chains thin until they're so light, they're almost invisible.

Loki jolts in shock, glancing at me questioningly.

He can be trusted. He let me out of the Moderation Room. He came here and saved Ra. Even now, he risks putting himself between Ra and me because he thinks that he needs to protect Ra. He's wrong about that but still, I didn't expect he'd do that for my lovers. Anyone who stands up for them, earns both my respect and as much freedom as I can grant.

"I thought Ra was your lover," Loki says, narrowing his eyes, "but right now the bars of his cage are glinting."

Ra snorts. "I'm no caged bird. But I am one who tends to cause explosions." He holds out his hand to Loki, who takes it with more gentleness than I'm expecting and pulls Ra to his feet. Ra molds his hair back into neat waves, adjusting the flowing lines of his suit that does nothing to hide his hard dick. He smiles. "My hero." *He's so milking it.* "I'm Atum-Ra."

"I know. I've seen you...about." *Is Loki blushing?*

I can't take it any longer. I need to hold Ra...*touch*

him...make sure that he's still in one piece and not like my parents...

I rush to Ra, wrapping my arms around him and startle a pained *oomph* from him. Somehow, Loki becomes tangled in the hug as well. To my surprise, he doesn't draw back. Perhaps, he thinks that it's his reward for the rescue.

He's earned it.

Ra cocoons me in his wings; I nestle into his soft feathers.

All of a sudden, my stomach lurches.

"Where's Kit? Oh Hecate, where's Kit?" I tumble away from Ra, and Loki falls against the cracked counter. I scan the room in desperation. My pulse pounds, and my temples still throb. "*Kit, Kit, Kit,*" I holler.

Ra pulls me against his chest. His nimble fingers massage the pain out of my temples.

"He's safe," Ra murmurs. "Nine-tails is the ultimate survivor."

I twist around to look at him. "You saved him first, didn't you? Sent him somewhere with your magic, which is why you're hurt?"

He shrugs. "By the Opener of the Ways, I couldn't let our resident fox-spirit explode. It would've been your slave bird here in his gilded cage..." Loki shoots him a glare, but his lips quirk at the same time, and so the effect's ruined. *Are they bantering?* No one normally gets Ra's sense of humor apart from me; it's why Ra prefers to spend time with his potions, rather than other gods. "...who'd have been stuck hoovering up the fluff for weeks."

"Where'd you send him?" I ask.

Don't say into the branches of the tree with Ratatoskr, the squirrel shifter. It took me kissing every one of Kit's nine tails from base to tip to get him over his insecurity that Ratatoskr's tail was better than his. Of course, that could be because Ratatoskr made up a *definitely not hilarious* chant about the differences between fox and squirrel tails, which had so many rude words in it that it should've been sung at a soccer match.

Ecstasy actually cackled when I told her, and wondered if this squirrel shifter ever came down the tree because she bet that he had the *type of cock she'd like to charm.*

Sometimes, my sister has a weird taste in men. I miss her.

Ra straightens his cuffs. "Not into the branches with the foul-mouthed squirrel again. I only had a moment to magic him away, but he should be in an alternate reality who worship foxes as gods."

I clap my hands. "He'll love that."

Ra chuckles fondly. "Since he already believes himself to be one, why not feed his delusion? And he'll be coming back to us in three — two — one..."

Kit tumbles out of the air in his fox form, and I catch him. He's so soft. He *gekkers* excitedly, pushing his nose against me and huffing.

I cradle him close, and he winds his tails to hold me even closer. "I thought I lost you."

"You can't lose your Kit." Kit's eyes are bright. "You'll always find me, my Infernal."

My throat is tight.

Loki studies Kit with open curiosity. "Huh, my sons once looked after a werewolf cub, until we set it free. We don't believe in anything being tamed but still, they'd love your pet."

Kit's eyes swirl with rage, and he growls. He darts towards Loki, who stumbles back with shock. I grasp Kit's tail just in time, pulling him to me and soothing down his bristling fur.

Ra slouches against the counter. "You have children, silver-tongue?" *Wait, Ra's using an affectionate nickname already for Loki…?* "Would they like a rabid fox-spirit?"

Loki grins. "Is he on sale? Then you have no idea how much."

Kit points his tail at Loki. "Your dick, my fangs — *snap, snap.*"

Loki hides his wince. "Your lovemaking techniques clearly need more practice. But my dick's never shied away from a challenge."

When Ra nudges Loki's calf with his bare foot, it's

more erotic than if he'd been on his knees in front of him practicing that technique. "Well played."

I think Ra's just pleased to have found a fellow crusader in his prank battle against my possessive kitsune.

Ghostly Asphodel petals rest on Kit's head; his new worshipers must've crowned him in flowers. I brush at them to distract his attention away from Loki, and Kit snuggles closer.

"How did you enjoy your fifteen minutes as a god?" I ask.

"I'm already a god if I want to be." Kit peeks at me from underneath his long eyelashes. There's something in his look that makes me uneasy. "Sorry."

"You know for you, there's a wide remit on that. Is it sorry for eating the last *three slices of cake* because don't think I didn't notice, sorry for the prank you played on Ra that turned his feathers rainbow colored or…?"

"Sorry about the spell that made it all go *kaboom*." Kit winces.

My lips thin. "You were in on this restore my magic nonsense that could've destroyed TOF and killed both yourself and Ra?"

Kit squirms uncomfortably. "Kit will make you a gift. You forget all about *kaboom*."

"*No*," I say just that bit too loudly. Then at Kit's hurt expression, I hurry to add, "I forgive you."

Kit's gifts always rest just on the psychopath creeper side of possessive, or perhaps, in kitsune culture, they're sweet.

"Kit gift," he repeats, happily. "Another poem."

To my surprise, Loki's eyes light up. "Okay, now I'm jealous. Please tell me what I need to do to get my own poem."

"Written in Kit's own blood," Ra deadpans.

"Kit's blood…?" Loki blinks. "You know, perhaps I won't adopt the weird fox thingie."

"His name's Kit," I say more sharply than I'm intending.

Of course, the effect is lost because Kit begins to recite the poem that he wrote for me on Valentine's day on beautiful white parchment, written magically in his own *blood*:

"The Kitsune sneaks towards the bed,

Sneaky, sneaky, sneaky,

The reaper raises her pretty head,

Licky, licky, lick—"

"Let's not share more of your…unique…words, along with our special love," I protest.

My cheeks are pink. I know what comes after the licking.

Listening to bad poetry is worse than listening to nails being drawn down a chalkboard and as Kit's lover, I should know. Having to *smile* while listening to that bad poetry, is like having to convincingly pretend that the screeching sound on the chalkboard is a Mozart symphony.

Painful.

"Oh, lets," Loki purrs. He's enjoying this. His magic is sparking with mischief. "So, modern poetry today is different than I was expecting. I'm entranced with the *sneaking* and the *licking.* I'm on tenterhooks. What's next? The fucking? *Fucky, fucky, fucky?*"

Kit bares his sharp teeth at Loki. "Not for an entire twelve stanzas."

"Well, slap my naughty wrist."

"It's not the part of you that I'm fantasizing right now about smacking," Ra murmurs.

I meet Ra's gaze in surprise. He nods at me, and I nod back.

Ra wants to make a play, and I trust him enough to let him.

Even though Ra's bruised and burned, he sweeps around to Loki and cages him with his wings. Loki doesn't struggle. His breathing picks up though, and he's frozen, unnaturally still.

"Thank you for saving me," Ra says. I can tell how hard he's analyzing what he says and filtering through options. "You didn't need to. The Bacchus cult have hunted and hexed you. If you'd chosen to leave me to be destroyed by my own spell, then I'd have understood. But you didn't, which means that as far as I'm concerned, you're welcome here." His hold on Loki tightens, and his eyes flash with fire. "But you hurt the woman who I love. You took from her and then spent a thousand years not caring to right that wrong. I need to know that you care now." My eyes blur with tears. Ra's always in my corner. It's a breathtakingly special thing to have someone in your life like that. "Do you have any idea of her suffering?"

"I don't know, is it perhaps anything like the suffering of the shifters at the hands of the Bacchants?" Loki snarls. "I can't change the past, and neither can your Infernal. But right now, I'm not your enemy." His gaze darts to mine; there's an openness and a longing in it, underneath the anger. I shiver. "Why don't you think about who your true enemy is, while I work on my true escape?"

CHAPTER SIX

Tree of Life, Autumn's Bedroom

S ome days, I call *Ra Special Massage Days*.

I wish that I can say I don't feel overwhelmed with stress or crushing anxiety that makes
my heart feel like it's *thud — thud — thudding* out of
my chest.

But that would be a lie.

For example, when I patrol the Eternal Forest for
hours to find the Shadow Traitors, need to rescue Oni
from a cage, reap only one of the Traitors and let the
other escape, which risks Oni's horns being ripped
from his head, and *then* discover Loki as a prisoner in
my tree after a thousand years. *And after all that,
almost lose my lovers in a magical experiment gone
wrong.*

On times like that, I'm overwhelmed with stress, and I call them *Ra Special Massage Days*. Except, the massage happens in the quiet of the night, when we're alone in our bedroom.

It's never something that I ask for: Ra offers it. He works my shoulders, until my chest is no longer tight and my muscles aren't knotted with pain.

The way that Ra cares for me is beautiful. Kit claims me as his in every breath, but Ra in every action. I never knew how much I needed someone to care for me, until Ra showed that he equally needed someone to care *for*.

Oni offers me wildness; Ra safety.

Each morning, before he goes to his workshop, Ra tidies our bedroom, making the bed and running me a bath. Only then, does he wake me up gently with a kiss (and on the best mornings, it's not on my lips). When I'm awake, he brushes my hair and oversees my bath.

It's a willing worship.

But he's *my* god, and I look after him, as much as he cares for me.

I relax back onto the satin pillows of the bed with a sigh. My back aches; I'm exhausted. The moon shines through the circular window over the low branch. The sounds of the night drift in.

The forest is restless tonight.

I drag the rich berry blankets over myself. It's cool

this evening. After Loki's talk about shifters, I can't help the shudder that I only just persuaded Ecstasy out of decorating with *Omega wolf skin* rugs, no matter how warm they are.

Will Loki truly try to escape?

He's tied to me by the hex and by carving his name in the tree. Yet his sons need him, and the guilt about that squirms uncomfortably inside me.

I needed my parents, and the Shadow Demons took them from me. I won't become like the things that I hate.

I'll talk to my sister tomorrow. Loki's not the same god, we thought that he was. After all, he saved Ra. I'm sure that I can make Ecstasy understand. If I ask her, she'll find a way to release him. Then everything can return to the way that it's been, and Loki can be free.

At least, I convince myself of that, but she hasn't released Oni or Kit.

I force myself to relax, breathing deeply. I love the room's familiar scent of honey; it even relaxes me at the sight of my huge scrolling desk, which is messy with paperwork. Our cult has power all around the world, and I'm the only witch without magic. It doesn't matter that I'm also the Infernal. I'm the one who's been reduced to desk-work.

Ecstasy is happy that my smartness is finally helping the cult, rather than causing trouble. Losing my magic didn't change my nature, but my sister never understands that.

For a while, I refused to work for the Bacchants. Ecstasy calls them my *rebellious years*, after she bound me to Oni, and we broke up. But then, I fell in love with Ra, and Ecstasy made things simple: if I wanted the cult's protection for him, then I needed to work.

I didn't believe her.

Yet when I refused to sort out their European finances, Ra didn't come back from his walk in the forest. *It was like Oni's disappearance all over again.* Then I received a magical picture of him alongside the financial accounts. He was being held by the Bacchants in Paris, and when I'd completed the French accounts, he'd be moved to Rome. Once I'd done the Italian accounts, he'd be moved to Berlin...

It went on like that for six months.

When Ra was finally returned, I held onto him like my Soul had been returned, and he held onto me like life. Yet he was so weak that he could barely lift his arms. A Soul-bird can't survive away from the one, to whom they're bound. Any longer and he'd have died.

Now Ra is safe only within the shadow of TOF but no further, and I work for the Bacchants. Once, they feared me but no more. I'm their servant, as much as Loki's mine.

My four-poster bed with ivy molded columns is

huge enough to fit at least five people. Oni asked Ra to create it with a wink, when he found out about Ra being my lover. It'd been his way of reassuring Ra that he was all right with our love and Soul Bond. Oni's generous like that. He lives his own life, independent of me. I wish that he could spend more time with me, but he's a demon. It's a miracle that TOF allows him inside at all (or evidence that Oni's special).

Even though Kit's a spirit from the forest, TOF has a soft spot for him. Kit shares my bed, just not in the same way as Oni. Hecate above, Kit's sexy, but officially, he's still a virgin. The rules drilled into him by Hestia as a fox-spirit cub hold me back. I'm not like the other witches but still, I fear making the final move with him.

What if he doesn't understand that he's free? *I couldn't bear that.* I'll give him as much time as he needs. *An eternity.* After all, that's what I have, right?

Magical fire blazes in a sizzling orb at the back of my bedroom, lighting the green vines that curve around the walls in a purpling glow. The fire also battles back the creeping chill. It casts shadows over Bacchus' shrine, which is built out of gold blocks in the corner. The shrine is covered with grapevines and phallic statues (all right, *wooden dicks*).

Oni says that Bacchus must be *compensating for*

something to need such huge dicks on his shrine. Kit merely mutters that Bacchus *is* a *huge prick.*

Number One reason for Kit being held upside down by his tails when my sister visits: *insulting our god.*

I don't much care if Kit does it, however, when I'm around. Kit's right, and I no longer want to think about the size of Bacchus' dick.

I strip off my top, before swinging around to the edge of the bed. I bend to unlace my trousers, dragging them off.

Bliss.

I don't need to bother to take off my panties because an Infernal is badass enough to go commando (or not to remember to do the laundry).

Then I squeak, as Caesar stalks into the room through the vine archway. Concepts of modesty are lost on a bear, as well as knocking. Who would've guessed? It's not like I care about them either. After all, in the forest with Oni, I spend as much time naked as dressed.

Good times.

Yet naked hugs are for Ra tonight, rather than Caesar.

Caesar rolls his eyes and gestures at his smooth, flat crotch, which translates to *no cock and balls, bitch. You made me like this.*

The bronze of Caesar's mechanical snout gleams;

he must've polished himself. He's proud like that. A patch on his back is duller because he can never reach it himself.

I drag on my only nightdress with a return roll of my eyes. It's our private way of communicating since we were kids. Along with growling. The nightdress is a personalized one (another of Kit's *special gifts*). I stare down at the picture of Kit in fox-spirit form attempting a ninja move on my chest. It looks all wrong like the Pokemon that no one's bothered to collect.

When Kit gave the nightdress to me for my birth-day, I stared down at it in astonishment.

"It's you…" I finally said, weakly.

Kit preened. "Who wouldn't want to wear some-thing with Kit on it? Just look at these ears!" He twitched them. Then he leaned in, conspiratorially. "When we finally," he licked his lips, "*you know…* You wear it and imagine you're with twins."

I bit my own tongue, hopping around in agony.

And now, I can never get *that* delicious *never knew I needed it but now I crave it badly* image out of my head, every time that I wear the nightdress.

Twin Kits.

Caesar growls, banging his heavy head against my knee impatiently

"Sorry, happy daydream," I say.

When Caesar stands on his hind legs and holds out

his paws for a hug, I smile and lift him onto my knee. I settle back against the wooden headboard and cuddle him. He growls, low and rumbling.

Why did the other Bacchants find him such a terror?

Oh yeah, all the chasing.

"Hey, you." Ra strolls into the bedroom with his golden wings furled. His cheek is still bruised, and I stiffen, even though I hug Caesar tighter. Ra waves his hand and his linen suit becomes more and more transparent, thread by thread, until it unpicks itself entirely.

It's moments like this that I can feel that he's a creator god. Yet he can unmake what he's created.

I'll never get tired of his beauty: caramel skin, powerful muscles, and strength that shines like the sun.

Ra's glass phoenix collar makes him look even more naked.

Witching heavens, I love him.

I don't care how goofy my smile is. I pat the bed next to me.

Ra lifts his eyebrow in his best arch attempt at *what me?*

It's spoiled, however, by the eager way that he launches himself at the bed, which bounces, and then crawls towards me. My stomach lurches. His aromatic scent catches me in its intoxicating hold. He grasps my foot and licks up its instep, kissing my ankle, before pressing his forehead to my knee.

He pauses, however, as he takes in the nightdress.

"And that's me done," Ra drawls.

We both burst into laughter.

Ra pulls himself to lie next to me. Magic flickers out of him, and a haunting recording of The Who's *Behind Blue Eyes* begins to play. It's a violin version with Ra's raw, sultry voice. Ra's personal recording.

Ra's own blue eyes meet mine. "Do you like it?"

He always asks that so carefully, as if it doesn't matter either way to him. Yet I know that it does. His songs are offerings like pieces of his Soul. People in his past trampled on them. How can anyone criticize — *attempt to destroy* — something that contains his heart?

I shiver, and chills run down my spine. The song is agonizing in its sadness and pain. *Ra means every word.*

He still believes himself the villain.

My breath hitches. I'm desperate to pull Ra into my hug with Caesar, and by the way Caesar is trembling, I think that he'll allow it. But it won't be the right thing to do. Ra doesn't need empty words or gestures. He may never change what he thinks; I'm pretty sure that neither *good* nor *bad* exist. There's simply good or bad *decisions.*

Ra won't believe me.

Ra makes plenty of good decisions, but there's also a darkness twisted inside him that I can't touch. He suffered under Mut. He has a right to his emotions.

I study his eyes, which are like flying into the freedom of the skies. "It's beautiful."

He lets out a breath, relaxing. I don't realize just how stiffly he was holding himself, until he sprawls back on the bed.

When we both start talking at once, Ra gestures for me to go ahead.

I stroke Caesar's ear. "So, today was interesting."

Ra smiles. "On the Eye of Horus, blowing up my workshop just felt like the thing to do."

I tap his nose. "Not funny."

"Given enough time, even tragedy is a little funny."

My brow furrows. "That's the thing. It was only a *near* tragedy because of our prisoner...guest... servant...whatever the witching heavens Loki is."

"He won't escape," Ra says, hurriedly.

"I know."

Ra presses his thumb gently to the crease between my brows, smoothing it out like he always does. "The Furrowed Brow doesn't lie. You're worried. But he's safely locked up..."

"It doesn't feel fair—"

"*In a spare room.*" Ra runs his thumb over my Furrowed Brow again. "He has a comfy bed and

127

everything. Although, Kit's taking first guard, so that *is* cruel and unusual punishment."

I nod.

Ra smirks. "Poor silver-tongue. He'll be Kit's captive audience for one of his lectures, probably on why nine-tails are so wise."

I wince. "Do you remember that one he gave us...*with slides*?"

The horror.

That's ten hours I'm never getting back. It doesn't matter that I'm immortal; I resent it. I glance down and even the Kit on my nightdress looks smugly mocking.

Ra gasps. "We're torturers now. Complicit."

"I can live with that." When I reach to adjust Caesar on my lap, I hiss at the pain in my shoulder. It makes me think of how Loki's arms must ache too.

There goes the guilt again.

Ra's expression softens. "Would you like a Ra Specialty Massage?"

I can't help the grin, as I twist to catch his lips in a grateful kiss. "Thank you."

I carefully lower Caesar to the floor, who growls in protest like a surly teenager. "Bed time for all bears."

At the opposite side of the room to the window, the vines peel back to reveal a low cave. TOF creates a home for each of us that makes us feel safe, as long as she accepts us and loves us. That she made the environment for Loki cold and dark, shows how much she rejects his presence in the tree.

Caesar prowls towards the cave, glancing at me with his sparkling amber eyes, before retreating into his cave for the night. It seals behind him.

"Now away with this monstrosity. Sorry, nine-tails." Ra whips off my nightdress, whirling it across the shrine; it hangs over a wooden dick like a flag.

"Disrespectful." I giggle.

"Necessary." Ra nibbles on my neck. "Now on your stomach, you."

"Feeling adventurous tonight?" I try not to look as enthusiastic as I feel, as I flip onto my stomach. "Or is this the massage...?"

Ra drops a tender kiss between my shoulder blades, and already I'm in melting mode. "Well, the night is young..." He straddles my ass, careful not to rest his weight too heavily on me. When he leans forward to ghost his fingertips down my neck, his hot dick rests on the hollow of my back like it was always meant to fit there, heavy and made for me.

A promise.

My skin prickles, as his magic skitters like static. I shiver in pleasure.

Ra's wings stretch out, shielding me in a golden sky.

I fold my hands in front of myself, resting my

cheek on them. "TOF truly doesn't like Loki. The Moderation Room was freezing. Even at the start with Oni, TOF was more welcoming than that."

"Hold on, are you surprised? Sphinx! TOF saw what you were like when Bacchus first brought you here. Shame we were out of banners and party poppers."

Ra works the heel of his hand between my shoulder blades, and I sigh.

Sweet Hecate, it's better than sex.

Don't stop.

Ra chuckles. "Are you approaching goo state yet?"

"Getting there."

"It's just that even if she was angry with him, Loki held such reverence for her." I'm under Ra's clever *clever* fingers, but I still can't forget my meeting with Loki in that tiny room and the hushed way that he spoke about TOF, resting his forehead against the vines like he needed the connection for his heart to beat. *Just how I feel about TOF.* "It's unexpected."

Ra snorts. "Everything about Loki is unexpected."

He digs his fingers deeper into the larger muscles of my back, where they're tight. I hiss.

Cauldrons and broomsticks, one day with Loki and already I'm tied in knots.

"Why do you always talk about our beloved tree as a *she*?" Ra asks. "Is it because you can't find a

branch that looks like balls because nine-tails discovered one a couple of years ago that looked just like a
cock." I push my ass up in protest, but Ra only
mouths at my neck; I can feel his lips curving into a
grin. "Ride 'em, Egyptian cowboy!"

I still, and he mouths me once more for good
measure. "TOF's a *she*. I can sense it."

Ra gives a happy hum that makes me tingle, as he
sweeps his large hands down from my neck to the
hollow of my back.

I force myself to keep the smile out of my voice.
"I even paint her wooden toenails."

Ra's hands still. "I paint *my* toenails. *You* don't
paint yours. So, does that make TOF male?"

Why's he serious all of a sudden?

"Black cats, if you feel so strongly about it…"

"*Loki*," Ra whispers. "He saved my life today.
He's powerful. By the Book of Thoth, his magic is
chaotic and shockingly beautiful. I'd like to take it
apart and analyze it. Okay, I desire to devour every
bright, *astounding* part of it."

"Perhaps, don't tell him that," I mutter.

Ra can be freaky sometimes like all my lovers.

Ra takes me by the shoulders, shifting so that he
can turn me onto my back. He lies so close that our
lips are almost touching. His heat warms me: a
living sun.

"I'm just saying that he could be more than a

servant." Ra's gaze is searching. "He could become a protector like me. *A Guardian*."

My eyes widen. I should've known that Ra would offer this. He's as generous as Oni.

He's never told me what happened in those six months in Europe with the Bacchants (protecting me again). Yet he knows that angering my sister is a risk to him and he's prepared to take it for my sake.

What I haven't yet told him — wasn't sure how to tell him — was that by asking Loki to carve his name into TOF, I've already made Loki a Guardian.

To become a Guardian in the Eternal Forest is a high honor.

I should've talked to Ra about it first.

How will Ecstasy react? I'm guessing worse than the fit she threw, when I deliberately ordered a thousand times the usual potion order of nettles to be delivered to her.

Paperwork can be powerful as revenge.

I bite my lip at the thought of what she may do. I don't fear her; I love her. But I do fear for my lovers. Still, I knew that making Loki a Guardian was the right thing to do the moment that I witnessed *his* connection to the Tree of Life. *His reverence.* Guardians are special not simply because they're tied to the tree, duty bound to obey and protect, as well as being loved by me.

They're family.

By adding their names, they take a sacred oath to become a Guardian of TOF alongside me. It was the only way to tie Loki to the tree that he respected and to reduce the cruel hex. I didn't want to punish or fight him, but I refused to risk my other lovers.

And I didn't want to reap him.

As a Guardian, Loki's no longer my prisoner, he simply doesn't realize it yet.

I wet my lips. "Excellent idea."

Ra captures my lower lip and sucks, as if in retaliation. When he lets go, he looks at me knowingly. "I knew it. He's already carved his name, hasn't he?"

"If I say yes, will you get back to sucking my lip?"

He kisses me but only chastely, and I sigh. "Tell him the truth tomorrow."

"Yes, sir."

Ra's pupils dilate. "Keep calling me sir, and I'll *bite* your lip."

"Promises, promises." When he nibbles on my lip, I gasp, then he swipes across it soothingly with his tongue. I capture his gaze with mine. "Am I making a mistake?"

He sits back, curling his wings around himself; his expression is suddenly raw and open. "Mut thought that *I* was a mistake. And bad. The other Egyptian gods think that I'm a rebel."

I squirm out from underneath him, pushing myself

up. I never touch him at times like this. He needs something else.

"They're all wrong," I say, softly.

Ra's gaze is sharp. "Then there's your answer."

My heart clenches. Do the Norse gods think about Loki the same as the Egyptian ones do about Ra? Except, I know that they do. I've heard the rumors. I knew them a thousand years ago.

Loki is the bad god. It's why I feared him being brought to the Bacchanalia as my offering.

Of course, I was proved right.

I stare at Ra, willing him to tell me that I'm not repeating the cycle.

Loki's a rebel god, but now I've made him a Guardian, he holds more power than he knows to hurt me, my lovers, and the Tree of Life.

He can bring about the destruction of the gods…Ragnarok.

CHAPTER SEVEN

Tree of Life, Autumn's Bedroom

I shudder at the thought of the end of the world and that I could've started it.

The magical fires in the orb blaze and flare, but I can't feel their warmth. Shadows swarm outside my window in a night that snarls with demons. My bedroom no longer feels as safe as it once did.

I wrap my arms around my middle, ducking my head.

Ra swings his legs over to perch on the edge of our bed like he's uncertain if he has a place there anymore.

I hate it.

"You mustn't ever forget how dangerous I am. If I wasn't bound to you, I'd tear apart creation. I *am* a

135

bad, rebel god," Ra says like these facts are as straight-forward and true as the beat of his heart. "By Seth, Mut and other gods weren't wrong about me. But I'm also a Guardian now. You granted me that. Do you regret it?"

"Never," I breathe.

"Then let's give Loki that same chance."

Ra opens his wings to me, and I dive into them. I burrow myself in their feathery softness, and Ra rests his cheek on top of my head. Then he winces.

I turn to look up at him and notice the bruise on his cheek. "Your turn for some pampering."

When I pull back from him, Ra looks like I'm stealing his favorite toy from him. "What…?"

Ra isn't the only one who looks after people. I care for my lovers as well.

I slip to my desk and pull a small tub of lavender healing paste out of a drawer.

Ra scrambles back onto the bed like I'm wielding a cane. Although, when we've role played sexy professor and naughty student, he's been more than eager…

"I'm all good," Ra protests, as I take my turn straddling him. His wings spread out onto the berry covers, until he looks like a fallen angel: *gorgeous*. "I'll stink, as if I've been rolling in flowers. What'll happen to my reputation?"

"Just see it as your penance for playing with

dangerous spells." I give my best impression of an evil laugh.

I even scare myself.

Apparently, I don't scare Ra.

"Where's Loki when I need him?" He asks in his best impression of a damsel in distress.

Insulting.

I open the tub (it truly does stink) and dab the lavender healing paste on his cheek. He holds still, even though I can tell by the way a muscle in his jaw is twitching how hard it is for him.

"If we do this, then don't freak out Loki like you do Kit," I command.

Ra looks at me with his most regal expression. "A god makes no promises that he can't keep."

I slam the lid onto the tub and toss it onto the floor. "I'm not asking Loki into our bed."

Ra stares at me. "Wow, when you get clarification for the question that you didn't even voice." *Why is my pulse beating so fast?* Ra needs to know where he stands. It's only fair. Ra's lips curl up at one side. "But just so you know, I'd be willing." My breath catches. *What?* "And as your Official Reader of Cocks, so would he."

"Don't be a mage's prick." I pull back from his hold. But he's not joking; I can tell. "Who says that I'm interested in my enemy...?"

Ra raises his eyebrow. "Are you really going to make me do this?"

I blink at him in confusion.

He crouches next to the bed and then reaches underneath it, which is where we keep our Box of Tricks. When we open the box, we always find the perfect magical toy to keep us both screaming and sweaty with pleasure all night.

Ecstasy gave it to me as a Soul Bond present. She can be a bitch but she can also be the most incredible older sister, the dark to my light. No one understands the intense importance of sexual pleasure more than her: *its power*.

Who else could've produced a sex toy box that produces exactly the right toy or props for your evening, before *you* even know what's right for the mood?

Except, instead of pulling out the Box of Tricks, Ra pulls out something else that I haven't seen, instead. It's a small green dossier with a love heart on the front with a Cupid's arrow through it and then in bold letters:

THE CASE OF LOKI'S ASS

I cross my arms. "Loki's ass?"

Ra shrugs. "Oni chose the name because you know, you have this thing about Loki's ass. You talk about it a lot. How many times have you checked it out since he arrived?"

"I haven't," *I lie*. "And Oni's in on…whatever this weirdness is then…? Traitor."

"Kit as well." Ra passes me the file. "It's a record of our love lives."

This isn't happening.

I flush, hurriedly flicking it open to a random page.

'*…Autumn makes beautiful breathy sounds, when I kiss down her spine. But she'll melt, if you kiss behind her knee…*'

I stare at Ra. "Do you know how stalkerish this is?"

"You say stalkerish; I say efficient loving."

I flick to another page.

'*…Autumn's left ear is more sensitive than her right ear. Her pupils dilate, when you pin down her hands but equally, when she pins down yours.*'

"How do you…?"

"I *know* you." Ra presses his hand to the file. "Like how your favorite place to make love is beneath the stars and your favorite vibrator from the Box of Tricks is—*"*

"I get it." I slam shut the file and hurl it onto the bed. "Have you memorized this record then?"

Ra traces my cheek with the tip of his wing. "Don't be cross, you. I wrote most of it." He looks down like he's trying to figure out how to explain. This time, I'm not helping him out. "We make notes and compare. Then we pass it between us. We love you and we share you. This is just one of the ways that we worked out how to do that. We decided that none of us wanted to have the advantage."

Ra, of course, as the one who shares my bed the most, is the one with the advantage.

In a twisted way, this is noble.

I lie down on the bed and hold out my hand to Ra. Gratefully, he takes it, curling next to me. He's just where he should be again.

"In a *competitive gods and demons* way that makes sense," I admit. "But I don't get the *Loki's ass* bit. Loki kink isn't my thing and I know that I'd have remembered if we'd ever had a threesome, so why's he in this obsessive record of yours?"

Ra kisses down my neck, and for a moment, I'm distracted. Then his words break through the haze of tingling pleasure, and I freeze.

"*Obsessive.* Pharaohs and pyramids, interesting choice of word." He licks along my collarbone. "How about the entire month that you asked me to dress in green, suspiciously like someone's eyes? Or that time you asked me whether I'd considered becoming a brunette? Or how about all the role play as powerful vessel and punished initiate? Or when Kit was the horse, and you rode him, running your fingers through his tail, telling him—"

"What a beautiful wild stallion he was," I whisper.

No, no no…

I squeeze shut my eyes. If I can't see Ra, then can I pretend that I don't recognize what he's saying?

Except, I do.

Ra kisses each of my eyelids; his breath ghosts across my skin. "And then there was that one wildly passionate evening, when you came so hard you almost blacked out, but then instead of calling out my name, you called out—"

"Sweet Hecate, I am obsessed," I groan.

"Everybody has crushes, it just depends if you're going to do anything about it."

When I open my eyes, Ra is looking down at me with a loving fondness that takes away my breath.

To be so accepted and quietly loved without having to give my heart, body, and Soul, as I'd been expected to with Bacchus, is beautiful.

I startle Ra by pressing a quick kiss to his plush lips. "You're amazing. I'm sure that I don't tell you enough."

"Likely." Then he tilts his head. "You're in love or at least lust with Loki."

"I'm not."

Ra rubs his crotch against mine, and I gasp at the sudden sparks of pleasure. "Too quick. Always remember to pause before a lie. You told me that you were intrigued with him, even before you met him. He has chaos magic just like you had. *Of course* you're attracted."

I bristle. If I hadn't lost my magic…if I could've been a Chaos Witch to match Loki's Chaos Mage… what would that look like? How wild, free, and powerful could we have been? Could he have answered all the questions that I had about chaos moments and the splendors that none of my cult understood?

Yet I don't have my magic.

I bite my lip. "I hate him."

Ra chuckles. "You don't hate anyone."

I can't help my answering chuckle. "I hate you now."

"Pause, remember?"

I push him, and he lets me, until I'm straddling him. I wiggle my ass over his hard prick, just to enjoy his *breathy gasp,* as its tip teasingly pushes between my cheeks.

Perhaps, I should start my own record on each of my lovers and share it between them.

In the sake of fairness.

I draw my fingers around Ra's phoenix collar, and his breath becomes uneven with desire. I circle my fingers across his nipples, lightly flicking and then encourage him to spread out his wings. "I'm going to kiss every feather, is that all right?"

His breath is rapid and uneven. "Only if I can

return the favor and lick between your thighs, until you come screaming *my* name."

Don't come yet…not yet…not yet…

I push my thighs together and kiss along Ra's wings, licking along his feathers, which smell sweetly of Frankincense. Ra writhes beneath me in pleasure like I'm sucking the head of his dick. It's delicious. A Sun-bird (or an angel's) wings are more sensitive than any part of their body. Mut used that to hurt Ra. I could spend eternity edging Ra, simply through worshiping his wings.

Ra clutches the bedclothes, as I kiss along his wings. I trace one finger lightly along his dick, which jumps, desperate. His gaze meets mine, as I pull his wingtip into my mouth and *suck*.

He hollers, arching.

A pearly arc streams from his dick across his stomach.

I suck him, while he continues to shudder. Then I draw back, before gently kissing down his wing, until at last, I kiss him on his lips.

Ra stares at me with an adoration that makes me blush. "You're so beautiful. *My life*."

"*My soul*," I whisper back, as I always do.

"Your turn," Ra grins.

"If you insist." I sigh, sprawling back and helpfully spreading my legs.

Ra kisses my stomach, before sliding down

between my thighs. I rest my hand gently on his golden waves of hair. I love messing up his neatness but this doesn't feel like one of those evenings.

That is, until he hikes one of my legs over his shoulders, and I gasp, as he teases the warm, wanting bud of my clit with his breath.

"Please let me taste you." Each word gusts against my clit, and my toes curl at the pleasure. Sweet Hecate, he's begging already. *I could come from his begging alone.* "Don't you want me to bring you pleasure? I'll do anything. Just let me worship your pussy."

Who could say *no* to that?

I tighten my hand in his hair. "Yes…Sweet Hecate…*yes*…"

He nudges his nose along my slit, and I quake at the sensation; he lifts his gaze to meet mine. Then he spreads my pussy wider with his fingertips.

"Ra…" I whisper.

I shudder at the first circle of his tongue.

"Ah, Kit's eyes are burned!" Kit screeches from the doorway.

I sit up, dragging the sheet over myself. I'm thrumming with pleasure like an elastic band that's wound too tight and is just about to snap.

Let me snap, please, please, please…

Now *I'm* begging.

Come back here tongue.

"Kit's dick is happy enough," I mutter, eying him. He's wearing matching pajamas to the nightdress that he bought me. He said that then I could imagine that I was sleeping with *triplets*. "It's waving to me through your pajamas."

Kit blushes and holds his hands over his dick that's tenting his pants.

Yet Ra merely peers over his shoulder at Kit. "Do we need to start putting locks on the doors? Don't Interrupt, Fucking in Progress Signs?"

Kit's ears press to his head, but he storms further into the room. "Kit's sorry. Kit broke the rules. Is Kit in trouble?"

I stand up, pulling Kit into an embrace. His long hair covers his face like a white waterfall. He's truly agitated; his breath is ragged.

"What rule did you break?" I ask.

I haven't given Kit rules. Hestia did, however, and Kit finds it hard to free himself from the past when he's frightened or anxious.

"Kit is a good guard and even bound Loki in ropes. Tight. But then Kit disobeyed." Kit rubs his cheek against mine. "Loki loved Kit's tale about the nine-tails. He asked to see more photos."

Ra groans. "And you left the room to go and get them, I suppose? Is Loki gone?"

Loki must be the first person who's ever asked to

145

see *more* of Kit's photos. I don't blame Kit for becoming excited.

Kit cringes, pressing his fingers together. "Worse."

"How can it be worse?" I regret my harsh tone, when Kit's tails droop between his legs. "He can't escape the tree. It's not a problem."

"But there was a pretty woman in the bed all tied up. Tight."

What...?

Ra smirks. "Why, Kit, you kinky little fox." I don't think that I've ever seen Kit such a deep shade of red before. "Don't bring your sex games in here; we have our own going on."

Ra waggles his eyebrows.

Kit breaks away from me with a growl, before stomping to the archway. Ra and I exchange a glance.

So much for my relaxing evening with Ra.

"Kit show you..." Kit curls his hand around a delicate arm and pulls a woman into the bedroom.

Silence.

Ra is as stunned as me. He strides to stand beside me.

The woman's wrists are indeed bound with magical ropes (I recognize them from our Box of Tricks and a fun session with Ra). She's stunning with silky brunette hair to her bottom, emerald eyes, and soft curves that even to me, look delicious. She's wearing a fire-red dress that's slit up to her waist, and her legs are flashes of pale perfection.

The woman ducks her head and looks at us from underneath her long eyelashes; she even flutters them at me with an innocent pout. "Please, let me go. I don't know how I got here. This crazy fox got frisky and—"

"Hey," Kit let's go of the woman's arm like it's burned him, "a nine-tail never touches anyone without consent, and Kit adores...worships...loves...only my Infernal." He looks at me desperately. "Please, don't..."

When the woman gives a sharp grin that's *so* Loki, I have to hide my own grin on Ra's shoulder.

"I believe you," I reassure Kit, before turning my most earnest expression on the woman (there's no doubt that it's Loki in shifter disguise). "Sorry about the mix up. Off you go then." The woman spins on her heel with her pretty little nose in the air. She even gives a victorious wiggle of her slinky ass (and I groan internally that my lovers are right: I *do* notice Loki's ass). I cross my arms, before calling out, "Oh, *Loki*..."

The woman stumbles.

Kit gasps in outrage. "*Bad* god to trick Kit! To think that I even called you *pretty*..."

I roll my eyes. "Bring him to the bed. I guess we'll do a sleepover tonight."

Ra nods.

Loki looks around wildly with a snarl that doesn't quite come off on the pink bow of his lips; it's more sultry than scary.

Before Loki can run, I thicken the crimson chains around him, and he sighs in defeat. It doesn't matter if he shapeshifts (I didn't know that he could change gender, but in female form, his Soul shines through so powerfully that it's simply like looking at Loki, as if his form is such a small part of who he is), when I concentrate, I can sense the hex still there.

The ropes are just for show. We don't need them.

Loki allows himself to be slung onto the bed. I pretend not to notice the way that his breasts bounce.

Kit points to Loki dramatically. "Bad, bad god."

Loki bares his teeth. "But I'm good at it."

"Did you think that the hex would be tricked just because you no longer have a dick?" I ask.

Loki smirks. "By the Norns, it was worth a try, and I'm seriously more special in this form than that. Want to find out?"

"Let's go. Huge group orgy. Right now." When I put my hands on my hips, Loki pales. *Never try to outbluff a bluffer.* "Wait, there's something I'm forgetting... Oh yeah, pussy or dick, you're still my eternal foe."

Loki manages to dredge up an off-kilter smirk (*bluff*). "Disappointing. And the kids don't say *foe* anymore. I'm more like your *eternal asshole*." We both grimace. Now there's an image that I won't be getting rid of anytime soon. "On second thoughts, stick with foe."

I drag the hated kitsune nightdress on (although my dislike at it is lessened by Kit's happy squeak of *twinsies*), and drag the blankets onto Loki and myself. Kit pointedly scrambles onto the bed on one side of Loki, and Ra takes the other side.

We lie together in awkward silence.

"You're not big on personal space then?" Loki raises his hands. "I'm at least getting out of bondage tonight, right?"

"*No*," my lovers and I chorus together.

When Ra sulkily glances at me, I know that he's thinking about what he's missing between my thighs (which is one of his favorite places). After all, he begged for a certain treat that he's being denied.

Ra scowls. "Now I hate Loki."

I share a secret smile with him. "I hate him too."

Loki squirms, trying to wrench his hair away, which is trapped underneath Kit. It serves him right for stubbornly not turning back into his male form.

To be fair, when he plays a trick, he *commits*.

"What is this?" Loki demands. "The Hate Loki Fan Club?"

"Kit is the President." Kit rolls away, until his back is facing Loki.

Loki will have some making up to do to Kit. You hurt the feelings of a kitsune at your peril.

When Ra nudges me with his shoulder, I know what he wants. Except, why is it so hard to tell Loki that he can't escape not because he's a prisoner but because he's a Guardian? Oh, and a servant. But I'll lead with the Guardian part because he already knows about being a servant. I just can't see him serving as my butler.

Being a Guardian is an honor that only a handful of people throughout time have been awarded.

I peer at Loki. I think I could tell it was him, even if he turned himself into a snail. It'd be haughty with a red shell and wave its antennae around.

"Look, we don't have time to guard a prisoner," I point out. "The Eternal Forest is too dangerous and we already have too many enemies."

I reach over Ra and gently undo the rope, which binds Loki.

Loki rubs his wrists and watches me warily. "Then don't. Huh, how could we solve this? I know, I'll take my pretty ass far, far, away."

He tries to struggle up, but Kit *thwapps* his tails across Loki, pinning him down, without even looking around.

"You're a servant, anyway," I say. "Not a prisoner."

"Lucky me." Loki's lips pinch. "I've always

dreamed of being the hot servant who's seduced by the dastardly duchess."

"Since you're a woman now, wouldn't that be the dastardly *duke*?"

Loki's eyes flash. "Bite me."

I clench my jaw. "Not one of my kinks."

Ra smirks. "Liar."

I nudge him with my shoulder. "Traitor."

Ra raises his eyebrow and mouths. "*Stop stalling.*"

I sigh, studying the uncomfortable way that we're lying together like a demon's wedding night. *And they're notoriously difficult.*

"I took a risk when I asked you to carve your name into the tree," I say. Loki coolly meets my gaze. It's Kit who stiffens. When I finally asked Kit to become a Guardian, it was the most significant night of his life — he finally felt worthy, valued, and *accepted.* I'll have some making up to do to my kitsune as well. "Because it means that you're now a Guardian of the Tree of the Life."

The anger slides from Loki's expression. "What does that mean?"

"That you're a protector," Ra replies. "Of the tree, forest, and Autumn. We're family and we look out for each other."

Loki hisses in a breath, and his gaze becomes open, although clouded with confusion. "You'd trust me with that? Honor me? You know that I'll always try to escape, so... Why?"

I pick at a thread in the blanket, unwinding it. "*Responsibilities.* I didn't understand what you meant when you said it at the Bacchanalia, but I want to now."

That one word has nagged at my mind for centuries. I've lived my life by it without even realizing.

Loki's breath hitches, and Kit cautiously glances over his shoulder at him. "On the World Tree, don't say that if you don't mean it."

"I do," I promise — *let him believe me* — Yet why does it matter so much that he trusts me? "Look, you have as much connection to chaos as me, more now. You'll have to earn TOF's trust, but I could sense your love for her. And it's the only way to lighten the hex." I drag out the thread, snapping it between my fingers, testing it. *Will it break?* "You can choose. If you're really into the hot servant fantasy, then fine, we'll go with that or you can willingly become a Guardian alongside the rest of us as an equal."

"I thought you said that I already was a Guardian," Loki mutters.

"In theory, smartass." I narrow my eyes. "But a Guardian has to be willing to become fully-fledged."

"Choosing between two bad choices is no choice at all."

"Are they both bad though?"

Why is my heart beating so hard in my ribcage? Why is my throat so dry that I can barely speak?

All of a sudden, I'm *desperate* that he chooses me...I mean, to become a Guardian, of course.

Loki smooths down his dress and closes his eyes like he's going to fall asleep without giving me his answer.

Hecate above, not a chance.

I nod at Ra, who nods back in our usual silent agreement.

Ra tickles the tip of his wing across Loki's nose, and Loki splutters, opening his eyes.

"Okay, okay, if you're not going to let a lady sleep, then I agree..." Like the dick that he is (even without one), Loki lets me wait a dramatic pause of at least ten seconds before he adds, "...to become a Guardian."

Joy thrums through me. I can feel the connection to the tree, forest, and realms winding out like an Infinity of possibilities. This was what I'd sensed in the Moderation Room. Perhaps, it's what I'd known back at Bacchanalia; magic has a way of recognizing its own. Loki squirms around in the bed, burrowing under the covers.

"Good choice," I say.

"Hey, happy times all around," Loki replies. "But

honestly, I've had a busy day of being kidnapped. I need my beauty sleep."

When I close my eyes, I can't help my own triumphant smile. "Tomorrow, you'll understand the difference between being my enemy and becoming a Guardian. You'll learn our secrets."

CHAPTER EIGHT

Petal's Garden

L oki kneels in the shadow of the Tree of Life, as if all the secrets of existence wind through the leaves that fall around him like tears, and he alone can catch and care for them.

Yet TOF has never shed her leaves for me. *What does it mean?*

The garden and ash tree are warded and invisible, unless you're a Guardian or Bacchant. The tree shimmers with ancient magic, twisting. TOF is giant; it's impossible to see her top branches, which disappear up into the clouds.

Loki's wearing a soft red t-shirt and black pants, and it's like he's shed something precious and secret

155

along with his suit. He could always have been here with me: a shadow life lived alongside mine.

Informal, he's disturbingly comfortable amongst nature. Just like I am.

I cross my arms and watch as Loki prostrates himself in silence with his forehead to the cold earth. His long fingers press to the base of the trunk with a gentle caress. He worships TOF, quietly and respectfully.

Beautifully.

When he whispers a blessing, I'm certain that I don't imagine the way that the wind rises both to mask the words and in whispered response. Perhaps, Loki's making his peace with TOF.

I hope so. I don't fancy freezing in dank darkness from now on.

Loki presses a small pile of nuts, which he collected like a busy squirrel (and I fought not to compare him to Ratatoskr and start Kit off on another rant about the comparative merits of their tails), as soon as we strolled out into the garden, to the base of TOF.

It's an offering. Simple and pure. My breath catches because there's no beat of drums, wild bonfires, blood sticky on my feet, or eyes swirling to amber. Nuts, rather than blood.

Would this ever have been enough for Bacchus? *Why does Bacchus demand so much from me?* Even for eternal pleasure, is it fair to demand my mind, body, and Soul?

I trace my finger over the band at my wrist. I don't need to snap it: *I don't.*

I settle on a wool blanket, which Ra laid out for me earlier on the grass in the shade next to his herb garden, which he's tending. I scrunch my nose at the warm, rich scents of the herbs — basil for money, saffron for success, nutmeg for luck — that Ra uses in his potions for the Bacchants. He should open his own magical shop. He's Ecstasy's Master Brewer.

"You don't have to do this," I told Ra, when Ecstasy put in her first order.

Ra held his hands together behind his back in a way so unlike his usual slouch that I was on sudden high alert. "One of the first lessons that I ever learned was to be more useful to someone than they are to you."

Ra never forgets that for a moment.

Ra's stripped to his light linen trousers, as he works with intent concentration. His skin gleams in the heat. A dome of light bathes our corner of the garden with warmth.

Ra can literally make the sun shine.

I glance at the darkness of the forests that surrounds our circle of light and shiver. Somewhere, out there in the trees, the Shadow Demons stir.

On the edge of the garden, where the trees have

encroached, are stone ruins. Vines and ivy have pulled down the roof and smothered the walls. The Guardian, who lived here before me and protected the forest, wasn't allowed inside TOF. *How lonely was she?* Before me, there was only one Guardian at a time. When I was first brought here by Bacchus, I was terrified that I'd be a hermit.

I'm not hermit material.

Yet somehow TOF understood that. A tree can be your friend, just as a forest can be so special that even the thought of something happening to it fills me with dread.

I'd die to save it, and it can't fail because it holds the true magic of the world.

I stare at the picnic breakfast that Ra made: scones, jam, cream, and strawberries. My favorite treat. Then I take a sip of coffee, which is my special blend.

Bliss.

Ra glances up at me, before wiping his arm across his forehead. "Eat up, you. It took me quite literally...*minutes*...to slice those strawberries." I laugh. "Tefnut's tit, we need to celebrate our new Guardian."

Ra glances thoughtfully at Loki, who straightens with a final stroke of his thumb across the base of the tree.

What else can Loki do with those skilled hands?

I cross my legs and pull Kit closer to my side, who's lazing in the sun. He's even undone the top button of his waistcoat. Let's not go witching crazy, he hasn't unbuttoned *two*. He's a well-dressed fox-spirit, after all. But his feet are bare; I love it when he frees himself like that. His sweet scent of apple blossoms winds around me.

Kit's ears twitch, and he opens his mouth. I roll my eyes but obediently place a slice of strawberry between his lips. It's worth it for the indecent moan of delight.

Food equals love for Kit. Hestia denied food to him to establish her dominance. I'll never do that.

This morning, I woke up in a delightful tangle of gods and spirits. Loki had transformed back into male form during the night but was still wearing a dress. I guess sleeping transformations aren't reliable.

Hex him for still making the dress look good.

Kit had turned to face him again as he slept, changing back into his fox form. He'd settled on Loki's chest, with his tails wound around his waist. I held back the snicker. He'd need to spray on Loki to declaim any louder that he was *his*.

In bed, Kit's a heat hogger and a snuggler. It doesn't matter how much he tries to resist it. He was held for too many years chained, cold, and alone. The surprise was how comfortable Loki looked sharing a bed.

I frowned. Wow, his reputation as a Don Juan must be true then.

Witching heavens, when did I become so possessive?

Except, didn't Loki say that he once looked after a wolf cub? I battled to hide my smile at the thought of Kit as Loki's cub.

I'm never telling either of them that. I value my ass.

Could I just take a photo though for prosperity?

When Loki finally stands from his vigil beneath the tree and wanders over to my picnic, he looks the most relaxed that I've ever seen him. At least, he looks less like he's imagining burning me to ash with his flaming emerald magic, while working out an escape route. So, that's an improvement.

Perhaps, he'll enjoy yoga...?

When Loki sits down cross-legged next to me, I rest my hand on his shoulder. He tenses but allows it.

Kit perks up, opening his mouth like he did for me.

He's optimistic.

"Feed me," Kit commands.

Loki snatches up a slice of strawberry and in what I'm sure is nothing but an act of playful mischief, slips it between my surprised lips, instead.

I don't moan. *Don't.*

"I'm not your servant," Loki replies.

Kit leaps to his feet. His eyes narrow.

Uh-oh...

"Shame," Kit purrs.

Loki leans back on his hands and looks at Kit with studied indifference, as Kit stalks around me, before sprawling in the warm grass next to Loki (who deliberately doesn't move to allow him onto the blanket).

Kit's move...

Ra pauses in his weeding of the herb garden to watch. His lips quirk in amusement.

I place down my coffee mug. Kit's playing with fire.

Kit...*carefully*...lifts one foot and rests it on Loki's lap. He waits like he expects it to be shoved off. Loki stares up at the sky, as if the light of the dome is fascinating and he has no idea what game Kit is playing.

He knows so much more than the rest of us. The knowledge of that is both thrilling and terrifying.

Kit...*carefully*...lifts his second foot onto Loki's lap.

Silence.

Loki still doesn't push Kit away.

Kit's feet are pale and delicate; they're an offering of their own. My fingers clutch the edge of the blanket.

Don't reject him...

Finally, Loki squeezes Kit's ankle in reassurance. "Am I forgiven for last night?"

"Is there grovelling involved?" Kit asks, suspiciously.

Loki hums. "Huh, there I was thinking a *wise* kistune like yourself would approve of a trickster like me. Where's the applause?"

Bubbling cauldrons, he's already picked up on the praise kink.

Kit holds his finger and thumb close together. "Tiny, *tiny* trickster applause."

Loki runs his finger through the open pot of jam (now in England, such desecration of the scone ceremony *is* the definition of chaos), and then sucks it off with way too much relish. "Sorry, do you want some?"

He dips his finger into the jam again and holds it out to me like a dare.

What in the witching heavens...?

"I'm not a pet," I hiss.

Loki's smile is wicked. "Hey, my mistake. I thought that you guys liked to be fed." When he dabs it against my lips, I gasp in outrage. "Seriously, you're kind of a messy eater. Do you want me to help you with that?"

Is it a bluff?

When Ra swoops towards me, he's a blur or feathers and possessive god. "She already has *me* on licking duty." His tongue is like velvet; my skin tingles at each swipe. Ra sits back on his heels but he keeps his wings caged around me. His sky-blue eyes are stormy, as he turns to Loki. "I'll miss you when you're gone."

Loki blinks. "I'm not going anywhere."

Ra's smile is long and slow and so, *so* dangerous. "Really?"

He draws out the word like a threat.

Loki blanches, fiddling with the hem of his t-shirt. He snatches up my coffee mug, as if it's the perfect distraction from the Alpha showdown.

I squawk in outrage because *no one* steals my morning caffeine shot.

"**BEST GUARDIAN MUG**?" Loki reads from the side of my *favorite* mug. "Who bought you this? Which one of these…" He uses my mug, sloshing the coffee goodness, to gesture at Kit and then Ra. "…was trying to earn a blow job?"

I hold onto Ra's hand to stop his snarling attack, but I can't stop the way that Kit's delicate foot grinds down on Loki's crotch.

Loki winces, but masks it, pretending to be engrossed in buttering a scone.

I wait until he's taken the first bite of his treat to reply.

"Firstly," I say, "my lovers don't need to earn BJs. I love sucking their cocks."

Loki chokes on the scone. Kit gives up his Heel Attack, and instead, rushes to pat Loki on the back. Kit won't admit it but he's attached to the new trickster god.

Ra chuckles, licking the final remnants of jam from around my lips, before sprawling with his head on my lap. I stroke his soft hair, and he kisses my thigh.

"Secondly," I continue, "*I* made the mug myself. Aren't you big on self-empowerment?"

Loki's lips twist like he's attempting to hide his smile. "Astounding: such confidence. Can you make one for me that reads **BEST GOD OF MISCHIEF**? Or how about simply **BEST LOKI**?"

"**BEST WANKER**," Kit mutters.

To my surprise, Loki laughs.

He strokes Kit's foot lightly all the way to the toes. "You expect me to disagree?"

"I expect you to play nice," I say. "Remember that discussion we had about the choice between *servant* and *Guardian*?"

Loki's gaze slides away from mine, and he nods.

All of a sudden, at the edge of the blanket, a single magical pink rose grows in front of me. When it blossoms, I smile.

My best friend who lives in the garden, Petal, was never going to be able to keep out of Loki's celebration breakfast. He thrives on drama.

The petals of the rose peel back, revealing a tiny but perfect man with a peak of shimmering rose pink hair and matching eyes. His skin is as soft as petals, and he wears tight pink leather trousers.

He smiles at me like I'm the sun.

There was a time, a couple of centuries ago, when I was pining for… I didn't know what. *Friendship?* I had the Bacchants, but they visited and then left again. They didn't understand my love for the forest or what it felt like to be trapped here.

Was it more than that? I can't think… *I won't*…

When I rebirthed Bacchus, I gave him my own life through my magic. I also gave him my own ability to *birth* life.

The forest is haunted by Shadow Demons. I'm immortal but just like a god that doesn't mean I can't die. How can I raise a child here?

So, why do I feel the hollowness of the loss inside me, the same as the loss of my magic?

TOF gave me a seed with instructions to plant it in our garden and water. I never expected a perfect tiny man to step out of the rose.

Petal: *my brave pixie Guardian.*

I love Petal as much as Ra, Oni, or Kit, just in a different way.

Loki's eyes widen. "How unexpected. You appear to have a pixie infestation."

Loki pushes Kit's feet off his lap and dives to slam his fist down on the rose...*and Petal.*

"*Don't,*" I holler, as my pulse thrashes in my ears.

I'll never forgive myself if something happens to Petal because I trusted Loki. Why do I keep forgetting that Loki's as volatile as me?

Petal squeals in outrage, however, and unfurls his glittering butterfly wings that speed him into the air with a spray of magic, so quickly that it makes Loki look as slow as a giant.

Of course, to Petal, we're all giants.

I yank on the crimson chain in warning. I don't want to use the hex but I will to protect Petal.

I hold out my hand, and Petal settles on my palm. "Loki, meet Petal."

Loki sits back on his heels. "Huh, I'm getting the vibe that he's less an infestation and more of a friend."

"*Beautiful best friend.*" Petal's voice winds into all our minds telepathically with a soft Welsh lilt. He's too small to be heard, and it devastated him (when he was first grown from the rose), that he was invisible because we couldn't hear him. Then he used his magic to communicate with telepathy. He's not invisible anymore. Kit and Ra edge closer like bodyguards. They love Petal as much as me and are equally as protective. When Petal turns to me, he presses his little hand to his chest like he's struggling to breathe. "*Loki, your enemy, in my garden? Are you tragically insane — all of you — godly, foxly, witchly insane — I'm alone in my sanity."* He pales. *"He's here to assassinate us. This is it, see. Flowers, I knew we were living on borrowed time. Mother Earth protect us, we're all going to die — agonizingly — slowly. Why? We're too pretty to be taken so young. I haven't even been kissed."*

I roll my eyes. "Deep breaths."

Petal nods, wrapping his arms around himself.

Loki peers at Petal with intense curiosity. "Is he a seer?"

Ra makes himself more comfortable on my lap. "No, just a drama queen."

Loki tilts his head, and his curls fall into his eyes. "And why can I hear him in my head?"

"Because my voice is perfect but also perfectly quiet," Petal replies, snootily. He flies up to kiss me on the cheek, before settling on my shoulder. *"Why the Loki infestation?"*

Loki's lips quirk. "Touché, pixie in leather pants."

Petal wiggles his ass in a disturbingly good lap dance on my hand, as if Beyonce's "Naughty Girl" is playing in his head, which only he can hear. *"Don't put me down just because you can't pull off this look."*

Loki smirks, pushing himself to his feet. "Who says that I don't look good in leather?"

He isn't going to...?

Loki transforms his pants into matching pink leather.

He does look good in them. *Hex him.*

Ra sits up like he's been pulled on puppet strings; it appears that his dick has the same problem.

Petal studies Loki haughtily (how does Loki know how to win over all the Guardians or else *manipulate them*?). Is he simply playing a long game?

"That's a lovely sight," Petal concedes. *"You can be my Official Wingman."*

Loki's brow furrows. "Wingman?"

Petal nudges my ear, sulkily. *"When's my marriage? It's like this, see, Autumn hasn't found me a lover, so I'm getting proactive. You're Wingman Number Two. Kit's my Number One for Life."*

Ra frowns. "What about me, aren't I your Number One?"

Petal waves his hand dismissively. *"Not a chance. You spend all your time bent over your work with your fingers in your potions or bent over Autumn with your fingers—"*

"Don't finish that sentence," I hiss.

Petal smiles sweetly. *"How am I ever going to find a wife for my gorgeous self if you're so busy all the time?"*

I flush with guilt. Yet who would I find for him? He was made by magic, and there are no pixies within the forest.

It's said that pixies were wiped out by the purge centuries ago. Petal doesn't know that. By the way that Loki's sad gaze meets mine, *he* does.

Don't hurt Petal. Don't tell him...

I hold my breath.

"Have you tried a toad?" Loki asks with a serious expression, even as he winks at me. "Or what about a mole, *Thumbelina?*"

Petal flies to snuggle on Kit's tail; it's where he hides like it's a bed, when he's upset and attempting to pretend that he isn't.

I narrow my eyes at Loki.

"Bad god — insane — impending deaths — end of world," Petal mutters. *"Just because I'm small and perfect doesn't mean that I don't feel."*

Loki catches my gaze. "I believe...end of world aside...that I was promised secrets about the Yggdrasil."

Ra raises his eyebrow. "Intrigued, silver-tongue?"

"Possibly."

I glance at Petal, who's no more than a flash of pink amid the gold of Kit's tail. "The Tree of Life is immortality. As it grows, it creates seeds that carry its essence out into the forest. The tree lives on endlessly through the saplings that grow up."

Loki stares out into the darkness around the garden. "This entire forest grew up from Yggdrasil like her kids, right? They're all connected. No wonder you love the Eternal Forest. Is that why it's connected to the different realms, and the veils are so thin here?"

I nod. "The Immortal Realms, Other World, and the underworlds. There are gateways to almost every land. It's connected in this one point, and where it meets is dangerous."

Loki's face is tight with concentration like he's *tasting* that danger with his magic; he sparks with it — alive and glowing.

He needs the risk. *He thrives on it.*

"To us Norse gods, Yggdrasil is also called Odin's Horse because he hung himself from it to gain knowledge, riding it like a horse." Loki scores the back of his hands with his nails almost like he doesn't know that he's doing it. "What can I say? We have a dark sense of humor. It's how Odin learned the secrets of the runes." Loki's shoulders hunch, and his glow fades. He suddenly looks smaller and younger. "Odin used me the same as he used Yggdrasil," he spits, bitterly. "He *rode* me into battle, as if I was little more than a slave."

Ra leaps up and cocoons Loki in his wings like the action of comforting him is as obvious and simple as breathing. After all, Ra knows what it's like to be possessed in such a way.

Loki as a war horse must've been deadly. Yet who freed Loki or did he free himself?

Loki startles and gently pulls back from Ra. When

his emerald gaze meets mine again, my breath is taken away by its sharpness.

"Who's riding Yggdrasil now?" He asks like each word is a dagger. "Honestly, I guess that it's Bacchus, since he has you installed here. And I want to know because I've learned through hard experience that whoever rides Yggdrasil, *rides me.*"

Sweet Hecate, how can he slice me to ribbons with such *truth*?

It would be cowardly to avoid his gaze. And I'm no coward.

"Bacchus uses TOF's fruits to feed the Bacchants and keep the spark of their immortality," I admit.

As if she was only waiting for my cue, TOF drops apples, pears, and plums, down on us like confetti. I yelp as an apple bounces off my shoulder. A pear strikes Loki's shoulder like a knobbly missile.

I did warn him about TOF's sense of humor.

Kit smiles in sly delight, however, snatching up a plum, as if someone's going to steal it from him, before offering it to Petal who bites from its juicy softness. Kit devours the rest with an orgasmic sigh. I don't blame him; TOF's fruit is literally food for the gods.

"And feed the Guardians too?" Loki asks with studied blankness.

I nod.

An unexpected burst of chaos magic explodes

from Loki. I scramble off the blanket in shock, as Kit shields Petal. Loki's eyes flash with rage. His magic winds from him like the branches of Fate that've become broken, corrupted, and *chaotic*.

The garden darkens. Ra twirls, fighting to bring back the sun. I gasp, clutching at my chest, but the air has been sucked from beneath the tree.

Come on, lungs, you've had enough years to learn how to do this. Inflate, deflate, inflate, deflate...

My vision grays, and white spots dance in front of my eyes.

I desperately attempt to yank on the hex that ties us. Why can't I? Am I already so weakened?

Witches above, how powerful is Loki?

I miss the warm feel of my Infernal Scythe.

"Sacrilege," Loki growls. I can hear every year that he's lived in the single furious word. "It's obscene. I've done many taboo things in my time but I'd never cross that line. Bacchus, your Golden God," *such a sneer, such venom*, "uses the blood of others to live, their bodies as vessels and pleasure. But now, he even takes the fruit—"

"You've said enough." Ra's knees buckle, but his eyes flash with an answering fire to Loki's.

"Have I?" Yet Loki appears to notice the darkness around us for the first time, as if awakening from sleep.

He shakes his head, balling his fist. Slowly, his

chaos magic retreats, the garden lightens back to sunny morning, a crow *caws* above our heads, and I can breathe.

Thank Hecate.

"Do lies protect your lover?" Loki says, more quietly.

"*See! Alone in my sanity!*" Petal drags himself to his feet, waving his arms to make sure that we don't ignore him. Is he reckless enough to fight Loki, even though he's the height of the grass? "*You're an idiot, Wingman. My lungs are perfect but tiny. Mother earth, didn't I say that he was here to assassinate us all?*"

Loki's gaze darts to Petal. "Sorry about the whole…"

He wets his lips, as if unsure himself how to explain it.

"Kit will make you sorry, when fangs go *snap snap* on your dick," Kit mutters.

Loki crosses his arms. "We've already talked about this, fox-spirit, don't feel bad about your lack of experience. I'm up for practicing, and then you'll get better at keeping your teeth to yourself."

Kit growls in outrage, and I only hold him back from launching himself at Loki, by winding my fingers through his long hair.

Loki's expression hardens. "Bacchus made a deal with the gods and demons, huh?"

I startle. "How'd you…?"

Emerald magic skitters across Loki's skin and then down the gossamer thin chain that binds us. I yip as it prickles me.

How connected are we?

"What deal?" He demands.

"In return for the trees' fruits and placing me here as Guardian, I was to become the Infernal," I reply. Why's it so difficult to tell him? Don't gods and demons always make deals? It's kind of their *thing*. "The Infernal Scythe is carved out of the tree's ash. In return, I reap for both sides. They give me the targets."

Loki stares at me for a long moment. "I think that's what the kids today call an *assassin*." I bristle. "I take it that there are consequences if you fail to reap."

I glare at him. "I don't fail."

"Indulge me."

"This mission today," I reply (*hideous howling, deformed faces*), "was for two demons. I have three days to complete it. This is day number two. If I don't, then my lover…ex-lover…I mean…"

"Are you making up your mind in the next millennium? You do have two days left."

"*Ex*-lover," I snap, "will have his horns broken off if I fail. I won't let his horns be taken like that."

I expect all my lovers to wince in sympathy but I'm surprised that Loki does as well.

Loki's eyes widen; he looks dazed.

"You're not free," he breathes. "You're a prisoner...servant...call me a Valkyrie's bitch, I don't care, you Guardians *and* TOF are the same as me."

I feel like he's slapped me. All the blood rushes to my cheeks.

He's wrong. He has to be wrong. *Then why does it feel like truth?*

"T-that's not... This is my h-home," I insist. Ra kneels next to me, wrapping me in his wings, but I'm still cold. "Being a Guardian is an honor."

"Where have I heard that before?" Loki taps his chin. "That's right: just like you told me that being a vessel for Bacchus was an honor. How did that work out?"

"Everyone serves someone." Ra traces his finger over his collar.

Loki's eyes are large and troubled. "Lie."

When he wanders towards the forest, I stiffen as he approaches the shadows.

Kit prowls to his feet. "You don't even know rules. Bet bad god was a naughty kid." He points imperiously at the trunk of the tree. "Stand in the corner."

This could go one of two ways: Loki or Kit in the corner (win-win on so many levels).

I don't expect Loki's hollow laugh. "You reckon that I could ever have been a *good* kid?" He ducks his head. "My sons are good. Once, we argued, and they told me that they hated me. I didn't blame them because I dragged them around in dirty tents without any friends or education. But they never went without food. There was often not enough. But they ate first. If I went hungry…?"

He shrugs like his starvation matters less than your demon ex eating your last piece of chocolate every single time he visits (true story).

Kit gasps, snatching up a slice of strawberry and darting to Loki. He presses it into Loki's mouth like he can erase the memory of his growling stomach.

Like a promise.

When Loki chews on the strawberry, his cheeks are flushed. "My sons were always frightened and on red alert. I knew that they didn't truly mean that they hated me but I didn't need them to say sorry. Because the moment that they said it, I forgave them. I didn't get it — unconditional love — until I had kids." His gaze scans me and then Petal, before lowering to the ground again. "I didn't love anyone, and with my mom, there'd always been all these conditions: *if* I was good, *if* I didn't shame her, *if* I followed her *rules*… I don't follow rules, right? So, I knew she'd never love me." His hand clenches. "There are no *ifs* with my sons. That's family. You don't simply stop loving." His lips quirk. "And no rules because I'm the god of mischief."

You don't simply stop loving…

I smile, as I catch Ra's gaze. I've tried to convince him of that: there's no *if's* attached to my love. I'm not like Mut. My love's eternal.

Yet I don't have a child, and the empty ache inside tells me that it's Loki's fault. Is that fair?

Now he's spoken about fatherhood with such passion and joy, however, I'm intrigued. I hope that his sons are safe in Rebel Academy. Did my parents love me as much?

I hope so.

Weirdly, I have a sense that Loki's a good dad, even if he's too busy right now pretending that he's *bad.* And that's high on the List of Sentences that I thought would only be forced out of me under pain of a Forever Pinching Bra Hex (which is one hex that I never want to experience again).

All of a sudden, a shadow detaches itself from the forest, sleek and agile. It moves towards Loki and Kit, who are standing too close to the boundary.

What is it?

I squint against the light but I can't see, and it's too late. If it's a Shadow Demon, I won't be able to save Loki and Kit in time.

They'll be torn apart.

CHAPTER NINE

Petal's Garden

My mouth is dry. I can't swallow. *Speak.*

I don't want anyone else to die.

Hecate above, don't die.

Ra snatches my elbows and pulls me up. I raise my hand, shading my eyes against the sun.

The shadow makes for Kit, but just as fast, Loki streaks to intercept it.

Is he crazy?

Yet now through the watery blur, I can finally make out that it isn't a Shadow Demon invading the calmness of Petal's garden. And it'll be Loki who'll be doing the tearing apart.

My horrified gaze meets Ra's determined one, as

his wings beat. But then, Loki's magic sweeps out in a wash of protective emerald, pushing us back.

Loki's protecting me, my lovers, and TOF…? Does he even realize that he's acting like a Guardian?

Loki knocks the forest creature onto his back, straddling him. He pins him down with his arm across his throat. The creature is like the beauty and wildness of the forest in one struggling bundle. Soft horse ears, along with nubby horns, poke out of his thick black curls that tumble all the way to the ground. They're so black that they gleam as if wet. A matching horse tail sweeps the ground. His narrowed silver eyes are pale like moonlight.

My beautiful forest creature.

He's only wearing green trousers that look woven out of moss with a silver flute tucked into the waistband like a sword. Yet I can't blame Loki because the creature does look wild and he *did* come running out of the Eternal Forest.

"Who are you, assassin?" Loki hisses like he's a second away from gutting him.

Kit falls back dramatically on the grass, hiding his face with his tails. "Save poor kitsune."

Kit never misses the chance for mischief. Perhaps, that's why Loki and Kit clash? It's the same as two Alphas fighting to the death for dominance. If you get two tricksters together, prankster sparks will fly.

"Get on with you, my singing's bad, but it's never

been accused of killing anyone before," Loki's captive gasps in a gentle Irish accent.

"Or are you a spy?" Loki says thoughtfully, pressing his arm harder. "Speak."

"Lay off! I could if you eased up on the choking," Loki's captive splutters. "Did I miss the whole negotiation stage because I know that's one of my limits."

"Let go," I holler, "he's..." *so much to choose from*, "...a Guardian."

Instantly, Loki pulls his arm away from his captive's neck like he's been burned but he doesn't get off him.

Perhaps, he's comfortable. *I* find that particular Guardian deliciously comfy to ride.

"Bard at your service." Bard holds out his hand to Loki like he isn't sprawled underneath him still.

Bard's always been quick to forgive: *too quick.*

Loki ducks his head. "How many of you asshole Guardians are there?"

Bard pats Loki's chest. "Why, you sweet flatterer, you." He flutters his far too long to be fair eyelashes.

"*Uh-huh.*" Loki assesses him. "You're the dangerous one, right?"

He's talking about my Bard...?

To my surprise, however, Bard's silver eyes flash in a way that thrills with danger. "Do I look dangerous?"

"Very."

"Well then."

I sigh. "Is this protective thing going to become a habit?"

Loki smirks. "Possibly."

Finally, Kit uncovers his face and rolls onto his stomach. "Are we having a moment because Kit finds this..." He points his claw at Bard and then Loki. "...hot."

I don't expect the way that Loki blushes. I'm not surprised at all by Bard's cheeky wink at Kit.

Ra hooks his arm around my waist and rests his chin on my head. "Objectively, they are hot together."

Loki huffs. "Omens and runes, I'm at the heart of a cult that worships frenzy and pleasure. What a surprise that you're—"

"Open minded," I suggest.

"Fun," Bard says.

"*Breathtakingly, mind-blowingly, fuckable*," Petal adds.

"Language," I scold without thinking.

Kit snickers.

When his protective magic fades, Ra and I stroll towards Loki.

When Loki leans forward to examine Bard more closely, Bard attempts to turn his head. Loki runs his thumb along Bard's long horse ear, and he presses it to his head in distress.

"What are you?" Loki has the same look that Ra

does, when he's trying to figure out a complicated spell. Except, he's trying to work out Bard like he's nothing but a problem to be solved.

I clench my jaw.

"A brilliant weaver of tales, once you buy me a few drinks," Bard says hopefully, before grimacing in pain, "and being squished right now by your godly arse. *Ow, ow ow*, my tail…"

Loki swings himself off Bard, who flashes him a grateful smile, as he sits up and runs his own fingers through his tail soothingly.

"Are you a Halfing familiar?" Loki asks like he's still trying to figure him out. He's not looking away from Bard's tail though. Do horse shifters have a *tail kink* or *tail envy*? I don't blame him: Bard's tail is gorgeous. I bite my lip. *Please don't let Loki find out about the hours I spend braiding it.* "Or did your shift go wrong? Transformations are tricky when you're running." Loki pales. "Valhalla! Did I cause an accident when I knocked into you? Did I—"

"Silver-tongue," Ra warns.

But it's too late.

Bard's cheeks are stained with pink. "I'm Bacchus' satyr. Here's the thing of it, the half-horse, half-man thing is kind of my look."

Loki's eyes become as cold as glass. "Of course, I was just thrown by the lack of fur and hooves." He caresses his hand through Bard's hair, but there's

182

nothing loving in the gesture. Bard cringes. "Giants and dwarfs, it's not like Bacchus to tolerate the imperfect. Why's one of his failed satyrs hanging around Autumn?"

"Enough," I snarl, dropping onto my knees next to Bard. "He's mine now."

"Whenever I can be," Bard says, quietly.

I knock Loki's hand away. At the same time, roses burst from the earth like a shield, blocking Loki from touching Bard.

"*Petal power*." Petal whoops.

I pull Bard into the kiss that I wanted ever since I realized that it was him beneath Loki.

Bacchus gave Bard to me as *entertainer and liaison* within the forest. *But he didn't know that we'd fall in love.*

I let the kiss tell Loki everything that I can't in words: Bard's different, not failed.

And he's loved.

Bard smells of the woods and ancient magic and he tastes of sweet wine. I chase the pleasure with my tongue. He draws me onto his lap, encircling my waist with his arms. I stroke my hands through Bard's hair to wipe away the feel of Loki's caress, and Bard moans.

He's always been the most receptive of my lovers. Is it wrong that a small part of me wants Loki to see that?

"*Now that's hot,*" Petal sighs. "*Find me a wife who kisses like that, see, and I'll be a happy pixie.*"

Bard and I laugh at the same time, breaking the kiss.

I rest my cheek against Bard's. "Sweet Hecate, as much as I love your visits, why'd you scare us all running in here like Shadow Demons were after you?"

Bard sobers. "By my horns, they...just a wee bit...not enough to freak out or anything...*were.*"

"What?" I whisper.

How many times have I told Bard that it's too dangerous for him to be alone in the forest? How many times has he laughed like it's a joke?

Bard tightens his arms around me. "It's the fault of this escaped demon She-Soul, the Shadow Traitor. The bad bitch is stirring all sorts of crazy amongst the other spirits and Shadow Demons. It's damaging the forest. My satyr arse only just escaped to reach the Tree of Life's safety. I could kiss the ground, but then, I'd rather kiss you."

I indulge him because...reasons (called *perfect lips*, as well as the fact that he only just survived to return to me *again*).

My fingers dig into his back, as I hold him, but it's Loki who I narrow my eyes at. "Still want to run into the forest?"

Loki looks like a caught rabbit. "I don't... wasn't...*huh?*"

"You walked over to the edge of the garden to plan for the best escape route." *It's not a question.*

Kit *tsks*. "Bad god."

Loki's look is inscrutable. "Possibly."

Bard's eyes are the palest silver and reflect my own troubled gaze back at me.

"Stay with me," I say, "until we've caught the Shadow Traitor."

"Are you inviting me to sleep the night?" Bard asks with a grin.

Yet my heart pounds, and my head is sick with worry.

Where's Oni?

I wish that he was here in the circle of my arms as well, instead of somewhere lost to me in the forest.

I rest my forehead on Bard's and will him to understand. "I'm *begging* you not to go back out into the nightmare of shadows."

Bard kisses my forehead. "Who am I to deny a lady? Yet by my ears, I've been brought up from the cradle in a nightmarish world, and there's no running from shadows because they'll always exist where the light can't reach."

BARD KNOWS THE FORESTS LIKE ONI, BUT UNLIKE Oni, he isn't a fighter. I've always hated Bacchus' rule that Bard isn't allowed to live in the tree with me but must remain a wanderer in the Eternal Forest, gathering information for me.

Loki isn't wrong about him being a spy.

All the satyrs belong to Bacchus. A long time ago, their tribe was defeated by Bacchus, but he kept them because they entertained him with song, dance, and tales.

Now they serve him; I'm relieved that Bacchus gave Bard to me.

I grant him the same freedom as my other Guardians. Except, Loki's making me wonder if none of us are free.

Even as a kid, I was confined inside a walled garden. To be still trapped now as an adult is nothing. My Guardians are my responsibility, however, and I'll do my best by them, as well as all the realms.

I just don't know what the *best* is yet.

After Ra herds the other Guardians inside, and Petal naps in his flowery bed, I spend the morning sprawled on the blanket in the garden with Bard, discussing the problem of the Shadow Traitors, until the sun is high in the sky.

I shiver at Bard's news. The She-Soul has stirred up so much unrest already.

How is it possible? *Such darkness.*

Did she continue her vendetta after death? It's disturbing. Is there nothing but never-ending cycles?

Revenge and hate, endlessly repeated? Am I part of it, woven into Fate?

After all, the Shadow Demons murdered my parents. By fighting back, am I playing a puppet part?

I shudder, and guilt squirms through me.

Mum, dad, I'm sorry. Please, just...I can't wrap myself in hate like Ecstasy does.

I wish that I could remember my parents' faces. Yet they're hazy. To Ecstasy, however, who was a teenager when they died, they're sharp as if she'd seen them yesterday.

She told me once that she dreams of them most nights.

I dream of the forest like I never lived anywhere tamed or so-called *civilized*. I see it through Oni's eyes; I am *Oni*. And when I wake, I wish that I could be with him again.

I once worshiped a god. I gave him all of myself. But then, he abandoned me. Now, my true loyalty lies with my Guardians, the Tree of Life, and the Eternal Forest. I'm dedicated to saving it from the encroaching darkness. The Shadow Demons hurt the spirits, terrorize the other demons, and drive the gods away. They slaughter the students of Rebel Academy who are foolish enough to invade the forest. The Shadow Demons are wraiths who suck away life and wither the trees. Everything dies in their path: flowers, plants, and animals.

My heart bleeds when I discover the stags, rabbits, and crows ripped from life.

I must save the forest from such unnatural death. *Who says that a reaper can't bring life?*

Bard turns to face me, encircling me with his arm. Our noses touch. I thread my fingers through Bard's long tail, and he sighs in delight. His tail is sensitive.

All of a sudden, I remember Ra's **Case of Loki's Ass** and how he reminded me of the game that I played with Kit as the horse.

Witching heavens, perhaps I truly do have a stallion shifter kink. Is that even a thing?

I don't know if I hope that it's actually just a Loki kink because that means I'm attracted to my enemy, and how can that lead anywhere good?

I drop Bard's tail, and he whines.

"So, the bad bastards are massing in the East of the forest," Bard explains. "Oni says—"

My eyes widen. "Oni? When did you see him?"

Bard's nervous breath gusts against my mouth; this close, I can see the way that his eyes crinkle with concern and calculation. "Your big, blue, horned bodyguard has been out searching for the She-Soul since yesterday. He hasn't even slept. Wasn't he following your orders then?"

Crack my cauldron, why do I keep forgetting Oni's obsessive devotion?

I flush, biting my lip.

Bard studies me. "Hello awkward my old friend." He tilts his head, and his ear flops over his face. I rub my cheek against it, and he smiles. "It's like this, see, I *might've* been running for my life, and our Oni *might've* saved my arse."

"He does that."

"Except, he never saves his own arse." Bard's warm fingers play down my spine. "He sent me here to tell you that he'd found the She-Soul and about the Shadow Demons. He has this wee plan…"

"I'm not going to want to hear this, am I?" I growl.

Oni's plans are even more reckless than my own.

"Everyone wants to hear my tales," Bard boasts. "All that'll happen is you bind the spirit of that stunning but scary Sun-bird of yours, bring the Infernal Scythe, and prepare for a hunt. Meanwhile, Oni and I make sure the Shadow Demons stay in the East like the brave warriors we are, so that you know where to find the She-Soul."

Can you die from fear alone?

"You're talking about being bait?"

"You've no poetry in your Soul." Bard smirks. "Bait sounds so—"

"Not a chance in the witching heavens."

Bard's smile is soft, but his silver eyes are sharp. "I wasn't asking for permission but cheers for the laugh."

I kiss him. Tender and chaste.

My eyes burn. "Don't die. Don't you dare. I forbid it."

Bard kisses me back, equally as tenderly. "Well, if you forbid it, then I'd better not die."

I laugh, even if we both know that it's more of a sob.

After lunch, I'll hunt the She-Soul and face the Shadow Demons.

CHAPTER TEN

Tree of Life, Bacchus' Kitchen

I stand alone in the dark alcove outside the kitchen, wiping my wet cheeks with the backs of my hands.

My Guardians don't need to see my pain; they have enough of their own. If the tears are gone, then I can pretend that they never wept from my eyes. I just can't shake my fear.

I grieve every day that I'm separated from Oni. He isn't the only one who feels the ache of our Soul Bond. Plus, I hate that Bard must still obey Bacchus' orders like all his tribe and can't choose his own path.

Is Loki right about Ra's *gilded cage*? Would I add all my lovers to it, simply to know that they're safe?

I wrap my arms around myself. Oni and Bard

swore to protect this forest. I owe them the right to battle for it alongside me.

I clench my jaw. *Nothing has felt the same since Loki arrived.*

It's as if his chaos infects everything around him, spilling out in the same way that my magic used to. I understand now why the other Bacchants feared me. Only, I fear myself now too because despite everything, this change after a thousand uniform years, which Loki has brought about, already thrills me. I desire to reach out magpie-like towards the glittering beauty of Loki's mayhem.

But what if it costs my lovers their lives?

I take a deep breath and steady myself, before I push through the door into the kitchen.

Unexpectedly, I'm hit by a dual wall of scents and sounds that intermingle in a way that's so delicious, I forget both my fear and grief. I sigh at the spicy aroma of garlic and onions.

Ra's an excellent chef, which is a good thing because I'm an excellent eater.

At the same time, my lips tug into a smile at the deep, lilting sound of Ra's voice, as he sings The Stranger's "Golden Brown."

I could lose myself in the worlds spun by his voice.

Ra always sings or hums when he cooks or brews potions. I don't think that he sees much difference between cookery and potion making. As a sorcerer, his magic is natural and not learned; it flows through him, as essential as his own blood. It's why he feels such despair on my behalf at the loss of my magic because to him, it'd be like tearing out his heart.

When I stroll into the kitchen, however, I blink.

Ra crouches over the spitting open fire with his wings folded back over his shoulders. He stirs the deep, bronze pot that hangs over the fire (and reason for the delicious smells).

Once, I told him about the humans' use of microwaves. Toads and frogs, that'd been a mistake.

Ever the inventor, Ra politely interrogated me for every detail of how they worked but then he asked, "Why?"

My brow furrowed. "Why what?"

"Why would the non-magical want such soulless food?" He gestured at the open fire; just the scent of its smoke, even if it stung my eyes, reminded me of Ra. *Our home.* "Sphinx! How could I prove my service with one of those?"

"You don't need to prove—"

He lay his finger on my lips to hush me. "Come on, you know you love to watch me cook. How else can you secretly check out my ass?"

I kissed the tip of his finger. "Guilty."

Mealtimes are even more special, when Bard plays his flute.

Yet this time, it makes me shiver.

Bard accompanies Ra, as if my lovers are flames sprung from the fire. They burn so brightly that they light up the entire tree. They chase away the last of the shadows, which haunt me.

Bard dances around Ra with a fluid but savage grace. His curls and gleaming tail sweep the floorboards on each twirl. When Ra sings the last note, Bard lowers his flute and tucks it back in his waistband like sheathing a sword. Then he sweeps Ra a deep bow. Ra abandons his vigil over the pot, and instead, in a burst of golden feathers, swoops on Bard, swinging him around in his arms.

Bard laughs.

Then they both look around, as I clap.

Bard shoots me a cheeky grin. "I'm here all night. Do show your appreciation in kisses."

I pat my lips. "I think I have a couple of kisses left in these."

I saunter further into the kitchen. It's the heart of the tree. *Vast.* Before it became mostly the place where Ra and I spend cozy evenings playing chess, or mornings trying to guard the last of my coffee from Kit, this was where the Bacchants congregated to worship Bacchus, as their chants of *dying-and-rising god* echoed up to the high roof.

They still do. But thank Hecate, only once in a witching moon.

And that's too often for me.

On the far wall, there's Bacchus' statue. It's the one that once stood in the Great Hall of the manor house that I grew up in: The House of Ecstasy. It's the life-size beauty of muscles and curls, over which all the Bacchants would swoon.

All right, so I swooned. On occasion. Bacchus is swoon-worthy.

Also, I've come to realize, a dick.

How could I've thought that I loved Bacchus simply because of a statue? In my defense, I was raised in a cult, kept a virgin, and cloistered away from men.

But my lovers now are real. Warm. *Alive*. Except, Bacchus' statue still watches over them, only he *doesn't* because whenever Ecstasy isn't here, I turn him to face the wall. It's creepy to be watched, even by a statue. Perhaps, Loki has a point about Bacchus. After all, the way I have him standing, it looks like *he's* been the *bad* god.

I attempt to mask my smile.

Right down the center of the kitchen is a giant, ash table, which grows from the walls of the tree with benches on either side. It can seat at least fifty (I know because the Bacchants eat and plot here when they visit).

Laid out in place of honor is a special witches vs mages chessboard, which Ecstasy gave me. We still draw most of our games, and none of my other lovers can beat me.

I frown, however, when I notice what's hanging from the roots of the back wall: *who's* hanging.

Loki dangles from the wall with his arms tied in vines above his head but in a casual sprawl like he's simply choosing to rest there.

How many times does something have to happen before it becomes a habit?

What's surprising is that Kit's bound in exactly the same way next to him but he's less casual and more flushed with shame like the good schoolboy who's shocked at being scolded by the teacher. His ears are flattened to his head; his tails droop sadly.

TOF has a serious soft spot for Kit. She never binds him in her roots, even when he pranks the witching daylights out of Ra.

What on Hecate's tit has gone on between them?

TOF only uses her version of time out — Reflect — to break up fighting between the Bacchants or in the early days, when Oni became too savage. Manners in the demon underworld aren't the same as those expected by witches.

Kit squeaks when he sees me. His pale cheeks flush an even deeper shade of red. He turns his head, as if that way I won't see him.

I slip onto a bench. "You know how Reflect works, nine-tails. Unless you want to hang about, while we eat the delicious meal that Ra's cooking without you..."

"That'd be the wrong choice," Ra drawls.

"...Then just say that you regret whatever you did. Then TOF will let you go," I encourage.

The whole purpose of Reflect is to make you think about what you've done. Not that I've been held in Reflect before....*much*.

Kit hates to be in the wrong. He has a drive to be perfect, and I understand it. The consequences for him failing used to be cruelly severe.

But can a fox-spirit truly regret anything?

The light of the fire catches the gold flecks in Kit's eyes like they're flames. "Kit broke a rule," Kit's voice is subdued. I force myself not to rush to him. He needs to say this, and I need to hear it. Kitsune are dangerous; I forget that. What has Kit done to Loki, when I should've been protecting the newest Guardian? I can't believe it; it doesn't feel real. I can get them both through this. *I'll find a way.* "Kit dishonored a Guardian by calling his hair silly."

"Hey, and all the other things," Loki protests.

I can't help it. I burst into laughter.

Thank Hecate. Is that all?

I'm panicking and planning ways to rehabilitate a rabid fox-spirit who's finally snapped and possibly bitten off Loki's dick, when in fact all Kit's done is throw around his usual level of sass. Is TOF getting stern to make a point about Guardian unity?

"TOF, give up on trying to force them to play nice." I pat the table to make sure that TOF is listening, and the lights pulse purple in protest. Her magic thrums through the ash. "It's just banter. I'd be checking their temperatures if they started being polite or calling each other *sweetheart*."

Bard grimaces, swaggering to the bench and throwing himself down on it next to me. He watches Loki's struggles with an amused twinkle in his eye.

TOF must've taken my words to heart (she's a good friend) because she lets Kit go.

Instantly, Kit dives to me, and I wrap my arms around his waist.

"Sorry," Kit whispers into my hair.

"*Ehm*, excuse me, what about the god with *silly hair*?" Loki protests, squirming against the wall.

"Well, go on then," I say.

Loki's eyes flash with outrage. "A kid's punishment? Hey, what's next? Shall I stand in the corner or lay over your lap for a spanking?"

"Don't tempt me." I refuse to acknowledge the blush pinking my cheeks. "But even though my Box of Tricks has a lot of fun scenarios for that, it also comes with a serious checklist that all my lovers fill out first. If you don't negotiate, you don't play."

Loki bares his teeth. "Huh, and there I was

thinking that you tied up first, and talked later."
Bastard...with a point. But I wasn't the one who did
the tying. He came gift wrapped. *Except, what did
Loki believe?* "Let me down."

"You're not one for reflection, are you?"

"You've no idea."

All of a sudden, TOF drags Loki up to the high
ceiling. Loki yelps, swinging like a pendulum.

I sigh. He's more stubborn than me.

"How long do you think before he caves?" Ra
chops herbs on the counter with the precision of an
artisan.

It's as beautiful as his singing.

I wince. An hour? *A day?*

I'm surprised that it's Kit who leaves the safety
of my arms (he spends his life finding ways to
wind around me and push my other lovers posses-
sively out of the way to get closer), and wanders
beneath Loki's swinging form. He tangles his
elegant fingers together, and his head is ducked as
if in apology.

In his fox form, he'd be lying on his stomach
whimpering.

"Kit was wrong to call your hair silly. Tell the
most gorgeous tree in all the realms that we shouldn't
have argued." Kit brightens, adding as if it seals the
deal. "Plus, Kit will gift TOF his tail fluff."

To my surprise, Loki's expression gentles. "I bet

Lady TOF would seriously like one of your special poems."

He's so in for a spanking. I'm giving him that checklist.

Kit nods excitedly. "Kit will write epic poem about the god of mischief who's *tricky, tricky, tricky*—"

"Oh, no spoilers." When Loki's laughing gaze meets mine, I struggle to hide my own grin. Then Loki sighs. "I swear on the Norns that I worship you, Lady Tof, and every leaf on your branches. That being said, you're crazy."

"Not helping," Bard singsongs.

"Odin's cock, fine," Loki snaps. "I regret arguing with another Guardian but I in no way promise not to do it again."

It's about as good as any of my apologies to Ecstasy. In fact, it's better than the one in which I sent Caesar on my behalf. How was it my fault that she didn't understand the difference between an angry and an apologetic growl?

Yet it must be good enough for TOF because she gently lowers Loki to the ground, releasing him.

When Loki snatches Kit's hands in his, my eyes widen.

Was Loki's regret a trick to attack Kit? *How many times will I fall for it?*

I'm ready to launch myself up, but to my surprise,

Bard winds his arms around my waist to hold me back. He's surprisingly strong.

"Why do you do this?" Loki murmurs. "Tangle your fingers together?"

I startle. Has Loki been watching Kit? Does he observe us all so intently? *Why do I hope that he does?*

Kit holds his fingers like that when he's nervous. Does there need to be a reason behind it? But then, I glance down at the band at my wrist. What if it's the same for him?

Kit's shocked gaze shoots to Loki's. I don't think he'll answer. Yet he doesn't pull away his hands.

"It's l-like s-someone..." At Kit's stutter, I'm cold in a way that aches my bones. For years, he wouldn't speak at all and then only with a stutter. I can't bear to hear it again. With an effort, Kit drags his fingers apart. ""Kit can i-imagine that s-someone is h-holding his hand."

My eyes widen. I'm frozen with horror.

How did I miss that?

"May I hold your hand?" Loki asks.

Kit nods.

When Loki takes Kit's hand in his, it's like a vow. Even Ra has stopped his precise chopping to watch.

"If you need me to take your hand," Loki says, rubbing his thumb across the back of Kit's hand, "just ask."

"Kit was alone. Never touched apart from to *hurt, hurt, hurt*. The w-witch never let me..."

When Loki's eyes flash with chaos magic, it's terrifying.

"Hestia," I say because there's no way in a world of bubbling cauldrons that I'll let Loki think I'd ever hold affection from Kit (*and why does it matter to me so much?*). "The bitch of a witch who owned him as a cub."

"Does this hurt?" With a compassion that I don't expect, Loki tightens his hold on Kit's hand.

Kit shakes his head. "Don't let go."

Loki smiles; it's the shy one that I've seen once or twice, breaking through. "I don't intend to." He pulls Kit to the other side of the bench to me. "But I do intend to beat this witch's ass at chess."

Ra snorts. "Anubis' dick, it's like a lamb to the slaughter."

Loki meets my gaze challengingly.

I don't need to warn him that no one has ever beaten me at chess apart from my sister, right? It'll be fun to wipe the smug off his godly face.

Kit snuggles next to Loki on the bench. "Kit lied," Kit whispers. "Bad Kit is jealous of your hair."

Bard laughs. "By my ears, they'll be calling each other *sweetheart* any moment."

Loki nudges Kit's shoulder. "Who wouldn't be? But then, I'm jealous of your tails."

Kit perks up, wrapping his tails around Loki. "Kit has the best tails in the forest."

Bard tilts his head. "Did I miss the vote?"

Not this again.

I swipe my hand over the chessboard and the magical pieces spring to life, ready to fight. "Let's play. I get the witches. You're the mages."

Loki inclines his head. "Obviously."

"I'll go first."

I always make the first move. You can take the chaos magic from me, but not the chaos. Chess is a battle; my blood sings with it.

Loki wags his finger. "Age before beauty."

He moves his pawn — *first*.

I gape at him, and Bard snickers.

All right, now I'm *really* going to destroy him.

I move to counter Loki. "You can steal my move and play tricks, but I'll still always counter you."

Loki's long fingers lovingly caress his knight, before he moves it. "And I'll outmaneuver you." He rubs my ankle underneath the table with his bare foot; I only just hold back the moan at the sensation. I bet Ra has that weakness written in the **Case of Loki's Ass**. "Who's your favorite villain?"

He moves a mage pawn who wriggles irritably.

"What?"

"Don't you talk during your chess matches?" His intense emerald gaze holds mine.

"Only if I want to lose," I complain. My witch hexes one of Loki's mages. *Good.* "That's street chess tactics. You play dirty, trying to distract."

"Is it working?" Loki gives a bloodthirsty grin, as his mage bishop curses mine.

This is turning into speed chess.

Time to turn the tables.

"Favorite hero," I counter, running my own foot down Loki's ankle.

He startles, before his grin broadens. "On the Valkyries, that's an easy one: Batman. Plus, a witch who can discuss the non-magical world without acting like a superior dick is a serious surprise."

Ra leans against the counter. "High praise."

I scowl. "Batman's not a hero."

"Get on with you, anti-heroes count," Bard offers like he's the referee.

I glance at the board. How have I lost so many pieces already? Loki's expression is placidly innocent. But I've only taken three of his.

I thrum with an excitement that I haven't experienced...*ever.* No one can go toe to toe with me at chess, even Ra. My sister is too close to me to count. We learned the game together.

Yet I'm not sure that Loki is even having to try.

When I go for my next move (the rook), Loki's long fingers curl around mine to stop me. I realize with shock that he's protecting me from making the wrong move.

He slides me over to a pawn that I've forgotten about with an amused twitch of his lips. "Sometimes it's the invisible fighters who others think weak, who are the deadliest."

I study the board. Can I pretend that he's wrong, even though he's right?

He's infuriating...and would it be okay if I lean over the board and crash my lips to his...? I mean, just as a thank you...?

"The Joker," I blurt as a way to control my bad lips and repay him by answering his question. "Savage, twisted, and—"

"Psycho." Loki hexes another one of my pieces, and I flinch.

Yet Loki never lets go of Kit's hand.

"I have a thing for psychos," I reply.

"Hey, you," Ra protests. "Said psychos can hear you and are slaving over a hot fire."

"And I appreciate it, my Song-bird," I reply. "I'm not too busy not to be stealing looks at your ass."

"As long as it doesn't exhaust you." Ra crushes spices in a heavy pestle and mortar. "Don't work too hard."

Bard rests his chin on my shoulder. "Are we losing?"

Yes....

"Of course not." I tilt up my chin. "Look, the Joker's a psycho but he *knows* that he's the bad guy and he admits it. Yet in his own screwed-up way, he challenges Batman to be better."

Loki's gaze flickers to mine and then away. "Huh, anti-hero and villain are friends then?"

"Batman knows he's not a hero too." I smirk. "He's a *bad* bat. And Joker's— "

"Chaos."

When Loki's foot slides up my calf, I bite my lip. My eyelashes flutter.

"Chaos," I breathe like the answer to a prayer.

"Check...and mate."

As if awakening from a dream, I straighten and stare down at the board in shock.

Witchity fuck, witchity fuck, witchity...

How did Loki do that and with a pawn that I didn't see, just like the invisible fighter he'd even warned me about? And why is a small part of my brain screaming that I never want to let go of someone who can outsmart me?

"Good game." Loki rolls his shoulders.

His lips curl at the corners. Is that what he looks like when he's happy?

"Teach me to play like that," I beg.

Loki's breath stutters. His gaze becomes suddenly vulnerable. Surely, he's been asked for help before?

I'm disappointed when his gaze becomes studiedly blank. "A magician never reveals his tricks."

"Let's eat." Ra prowls to the table, placing down a bowl of fish stew with lentils in the middle. I lean over, taking a deep breath of the rich aromas of garlic and onions. Bard leaps up, helping Ra to carry over baskets piled with flatbread, tankards of beer, and salad with my favorite relish, as well as piles of plates and utensils.

This is Egyptian food adapted by Ra, but it's also what he prepares to pamper me.

I shouldn't have hidden my tears. My pain was my Guardians'. Ra always finds small acts to prove it.

Ra passes the plates, while Bard passes out the beer. I push the basket of flatbread across the table to Loki and then, without thinking, lean across to press a kiss to his cheek like I would with any of my lovers.

It's fleeting, relaxed, and familiar. Easy like I've been kissing him for centuries.

Loki's eyelashes flutter, before we both draw back in embarrassment. We avoid each other's gazes, as if the moment didn't happen.

Black cats, it's better that way. Safer.

"Now we're getting to the good stuff." Bard takes a hefty swig of his beer. "Drinking and telling tales like all good warriors should."

Kit groans, covering his head with his tails. "Nine-tails says no tales."

Bard pretends to ignore him (he's had plenty of practice). "Tales of brilliant derring-do, with dragons, demons, and djinn, which'll blow your..."

All of a sudden, the tree shakes. TOF pulses a warning. The vines in the walls squirm and writhe. A deep rumbling rolls through the kitchen. Ra throws himself over the food, covering it with his wings to try and save it, as the tankard spills and plates crash to the floor.

Bard tightens his hold on me, as Loki grasps harder to Kit's hand.

I know what the signs mean. Nothing but grief and pain for Loki: the enemy, who I can no longer even pretend *is* my enemy.

Ecstasy's coming home for a visit, and her rage that's already rumbling through the tree, floods me with fear for Loki.

CHAPTER ELEVEN

Tree of Life, Bacchus' Kitchen

The kitchen rumbles with the leader of the Bacchants' displeasure.

Ecstasy always likes to make an entrance, just like our god.

My thigh presses against Bard's under the table; the solid feel of him steadies me. Puddles of beer darken the ash table. I wrinkle my nose against the malty scent, as my fingers are drenched in the sticky spill. Yet I can't lift my hands from where they grip the edge of the table so hard that my knuckles whiten because Loki's face is ashen.

He's been hunted by my sister, hexed, and caught. *He knows what comes next.*

Yet I can't bear to see him wear such an expression. How can I comfort him? He's made it as clear as glass (or a glinting chaos moment) that he hates lies, even *white* ones meant to shield from painful truth.

Ecstasy's ancient, powerful, and my leader. Once, I was stronger than her. But without my magic, I'm one of the lowest serving Bacchants, who's relegated to paperwork, in between my reaping.

If I wasn't Ecstasy's sister, would Bacchus even have granted me immortality alongside her, or instead, would I've been left to die a mortal's death, turning to ash a millennium ago?

Anticipation — *sister, family, and safety* — wars inside me with fear for Loki.

Sweet Hecate, why do I always have to be torn apart?

For centuries, after the Bacchanalia when my magic was ripped from me, Ecstasy grieved, alongside me. Her grief turned to rage, however, in a way that mine never did. She was driven by hunting Loki; she dreamed of hurting him and his descendants.

Her revenge.

I worry that she lost as much as me.

I should've thirsted for the taste of Loki's tears as well. Yet I had Oni, who showed me a new way to live and love, discovering how to still be wild within the forest. Without Oni, would I've become as eaten away with vengeance? Would I still worship Bacchus?

Hecate, let Oni be safe from the Shadow Demons.

Ecstasy's magic prickles across my skin. The room shakes, and the plates rattle.

All of a sudden, roots curl out of the floor at the head of the table, curling up into a bone-white throne. I swallow at the sudden scent of mulled wine that washes over that of the beer.

Kit growls, transforming in a spray of golden glitter into his fox-spirit form. He winds around Loki's neck protectively. Loki's magic hangs heavily in the air, dark and oppressive.

I pull on the hex warningly. When Loki's hurt gaze lifts to mine, I wince. I find myself nodding at him in the secret system that I use with Ra: *control yourself.*

When Loki looks back at me blankly, I almost bang my head on the table.

He doesn't know the secret system...*yet.*

There will be a *yet.*

I can't shake the sense that Loki should've lived his life with me, even though I know he hasn't (*so, no blaming an Infernal for the occasional slip*).

Then all thoughts are driven from my head, as branches of purple coil like sinuous ivy over the edges of the root throne and tangle into the shape of Ecstasy. Magically, the foliage melds into her purple toga, which she smooths down. Her large, hazel eyes glow with predatory danger, but she merely fiddles with the moth brooch that pins her dress like her hand isn't shaking with rage.

As if she isn't aware that I know.

Her cat familiar, Pocus, curls in her lap. His slinky fur is so black that it gleams. A pentacle collar clinks around his neck. Ecstasy's fingers claw hard into the scruff of his neck, holding him in place.

Pocus narrows his eyes at me.

He's a Halfling, which means that now he can now spend most of his time in his gorgeous lithe Korean vampire form (with the addition of the most adorable cat ears and tail). Ecstasy only turns him back into a cat as punishment.

Or when she's truly angry.

No wonder Pocus is baring his fangs at me and bristling his fur. He's suffering because I've pissed off my sister.

Yet how did she know that she'd discover Loki outside the Moderation Room or…*about the rest?*

I sneak a glance at Bacchus' statue and the curve of his stone curls.

Can a statue eavesdrop? *Has he been spying for Ecstasy?*

I shiver, and Loki shoots me a concerned look.

"Darlings, I'm home." Ecstasy's voice is educated and American. I used to wonder why she relocated to America. She claimed that it was to *make her name* amongst the covens there. Well, she managed that but now, I realize that she was also tracking Loki. She taps her long nails on her knee. "What's a *half-breed* doing at your table?"

Even though she speaks quietly, her voice echoes around the vast kitchen like a scream.

"Well, he was about to eat lunch." I force myself to shrug casually. "Ra's made his delicious fish stew. Shall I pass you a plate?"

Ecstasy strokes Pocus' back, as if it's the only thing keeping her from leaping out of her throne. Pocus settles his chin on her knee. "I'll pass on breaking bread with my enemy. For a thousand years, the Bacchants and I have dedicated ourselves to hunting his cutie pie ass across realms and the shadowy places in between, where chaos reigns. I tore apart worlds to deliver him to you, little leaf, but you're..." She glances around the kitchen at the simmering pot, warm bread, and spilled beer, "... playing house."

Why did she have to use my nickname?

I'm frozen back to childhood; she's sister, mum, and dad wrapped into one.

"And playing chess." When Loki's hard gaze meets Ecstasy's, a tremor runs through him, but he raises his chin defiantly. "Oh, and *I* won."

Godly show-off.

"Still untamed, talking out of turn, and a *liar*." Ecstasy's lip curls. Loki flushes, and I can't help the twinge of pride that she doesn't believe I can be beaten, which is edged with outrage on Loki's behalf. "Has my scolding about tidiness finally got through to you, and you've coiled the chains and whips under the table for the sake of neatness?"

"Chains and whips?" I ask.

It's not our turn to host the *Witches of Kink* this month, right?

I know that I've been caught up in my reaping, but I'd remember if Ecstasy was taking the tree over for one of her events (which are legendary amongst the covens). Also, one of the nights of the year that Ra and Kit stay firmly in my room with just me and our Box of Tricks.

We don't *play* with other witches.

Ecstasy cocks a haughty eyebrow. "Why would a *prisoner* be out of the Moderation Room without them?"

"To be fair," I force myself to prise my sticky hands from the table and point to the back wall, "Loki was hanging from there this morning."

"And the ceiling," Kit adds.

Ecstasy's expression darkens, as she studies the possessive way that Kit clings to Loki.

Sweet Hecate, that's not good.

"Mother Earth, save us," Bard whispers. "She's going to transform us all into footstools or perhaps, floral armchairs that sing merry tunes from beneath her power tripping arse. I don't want her sitting on my face again."

He scrunches up his nose in distaste. I don't blame him. That *is* one of her favorite punishments.

Then Ecstasy's gaze settles on Bacchus' statue, and her magic sparks. I yip from the smarting sensation. She waves her hand, and the statue twists around, until it's once more facing the room.

Watching me.

Creepy.

My brows furrow. "Wasn't Loki a gift? I discovered him tied up without even a note. Can't I play with him how I want? He's mine."

Don't look at Loki, don't look, don't...

I hear Ra's shocked intake of breath, however, and Kit's growl. I feel how Bard pulls his arm from around my waist.

I'm sorry. Hecate above, I don't mean it. Please trust me.

"Why aren't you breaking him?" Ecstasy's howl promises darkness and pain.

I meet her anguished gaze and I wish that I knew what to tell her.

Why aren't I?

Yet all I see when I look at her hand fisting in Pocus' fur hard enough to make him yowl, and the way that she shakes with as much distress as anger, is that *she's* breaking.

A shadow crosses her expression: *fervor and obsession.*

When she stalks to her feet, and Pocus scrambles off her lap, my eyes widen.

"The half-breed is the prisoner of the Bacchants and not yours," Ecstasy hisses. "He's the eternal offering."

Ra leaps onto the table, scattering the meal in a *clatter* and *clink* of bowls and plates. His blue eyes flare, and his wings burst out like a golden shield. He has his reasons to distrust the Bacchants, after they kidnapped him.

Sweet Hecate, how is it different to what they've done to Loki?

Kit flies in front of Loki with a fierce determination, whirling his tails, as if he can mask Loki from Ecstasy.

My breath hitches. *They're preparing for battle to protect Loki.* My heart clenches at my lovers' (bravely stupid) loyalty.

When Bard begins to stand (*witches above, what does he intend to do, Pied Piper Pocus with his flute?*), I shove him back down, and instead, stand up myself.

It won't do any good. Bacchus has control of TOF. When Ecstasy is here, as leader of the cult, she has the ultimate power. Yet we'll still try.

"Don't." Loki's tone is clipped. "Valhalla! Don't you understand what's happening? Seriously, just get out of here, *please*."

The realization sears through me. As much as we're attempting to protect Loki, *he's* protecting us. Plus, he doesn't want the other Guardians to witness his torture.

I pale. How many times has he been hurt by witches?

Well, I swear by the roots of the Tree of Life, *that* won't be happening again.

"Funny thing we have around here," Ra drawls, even though his wings vibrate with agitation. "It's called loyalty, silver-tongue. We won't leave you to be—"

"Out. Now," Loki hollers.

Silence.

I nod at Ra, and this time, my lover understands because it's Ra, and he always does.

Magic ripples in waves across Ra, as he meets Ecstasy's gaze like one predator sizing up another. "Perhaps, you should remember that a god is still a god, even if his wings are clipped."

Reluctantly, Ra folds his wings. Then he jumps off the table. He snatches Bard by one hand to pull him after him, and then to my surprise, Kit's paw in his other, sweeping out of the kitchen like it's a regal procession.

Loki smirks. "Ra has style."

Ecstasy prowls around the table to Loki, and he stiffens.

I jerk at the same time as Loki, as Ecstasy directs her magic at him, and the crimson chains become as heavy as they'd first been in the Moderation Room.

She placed the hex on him, and so she can control it too.

Loki gasps, ducking his head. I want to hurl.

Pocus leaps onto the throne, pretending to sleep. It's a trick he plays, whenever he doesn't want to watch.

Reassuring.

"Do I need to gag you?" Ecstasy asks. She pushes back her midnight tumble of hair. "Your lips would look good stretched like that but then, your sons' would look even better."

Instantly, Loki straightens; his eyes are wide and frantic. "Don't you dare touch… On fear of Ragnarök! You don't need to threaten… I'll do whatever you want, just don't…"

"Then sit still."

Loki freezes.

"Good puppet," Ecstasy croons with mock-tenderness like praising a dog.

"Stop it." My legs are shaky; my mouth is dry.

I should want this. It's our sisterly moment of triumph. Yet how can she terrorize Loki with the threat of hurting his sons? He's a good dad. He loves them. I sat and listened to his stories about them.

I can't allow this.

"His sons are innocent," I insist. "Hecate above, they didn't destroy the ceremony or harm me. Just leave them out of this and let them go. After all, we have Loki now, right?"

Ecstasy wraps her hand in Loki's curls, wrenching back his head. He hisses but doesn't resist.

My eyes widen. Since my sister has control of his sons, of course he won't fight her — he's caged.

"Little leaf, you're the smartest witch I know, so why are you acting dumb?" Ecstasy shakes Loki by his hair, and he bites his lip not to make a sound. "I took the job at Rebel Academy as a cover. Do you think that I enjoy playing *Professor Bacchus* in such a deadly academy? I have to watch my students die and try to save others from fates worse than simple death. But all of it is worth it to cause agony to the god who destroyed the House of Ecstasy. Loki's sons are the hostages. *Bait.* The Enemy You've Hurt the Most hex is based on ancient karmic energies. Loki's binding to you is fair by all the rules of the universe. He hurt you and until he undoes that hurt, he won't be free."

I can't help it. I *ping* the band on my wrist. "Wow,

that's a shame. Then he'll never be free because even with my magic, I was never able to time travel. I mean, I've heard it's possible but only when the Fates intervene. The Fates have had their chance and no intervening. You can't undo this…hollowing out…of my magic."

When Ecstasy traces her long nail down Loki's arm, he flinches. "I said, don't move." I'm surprised, when the Leaf Tattoo on my arm (in a mirror image to the place that Bacchus is tracing with her finger on Loki), warms. "What if I told you that there's a way to be free of the hex?"

My heart thuds in my chest. I can't catch my breath.

Does she mean…?

"Don't say that if you don't mean it," I whisper.

Ecstasy's expression gentles. "I only want my little sister healed. I've been searching for a way to restore your magic, ever since you lost it. If we repeat the ceremony, then honestly, there's a chance with Loki and you playing your parts, that you can be whole again."

But I'm not broken, am I?

My hands clasp around my womb.

Whole.

But what's Loki's part in the ceremony? I was too incited with frenzy and pleasure to understand more than flashes the first time around.

Loki attempts to shake his head at me desperately, even though Ecstasy tightens her hand in his hair.

Yet my mind is filled with the possibilities. My magic returned without the need for Ra's deadly experiments. My power. Being able to protect my lovers and the forest.

Could I even leave the Bacchants?

"What do I need to do?" I mutter.

Loki hisses in frustration, closing his eyes.

Ecstasy grins in triumph. "For the best chance, you need to have full submission from your offering. You should Soul Bond with him."

"Flattering proposal, but I refuse." Loki's eyes flare.

I stare between them.

Soul Bond? It's more than marriage. It's the closest and most intimate connection that there is. I was forced into it to save Ra's life. I don't regret it but I'll never repeat a Soul Bond, unless it's willing. Plus, TOF won't allow it.

I press my hand to my Leaf Tattoo, which warms like I'm touching Ra through it. By my Soul Bond, as the Infernal, I can draw Ra's shifter spirit from him to reap alongside me. He's the most devastatingly glorious Song-bird in spirit form, and he looks like he could burn down the world.

I'll never tear Loki's spirit stallion from him without his consent.

Loki looks at me like he already knows this and believes in me. His trust is terrifying, when it's my sister, who's cruelly twisting his head back by his curls.

I shake my head. "I won't Soul Bond unwillingly, and it's not possible to trick TOF. She can tell if it's forced without a real connection; it won't work. Ecstasy, you've never...you haven't bonded. Hecate's tit, you don't know the intimate closeness; it's like you're inside each other and to even think of forcing that is a violation. We'll find another a way."

Ecstasy's eyes blaze. The room shakes, and vines squirm from the walls, writhing. Bacchus' statue bleeds honey.

I stare at her, shocked.

"If Bonding's like you're *inside each other*, then you won't mind being locked together in the Time Cave," her voice is low and deadly. "You need to connect...? Well, then you'd better do some speed dating. Once you share Loki's memories, then you'll be *intimately* acquainted enough to Soul Bond." *Please, no.* She's never spoken to me as if I was just another Bacchant to be ordered around or worse, one of the Bacchants' men. How have things crumbled so fast? "Bacchus is a god of dark pleasure and frenzy, darling, and you've finally got a chance to return fully to his ranks of worshipers. Think about whether you want to blaze back to power with your magic or remain forever trapped in the past. Displease me, and you'll no longer be the Infernal. My magic granted you the power of the Infernal Scythe, and I can take it away."

CHAPTER TWELVE

Tree of Life, Time Cave

I should be spending my time trapped in the Time Cave making the biggest decision of my life: betray my beliefs about taking an unwilling Soul Bond in order to rise on the wild waves of my chaos magic back to my rightful place as the most powerful of the Bacchants or lose my last connection to magic and the Infernal Scythe.

Instead, all I can think about is how desperately I need to piss.

My life sucks.

Gods and demons tremble beneath the Infernal, but sadly, I still don't have control over my bladder when I'm trapped inside a cave for hours.

I knew that Loki would be trouble. It's totally fair

to blame him. *It is.*

The cave is tiny and cramped. It's beneath the tree; a tangle of arcing roots. I scrunch my nose against the earthy, damp stench. The only light is the glow of Loki's emerald magic. Loki and I bend our heads to fit. My neck aches.

Witching heavens, what I'd give for one of Ra's neck massages.

So that we're not crushed against the walls, Loki and I are forced to sit with our legs around each other's waists; Loki's leather trousers are sticky against my skin. Perhaps, I should invest in some baggier t-shirts. I rest my arms around Loki's shoulders, and his arms curl around my waist.

Ecstasy did want us to become *intimate.*

Loki's cool fingers trace soothing circles on the hollow of my back almost like he doesn't know that he's doing it.

My bladder gives another twinge. It aches from holding on too long. I redden.

Don't think about needing to take a piss. *Don't.*

Waterfalls, gushing taps, and showers of rain.

Drip. Drip. Drip.

Hex you, traitorous brain.

I focus on Loki, desperate for the distraction. He's humming a lilting melody that shivers down my spine like melting ice.

My brow furrows. "You're calm."

Ecstasy is Loki's worst enemy. She's trapped him. He could be forced to Soul Bond. Yet is this calm nothing but a mask or a quiet strength that I haven't seen before?

Ra would admire it.

Loki's eyes are bright and piercing in the gloom. "And *you're* squirming."

I blush.

Hecate, strike me down now.

"What are you humming?" I ask.

"It's an ancient Norse lullaby that I'd sing to my sons. It'd sooth them when the witches hunted us, and we had to hide in caves."

I bite my lip. What can I say to that? *Plus, was he humming it to help me?*

"Sorry," I whisper.

He stops tracing circles on my back, and I instantly miss his touch. "Honestly, I don't regret what I did at the Bacchanalia, so why should you regret having me hunted? It's natural. When two true chaos forces come together..." He tilts his head, assessing me like I'm a puzzle that he's desperate to solve. "... By the World Tree, they never have before. It's kind of thrilling to find out what happens."

"Have you had much excitement before trapped in caves?"

Loki's magic prickles across my skin, even through the hex that weighs him down. "Valhalla!

You've no idea. But order's the eternal lie. The myth spun by gods. The truth is that neither god, demon, nor man know what will happen. Even the Fates can be broken and rewoven by the Norns. We're all trapped in a meaningless existence, but the only certainty is *change*. Dazzling, brilliant moments that can be snatched by those with the skill to see them. *That's chaos*."

I stare at Loki, frozen.

All these years, alone. Hoping, wishing, *desperate* for someone else to understand what's going on inside my head and thundering through my magic. *And Loki has just voiced it all without me even asking.*

He's the other half of me: we should rage together in our chaos. *I need him.*

I rest my forehead against his, tightening my legs around his middle and sliding my fingers along his silky skin because I don't know how to tell him that.

It's too much.

"Why were we ever enemies, when we're both made up of chaos?" I murmur.

Loki's surprised gaze meets mine, before he firmly pushes me back.

"Huh, how many ways to answer that." His breath gusts against my cheeks; he smells of sweet strawberries. *Hecate's tit, I wish that I could take back my words.* "You chose to make me a Guardian of Lady TOF, which means that I'm no longer your enemy.

But why *were* we enemies...? How about that your cult hides behind chaos to feed their frenzy and ecstasy. I'd have watched your orgies, which only pretended at worship, with nothing but amusement, if you didn't drag in the unwilling for sacrifices and..." A troubled expression flashes across his face, before he can hide it. "...worse."

A sick feeling twists in my gut. Does he mean during the initiation? Whatever the *secret* is about the caves? Are the initiations still happening? These *sacrifices*?

What's the secret?

Yet when I open my mouth to answer, my bladder gives another twinge. I grit my teeth against the pain but can't help squirming. Unfortunately, it comes across far more like a lap dance than a potty dance.

Loki startles, as my crotch rubs against his. I'm not imagining his hard, thick (and godly-sized) dick in his pants.

Loki's smile is slow, smug, and infuriating. "I know that I'm irresistible, but now isn't the time to seduce me. I kind of like to be courted. I'm old-fashioned like that. Sorry if you're a little *frustrated*."

He draws out the word out in a way that can't help but draw my attention to his lips (and make me imagine what his tongue would feel like licking between my thighs, rather than *frustrating* me).

I narrow my eyes. "You truly are the god who puts *cock* into *cocky*."

Loki grins. "I'm flexible, but I'd rather put my cock into—"

He snaps his mouth shut hard enough that I wonder if he's bitten his tongue. Then he flushes.

I smile, *smugly*.

My *unique* lap dance has broken Loki's *hard to get* act. Perhaps, needing to piss is a superpower?

Loki taps his fingers on my back, impatiently. "Enough games. If you're going to force a Soul Bond…"

I stroke my fingers through his curls; they're as soft as his gaze is hard. "I won't."

I'd made the decision, even before Ecstasy shut me in here. Nothing that happens will change that.

Loki scrutinizes me. "Strange witch that you are, I believe you. But would it work? Will it restore your magic?"

"I already told you. I'm not—"

"Huh, I'd have thought that Ra and you would understand about the difference between reality and *theorizing,* or does he invent and experiment, while you kill and reap?"

Instead of tightening my hold in Loki's hair (*so tempting*), I bring my other hand around to feather moth-light touches down his cheek. "Intelligence and strength can't go together…?"

"Rarely." He considers me. "I can't resist, when they do."

Warmth furls through me. I love how smart and strong Ra is. It's Ra's strength to have survived, as much as his power. For some reason, I know that Loki means this too.

"In *theory*," I can't resist rubbing my nose against Loki's to emphasize the word, "even if we become *intimate* enough in here for TOF to accept the Bond, I don't think that it will. We both know chaos magic doesn't work in such a simple way, and when it was drawn out of me to give Bacchus his life, I knew that it was gone." I shake, consumed by the horrifying sensation of its loss. "Repeating the ritual without taking Bacchus' life, won't *fix* me. How would Ecstasy even come up with this and be so certain as to…? She's never treated me like this before. Hecate above, I hope that I'm wrong but I think Bacchus is…" Am I truly going to say this about my own god? *It's blasphemy.* "…tricking my sister."

"He told her about the ceremony," Loki guesses. "He lied that this is what needs to happen to restore your magic. Tyr's beard, your sister's the *puppet*."

I want to defend her, but Loki has a point. The only question is *why* Bacchus wants this.

Am I daring to question my god?

All the Bacchants fancy themselves in love with Bacchus, but Ecstasy adores him still like she did as a teenager: pining, desperate, and lonely. She's still the Cock Charmer, but she's never married.

She's remained married only to Bacchus.

Does she play rough with men as a result, seeing them as nothing but *sacrifices to Bacchus and pleasure,* as she's always called them? I never understood what she meant. Now I wish that I'd questioned it more.

Loki's tongue darts out to wet his lips. "So, we have an asshole god tricking an asshole cult leader on one side. Let's twist the problem on its head. What's the consequence if we *don't* do this?"

My heart thuds in my chest. All of a sudden, the cave feels much darker.

"I lose my Infernal Scythe and my last ability to wield magic."

Loki hisses, and I know that I don't need to say more because he understands the devastation of that.

"How do we reap this dickish Shadow Traitor, who's stirring up unrest amongst the Shadow demons then?" Loki arches his eyebrow.

"Can't," I force out. The thought spears me: I'll be useless to defend my tree, forest, and lovers. *Oni.* "My demon lover is out there alone right now with them and I…"

Loki *hushes* me. "Looks like we're Soul Bonding then."

All right, what…?

ROSEMARY A JOHNS

"You. Me. Together." He smirks but glances down. His butterfly eyelashes rest on his cheek. "If it's not *unwilling,* then we'll have punched Bacchus in the dick. Remember what I said about change and choice? Pick your own path and take it."

I blink. "That's the least romantic proposal that I've ever heard."

Loki's lips twitch; his gaze is playful.

He untangles my hand from his curls and raises it to his lips. His kiss is feather-light, but I still shiver. Then he places my hand over his heart. I can feel the rapid *thud — thud — thud.*

He's nervous and just hiding it. It's weirdly sweet.

"Autumn, in the name of the World Tree," his voice is deep, shaking me to the core, "will you take me, Lopter, as your Soul Bond?"

When he places his own hand over my heart, I know that he can feel that it's beating just as rapidly as his own.

"With all my Soul," I murmur.

"The official ceremony is just words and ancient magic," Loki replies with an intensity that captures me and holds me breathless. "I long ago swore that no person or creature would belong to me. Yet we've merely entrusted each other with our spirits. I trust you to keep mine safe, and I shall treasure yours." Loki hesitates, looking suddenly uncertain. "Ra and you are Soul Bonded already. Are you

232

certain that he'll accept this? I won't come between you."

He means it.

I stroke along the outline of his heart. "It's not my story to tell why I'm Soul Bonded to Ra. If he wants to share with you, then it's his call. But Hecate above, I swear that I don't love my partners more or less for being Soul Bonded." I glance down. It's all so natural with my other Guardians, but then, none of them started out as my enemy. "I once asked Bard if it was mandatory for satyrs to live in harems. He replied that it wasn't mandatory *just inevitable* since they were all *horny and had a lot of love to go around.*" Loki laughs; his eyes are beautiful when they light up. "Oni's my demon bodyguard, and it kills him that we can't be together, even though we're Soul Bonded. But right now, that'd be taking advantage of his position. We still love each other though. He's more likely to ask me for all the kinky details of my night with Ra than to get jealous, unlike Kit who's—"

"A possessive ball of fluff?" Loki's lips quirk.

I nod. "Fox-spirits can't Soul Bond, which is something that makes him feel…"

"Like you love him less," Loki says with sudden understanding. "Like he belongs with you less."

"Add insecure *virgin* ball of fluff. So, no matter what tricks he pulls, you'll treat him with care and gentleness." I sigh, as I think about the beautiful kitsune who can

233

never truly believe that I want him. "I need all my lovers, and they'll welcome you as my Soul Bonded. Didn't you see how they were ready to go into battle for you?"

I bite my cheek to stop myself adding that Ra was equally ready to let Loki into our bed.

Is it too soon? *I'm calling too soon.*

Loki's gaze becomes anguished. "Why would they risk that for me?"

"Easy. You're a Guardian."

Loki's face is soft with wonder.

All of a sudden, the roots pulse. Then blurred images swirl, as if lost in tears along the roof and walls of the cave.

Loki clasps his arms around me again. "What in Odin's name is happening?"

"The Time Cave, may it be cursed with the Hex of Burrowing Moles, is powering up. It drags memories from you and then forces you to relive them. If it's mine, then we'll both feel the same sensations, thoughts, pain or pleasure, as I did at the time. You become that person. Same deal, if it's yours. I guess this is what Ecstasy wants to teach us to become—"

"On fear of the Valkyries, I forbid it!" Loki howls. For the first time he struggles, as if there's anywhere to go. "This asshole cave isn't rummaging around in my *private*," he hollers up at the roof like the cave will listen to him, "memories."

His eyes are feverish with panic, and terror, and then…

I'm dragged away from him, falling into the past memories, which the Time Cave has ripped from one of us.

Ra will be really pissed at me, if his first time screwing Loki is through a past version of me.

Life as a witch is sometimes freaky.

My gaze becomes hazy, and my mouth is dry. Then my eyes focus again, but I stagger over onto my ass. I squint, blinded by light. Everywhere is vast and golden: a hall with gold arches, columns, and floors. I stare down at my tiny hands.

I'm a kid, and the only thing that's not golden. I wiggle the toes of my bare feet and stroke my hand down the scratchy, coarse wool tunic and pants, which are like a servant's.

I snatch my hand away quickly, at the feel of a dick that I didn't have before.

This isn't my memory. *It's Loki's.*

Why would a god or a kid be a servant?

My mind becomes woozy, and I scramble to hold onto my own thoughts. I stare at the floor. Why am I sitting down? This is Odin's Hall in Hlidskjalf.

Was I slapped for slowness at my duties again? Have I fallen?

It doesn't matter. I'm sitting, rather than serving.

I'll be whipped for this. Heimdall will have seen. He always sees. *Always tells.*

My heart beats too rapidly, and I wipe my hands down my tunic, trying to steady them.

Hide. Mask. Survive.

On fear of the Valkyries, none must know of this panic. Fear is beneath a god.

I push myself to my feet, ducking my head. My long brunette curls fall into my eyes. I brush them back, wishing that Laufrey (*never mother... Please mother, look at me*), would allow me to cut them. But she said that the All-Father prefers them long, if I'm to continue to work on seidr magic with him.

Why then did Sif spit at me yesterday that I was an *ergi*? How can it be unmanly to work the same magics as the All-Father?

I didn't hide the way it hurt though, blushing. I'll never let it show again.

My temples throb; the forges outside the palace are already ringing with the sound of hammers. It's only breakfast, and Asgard is awake and bustling with life and purpose. My stomach, however, is empty, hollow, and achy. Yet at least I have a purpose. I should be grateful to the royal family. They're giving me a roof over my head, an education, and a job.

No one else would do all that for a monster.

I push myself up with new determination. I'll

make Odin proud. I sneak a peek at him. *Did he see me fall?*

Gods do not fall.

Odin sits at the head of the grand royal table with his two ravens on his shoulders, Hugin and Mugin. I poke out my tongue at them, and they *caw*.

They'll peck me later. They always do.

Odin: The Blind Guest, Greybeard, the Furious one, and the All-Father. I repeat it like a mantra.

Knowledge is power.

Odin's craggy, one-eyed face looks ancient, but his robes are worn and tattered. He's back from one of his solitary journeys through the Nine Realms. His old man act is just a mask; he teaches me about those.

Why did I miss him? I'm an *idiot, idiot, idiot…*

I snatch up a golden plate from the side, which is laden with cheese, breads, jam, apples, and grapes.

My stomach growls, and I'm dizzy with hunger. Would Odin miss a single grape…? *Just one.*

But Heimdall will see. He always sees and then he tells.

I grip the heavy plate between both hands, focusing not to stumble. There's a warm hum of chatter and laughter from the table.

The royal princes sit next to each other. Baldr's practically a man and the most beautiful god in Asgard, everyone says it (even Sif). His skin is paler than mine.

He's kind.

I don't have to be scared with Baldr.

His younger brother, Hod, is blind and sits next to him. Baldr is especially kind to Hod.

Omens and runes, I wish that I had a brother.

When I pass Thor, the youngest prince, who's taller than me (and boastful with it), he shoots me a secret smile.

I bite my cheek hard not to shoot one back.

I'm tutored alongside Thor, so that I can help him study. I love his secret smiles, but I love his wide, sunny ones that he keeps for his *real* friends best. His flashes of rage — when lightning flashes in his eyes — are scary. But he never directs them at me.

I slide the plate in front of Odin.

Don't notice me. Be invisible. A shadow.

If I don't breathe, can I cease to exist?

I slip away from Odin's harsh presence (and the pressure of his wild magic that calls to my own). I press my nails into my palms, willing my chaos not to spill out.

Please, please, please...

My back still aches from the stripes of my last beating. And Heimdall will already tell about my clumsiness this morning. How many strokes will that earn?

Ten? Twenty? More...?

I lift up the next plate, which is heavy with

strawberries, rather than grapes, because they're Baldr's favorite. I breathe in deeply the delicious aromas. It's torture when I can't taste, but the temptation to at least smell their sweetness is too great. If I'm good, I'll get porridge in the servants' halls after.

Just one strawberry slice…

I bite my lip hard enough to bead blood.

When I look up, I make the mistake of glancing at mother…*not mother*…Lady Laufrey, who's dining with the royal family.

Idiot. Idiot. Idiot.

She's beautiful just like I daydream at nights in my room in the servants' halls. Her dress overlaps in crimson silk like falling leaves, and her flaxen hair gleams in the light. Her head is turned away. She never sees me anymore.

I'm invisible.

Hide. Mask. Survive.

I can't resist. I haven't earned the right to see her in months. I sidle to her side, balancing the plate on one hand.

"Lady Laufrey," I whisper, tugging at her dress.

Mother…*Lady Laufrey*…stiffens but she doesn't look down. Instead, she clasps her hands in her lap and begins a determined conversation with Hod about the merits of different dwarven craftsmen.

Perhaps, she didn't hear me or…

239

Tears wet my eyelashes. Perhaps, she doesn't want me at all.

"Thor, I hear you're studying about Yggdrasil this morning," Baldr says, softly. I look up and catch his eye. He's talking to Thor but he means the words for me. It's a trick he uses. I hate that it means he noticed my idiotic weakness for family but he knows that I'm obsessed with learning about Yggdrasil. "Won't that be something to look forward to?"

Thor rolls his eyes. "Boring."

Thrilling. The World Tree, which let's me hear the song of the Realms and whispers to my Soul.

One day, I'll escape from Asgard and slip through the tree's shadowy branches and roots, walking through the skies, snatching brilliant fragments of chaos, dancing with mischief, howling out my mayhem, rather than bottling it inside.

My heart thuds with excitement; I can't hide my grin.

Without thinking, I push the plate that I'm holding in front of Hod. Then I freeze.

When Hod reaches for a strawberry, I panic.

By the Norns, he becomes ill when he eats them.

I slap away Hod's hand. The *smack* rings through the hall, along with his gasp of pain.

Valhalla! What have I done?

Idiot. Idiot. Idiot.

I cringe back, hugging my arms around myself.

I've struck a member of the royal family. *A blind child.*

I can be executed for this.

My breaths are ragged. My magic spikes from me in agitated waves. I can't mask or hide my fear.

Odin rises from his seat. His expression is thunderous. He looks like he could tear apart worlds to avenge his son.

I'm sorry, sorry, sorry…

But I've lost my voice. I can't make myself say the words. Fear swallows them.

Omens and runes, I'm desperate to run but I have nowhere to go. *Can I hide under the table?*

Thor's frightened gaze meets mine.

Lady Laufrey slips her arm around Hod's shoulder like *he's* the one who needs the comfort. He holds his hand like it's been caned (and that is painful, as I know well), but there isn't even a pink mark on it.

My hand was slapped like that when I was half his age, and I was never hugged after.

I'll lose my head for this.

I stare hard at Lady Laufrey like maybe…*just this once*…she'll speak up for me.

Mother, help me. I'm still your son.

Instead, she tightens her hold around Hod.

When Odin studies me coldly, I wish that I was invisible again. "By the World Tree, I've taken into my home an idiot. Would you kill my son, jotunn?"

The silence suffocates me.

I frantically shake my head. "No, no, no… I w-wasn't…"

"Have I allowed a snake to slither into the royal household? Do you dare attempt to *assassinate* my precious son, taking advantage of his blindness?"

"I d-didn't… It was only…"

"As your hands have trespassed," Odin's judgment rings through the gleaming halls, "they shall be cut off."

I shake. Tears course from my eyes. I don't care that I don't look like a warrior.

He's going to take my hands.

How can I use my magic properly or brew potions? How can I work as a servant? Will I be cast out? Homeless and broken?

"Please, I'm s-sorry," I gasp.

Odin strokes his beard. "I can be merciful. By the runes, you're still the most powerful Shifter God, who I've encountered. You'll lose one hand, so that you can work your seidr. Choose: will you lose your right or you're left?"

I can't help it. I hide my hands behind my back. If I just clasp them together, tangling my fingers like someone else is holding them tight, then he can't take them.

He can't steal my hands.

"I should've known that Hod's hunger would mess

up the trick." Baldr's gaze meets mine in warning, before it raises to the All-Father's. "I requested Loki to give a demonstration of the siedr that he's been learning, as so few are blessed like you, Father. He was going to move the plate across the table by magic. I forgot about Hod's aversion to strawberries. I'm sorry."

Baldr doesn't lie. He *never* lies. *Except, he's just lied to save me.*

And Heimdall loves Baldr more than any other god. Even though he'll have seen the truth, he'll never tell on him.

I stare at Baldr in shock.

Hope is a fool's game but it floods me. Why would anyone help me? I'm a half-breed. Frost Giant. *Monster.*

Yet Baldr has, and Thor's shooting me that secret smile again.

When Odin stalks towards Baldr, I stiffen.

By all radiance of the Rainbow Bridge, believe him.

Crack — Odin slaps Baldr across the cheek.

The red hand print is stark against the paleness of Baldr's high cheekbone. Baldr tilts up his chin; he doesn't lower his gaze.

Thor jumps out of his seat, as if to defend his brother.

"Don't ever risk Hod over a servant's trickery and

mischief again." Odin's glare swings to me. "A day without eating will teach you both a lesson about carelessness." I tighten my arms around my rumbling stomach. It's only another day. Once, I went a week without food. But why must he punish Baldr for my mistake? If only I could take his punishment as well. Odin's single eye narrows. "Don't think you fool me, jotunn. I see your deceits and rebelliousness. I taught you the mask; I know the bad boy beneath it. *The liar.*"

But *I* haven't even lied...

All of a sudden, I collapse. My mind becomes hazy. The golden walls blur like my vision is wet with tears.

Then I blink and I'm back inside the Time Cave, pressed against Loki who's shaking, and my vision really is blurry with tears.

For the first time in an hour, I don't feel like I may wet myself. The shock has driven the need away.

Instantly, I drag both of Loki's hands up to my lips and I kiss them over and over and...

He could've lost one of his hands.

I gasp at the shock of it. Then I kiss the backs of his hands, across the knuckles and down to the tips of his fingers. I turn his hands over and kiss across his palms, as if I can banish the memory.

When I finally glance up at Loki, his eyelashes are matted wet, but he's laughing.

"Are you done with these now?" He wiggles his fingers.

I shake my head, holding on tight. "Never."

"Hey, far be it from me to escape a hand worshiping."

I lick his palm in retaliation, and he wrinkles his nose.

"How could…?" I shouldn't have seen Loki's past like that without him wishing to share it but now that I have, I understand the masks that he hides behind. But I don't understand why he was treated like that. He has a mum (who wins Worse Norse Mum Award), and he was powerful with magic. "Why were they such dicks?"

It's hard to find the clever words, when only moments before, I was stuck inside the mind of a kid, and am thrumming with the urgent need to knee Odin in the balls.

"Not all of them were." Loki's eyes gleam with the tears trapped at their corners. "At least two… maybe three…didn't suck, and the others had their reasons. When you're invisible, you learn every nasty, dark truth that people want to keep hidden. Do you want me to share?"

Sweet Hecate, yes.

I don't need to be shielded and protected in a walled garden, TOF, or the Eternal Forest. I battle dangers every day, both demons and gods. Why shouldn't I know what truly happens within their realms?

Will Loki tell me the truth of the caves?

"The truth," I say.

"Trust you to believe that the god of lies would tell you that." His grin is sharp. "Time to rip off the mask and reveal the secrets of the gods."

CHAPTER THIRTEEN

Tree of Life, Time Cave

L oki holds my gaze like he's challenging me to look away. Wreathed in the shadows and silence of the cave, I'm spellbound.

Even if I still had my magic, I wouldn't be able to break his gaze.

This moment.

"I stole the secrets of the Aesir gods, hiding them magpie-like inside," Loki says like the words are torn from him, "because for the first three years of my life *I* was a secret." My breath is ragged. I entangle my fingers tighter around his. "Mom hid me, until I was discovered and Odin showed me mercy in the only dickish way he knew how. After all, I was Farbauti's monstrous seed, birthed into

Mom's shame. *Her ruin.* She kept me in a dark, hidden nursery: her secret Frost Giant baby." My breath catches. "It must've amused Heimdall to watch because he didn't tell Odin, until my magic became too uncontrollable. Then I was separated from Mom and taken away to be a servant and companion to Thor."

Frost Giant...

I've heard whispers of their wickedness, as they prowl the frozen wastelands of their realm, Jotunheim. Yet also their devastating beauty, which inflames you with obsessive love.

Witches above, I never dreamed that I'd be ensnared by one.

Loki flushes, ducking his head, until his curls hang over his eyes.

Merlin's cock, how long has this silence drawn on? Why haven't I said anything? I'm not rejecting him.

He's beautiful. *I am obsessed.*

Yet I don't care if he's a god, Frost Giant, or badass pixie (Petal's both adorable and dangerous).

He's *Lopter*. That's enough.

When he attempts to pull his hands away from mine, I hold on firmly. "You'll never need to hide. Not from me. Tell me about these Frost Giants."

Loki's eyes narrow like he's searching out the lie in my words, but he stops pulling away from me.

"Frost Giants are the *enemy* of the gods. They're nature, the bleak wild, and chaos."

"Sound like my type of giants."

Loki gives a slow grin. "We do, don't we?"

He pulls me closer with his legs, and I gasp. His eyes brim now with predatory danger, which I'd take any day over the distress, which was reflected in them, when he spoke of hidden nurseries and secret shame.

All of a sudden, the air chills, and his skin cools. Loki's breath and mine puffs into the air like mist.

Loki smirks. "I'm more of a show than tell sort of guy."

"I think you like to *tell* just as much as…"

He rocks against me, and I break off with a gasp. His hard dick rubs against me through his pants in just the right way to spark pleasure cascading through us both. We shiver.

Is his dick as cold as his hands?

Both his cool fingers and cold dick have definite possibilities.

Loki's gaze is amused when it meets mine, until I drop my hand to hover over his crotch like a question.

His lips pinch. "You don't have to. I could warm back to my godly form."

"Don't you witching dare," I insist. "And I *really* want to."

Has he ever been touched by…*anyone*…in his Frost Giant form?

By the way that his expression becomes as fragile as spun glass, before he hides it behind a shuttered mask, I'm going with legendary lover as a god, but *virgin* as a Frost Giant.

I'd better not mess this up.

"Who am I to deny my future Soul Bond?" Loki's magic shimmers, and his leather trousers vanish, revealing his milky skin and large, *perfect* dick. "Especially as there's begging involved."

And he's still haughty and infuriating.

"There'll be begging involved," I murmur, "but it won't be me doing it."

"I beg to differ..." He breaks off, stuttering in shock, as I grip his dick, tracing its silky coolness.

His cold is different to Ra's heat. What will it feel like to experience both together?

Now there's a fantasy that keeps on giving.

Loki hisses through his teeth. Is he always this sensitive or only in his Frost Giant form?

This'll be fun.

I twist up and down the shaft lightly, before tightening my grip and watching Loki closely, so that I don't miss the way that he stiffens and bites his lips, whenever I discover something that feels even more intensely good. I circle the head of his dick, and he moans. Then I swirl over his slit, rubbing the precum over his shaft.

"Harder, faster, anything...on the World Tree,

just...*please*..." Loki's pupils are dilated, as he thrusts his hips towards me.

My skin tingles at his desperate need.

"Demanding," I chide. Instantly, I pull on his balls with one hand, as I stop touching his dick with my other. "You did want there to be begging involved, and I promised that I wouldn't be the one doing it."

He looks at me like I've just announced Ragnarok.

His abandoned dick bounces hard against his stomach, sadly.

He gives something that sounds caught half between a sob and a laugh. "Tease."

I run my finger down his chest. "You love it." *So do I.* "Or am I wrong?"

"Not wrong." Loki struggles to slow his panted breathing; he's on the brink of coming, and I almost give in and let him tumble over. I will if he asks. *Nicely.* "I adore delicious...gorgeous...cruel...teases."

I coil his curls between my fingers. It's weird that I can do this at last. Yet it feels like he's a rare but hunted creature, which I should always have been protecting.

Loving.

I kiss him lightly. "And it looks like I adore Frost Giants."

Loki stiffens like it's an insult. His eyes become cold at the same time as his skin warms, and the chill disappears from the cave, as if it was never there.

I miss it; I miss the side of Loki that he's hiding.

At the same time as the cold vanishes from his skin, it appears in his eyes. "I take it that you still want to know the gods' secrets?"

I frown at his abrupt tone. "Screw the gods."

"They're too busy screwing the rest of us," Loki replies, low and dangerous. His magic prickles across my skin. He's deadly like this. "The secret of the gods is that they're not *good*. The assholes are brutal dicks with more vices than the worst villains of any other world. Honestly, they've lived so long that they no longer understand that we're still accountable for our own consciences and they hate me because…" His laugh is bitter. "Well, there's a troll load of reasons for that. I have a habit of ferreting out their secrets, however, and then holding up a mirror to their faults. They're so weak that they'd rather smash the mirror than face themselves."

All right, now I understand why in the alternate reality that I accidentally visited, Loki was punished with snake venom for *badmouthing* the other gods.

"Risky strategy," I suggest.

Loki shrugs. "Hey, I'm a rebel god. Plus, when you're the outcast, sometimes all you have is words."

"What kind of vices are we talking? Stealing each other's special coffee or chocolate because Kit is entirely guilty of that as well or…?"

"Kidnap," Loki lists off on his elegant fingers,

"forced marriage, malevolent sorcery, oath breaking, warmongering… Oh yes, and *murder*."

I grimace.

Crack my broomstick, remind me not to accept any invitations to Aesir parties. At least, not unless I take my Infernal Scythe and pretend that I've come in reaper fancy dress.

It'd be an acceptable use of the scythe to reap a couple of these gods, right? How about two from my God Hit List?

What about just Odin?

"*Oww*… Hair tugging happens to be one of my kinks too, but murder doesn't get me in the mood. Okay, sometimes it does but not right now." Loki raises his eyebrow.

I stare at Loki blankly and then at my hand, which is still fisted in his curls and yanking like I'm imagining reaping certain one-eyed gods.

"Sorry." I let go, smoothing down his ruffled hair. "So, how did they become such dicks?"

Loki's lips twitch. "Because after thousands of years, they've forgotten that it's their decisions that make them who they are. I'm bad, but I can still do good. But they believe that the Norns weave their path. It's kind of hard to control your baser side and desires, if everything's been decided already. *That's* why I'm the outcast: I'm chaos, which is change.

These bastards shake in their godly boots and would rather stay the same until Ragnarok."

I study him. "Then why were you trying to help them?"

He blinks. "What?"

"You could've stayed quiet and safe, but you didn't."

"You don't know me," Loki snarls. The tremors that shake through him, shake me. For the first time, since we were first shut in here, I'm way too aware that I'm trapped beneath TOF — *alone* — with a god, who my sister is keeping prisoner. *A bad, rebel god.* "What do you think it was like to be caught between both worlds? Memory is sacred. Just because you saw one fragment of my life, doesn't mean that you can judge it. Odin saved me from Mom. He taught me magic, shifting, and cunning. Thor, Baldr, and Hod weren't my family, but they sure as Valhalla felt like it. I take it that you have a cozy notion that the Frost Giants were my family? *Dad abandoned me.* I have no Frost Giant family. My loyalties are—"

"Divided," I say. I rub my hands up and down his strong forearms, playing with the edges of his t-shirt, until his tremors gradually fade. "Hecate above, I get it. Do you think that you *know me*, just because you saw me at the moment that I became a vessel to be hollowed out and possessed? I was trapped as well and kept behind closed doors as Bacchus' virgin. The only person that I had who loved me was my sister. She forgave my spilled magic and mischief. She could keep up with my constant demands for knowledge and chaos. But I'm not an idiot. I know now that she betrayed me by allowing me to be used as a vessel and then, by hiding me away in the Eternal Forest. Loving a sister, it's a battle. I owe the Bacchants everything, but they're brutal like the gods. Bacchus' spirit possessed all of us, after all. It changed us; Ecstasy more than anyone. But they're still family."

"Our family and pasts don't make us who we are but they sure can screw us up."

I tilt my head. "All right, that wins the *sentence that didn't go where I was expecting* gold star."

"Never be predictable." Loki's eyes sparkle. "For a long time, I was wild and self-destructive. In short, I was a total dick."

"Sorry, *was…?*"

"You're lucky that there's not room in here to spank you," Loki growls. Doesn't he mean *unlucky…?* Warmth floods through me. I cough to hide my blush. "The thing about having a kid is that it doesn't matter if you're screwed up, they still need their diaper changed, to be fed, or kept safe from the witches hunting you. You have to remake yourself for the new life, for which you're miraculously responsible. It's the greatest chaos moment of all."

When he vanishes his t-shirt, I roll my eyes. "That

was a killer chat up line: babies and hot men being redeemed. But Little Loki," I tap the head of his dick (and Little Loki is still at full attention in deluded hope), "is not getting lucky. Ecstasy's traditional about First Nights after binding ceremonies. The wait will be worth it."

"If you ever call my dick *Little Loki* again, the wait won't be worth it for either of us because you won't be touching it." Loki's jaw clenches. "And I vanished all my clothes because I want to show you something."

I widen my eyes at him innocently. "So, not Little Lok—"

"Not my dick," Loki hollers, and the phrase echoes around the cave.

Silence.

Then I giggle, and Loki snickers.

He reaches for my hand, resting it on his pale skin. I gasp, as whorls rise, glowing with green magic. The patterns *carved* into his skin are beautiful. Hidden. Secret.

But Loki's choosing to show them to me.

Loki's thumb runs across my knuckles; his heart thuds fast and hard. "They're runes. It's not only secrets that I carry magpie-like inside. Honestly, the best magic that I've ever woven, was a way to hold important messages of my life with me at all times in the most intimate way. They're part of me, but I never thought that they'd be from those who truly loved me. So, I'm blessed." He glances around at the walls. "Hey, we're in the Time Cave. You should understand about the power of memories. By Mimir's Well, to me they're…"

"Worth carving up your own skin?"

"Worth bleeding for." Loki moves my finger to trace the rune. "Worth the pain and worth the scar because that's what memories are."

This is ancient magic used in a creative way. It's brilliant, but at the same time, dark and damaged. It's so *Loki* that I press my fingers harder against the rune. To my surprise, the rune twists out alive from his skin, along with Loki's voice singing a lilting song.

It's the same melody that he hummed earlier. There's a soft love to his tone that surprises me — it's gentle.

Then a kid's voice (Hecate above, the boy couldn't be more than a toddler, could he?), says, "Ni-ni, dadda. Me sleep."

My eyes prick with tears. It didn't feel real before.
Loki's a dad.

He has a kid — *kids*. Of course, they're old enough now to be in the Rebel Academy (at least eighteen), but he raised them, and even though he had no dad and no example from what I saw of love as a kid, here he was singing to his own one.

"My singing's not that bad." Loki's hand tightens

around mine; he hasn't missed the tears gleaming in my eyes.

"Debatable."

"Well, how can I compare with the mighty Ra? Although..." Loki gives me a cheeky wink, before he presses his hand over a different rune, which wriggles to life.

Loki's voice (sounding younger but equally sassy) drawls from the rune, "Remember you're badass."

Bubbling cauldrons, even his past self was arrogant.

When I raise my eyebrow at Loki, his eyes twinkle.

"What?" He asks. "It's important to have positive affirmations."

"And to think that you took the piss out of my **BEST GUARDIAN** mug."

Loki chuckles. "If you're expecting the god of chaos to be consistent, you're in for a serious dose of disappointment."

I press my hand to a sweeping rune that runs across his lean but perfect abs, and they rise into the air in a set of stumbling (and painfully wrong) guitar chords.

I wince. "Looks like your guitar playing is as epic as your singing. Ra's winning."

Loki arches his brow. "I don't play guitar. And who said that this was a competition?"

"Sorry, I forgot that you weren't Kit for a minute. So, who's playing?"

When Loki's expression gentles, I know instantly that it's one of his sons. He doesn't answer for a moment, and he looks lost deep inside himself, as if he's struggling to come to a decision.

"I only have one son," he finally says.

I blink. He's lied.

But why...?

I don't pull away from him though because there's something about the way that he says it, which makes me kiss his cheek. He needs to know that I'm here for what he says. That I'll listen, understand, and not judge. That I won't reject him and his son. The shock and then fragile hope in his eyes, tells me that it's the right thing to have done.

"At least, the world would see him as one." Loki wets his dry lips. "But I have three sons, and by the runes, I love them all equally. It's not uncommon amongst gods for multiple gods to exist within one body. Their personalities jostle for control." He gives me another searching look. "Sleipnir is the dominant god. He's musical, smart, and loving. He's the one who was desperate to learn guitar; the rune is a recording of the first performance that he put on for me. Jormungand is more laid back and creative. Fenrir is hot-tempered but he's protective of the other two: a fighter. Every day, I took pride in their strength. I don't know whether it's because they're sharing a body, but they've aged at many times the speed of any other Aesir child. Although it could be because they were unlucky enough to have me as a dad. Honestly, it worries me to see them burn through their immortality. We were never apart, until they were snatched." His gaze slides from mine. "I miss them."

He's told me their names, and names have power. He truly does trust me. I swear by every star in the witching heavens that I won't betray it.

I glance at the magical tattoos on his arms: eight-legged horse, gleaming serpent, and snarling werewolf.

"You won't miss anymore of their lives. I promise that we'll get your sons. Then you'll be together again," I swear.

"Even though you and I are to be Soul Bonded?" Loki asks, carefully.

"What am I, the wicked step-mum?" I demand. My chest is tight and my guts roil. I never had anyone outside the Bacchants. Then I was Soul Bonded to Ra, and bound to Oni, Kit, and Bard, before TOF gave me Petal as a seed. Yet Loki's talking about family in a new way. Why do I crave this *change* with sudden, desperate crushing need? "If they're your family, then they're mine."

Loki's smile is brilliant and shy all at once.

I can't help asking, "Can I record a message?"

Loki's smile fades, however, and he disentangles our hands. The runes fade back into his skin like secrets that were never there.

"Not yet," he replies, tersely. He softens the rejection that twists inside me, however, by adding, "We'll know when it's time, and I have the feeling, that it'll be the most special message ever carved into my flesh."

For these savage gods that was romantic.

My lips quirk. "Just wait until it's Kit's turn. He'll probably write a long, *long* poem about your hair."

"He'd better use my dick then. Aren't decorated dicks popular nowadays?"

How does he manage to say things like that with a straight face?

"Only if you don't mind knife play on Little…" At Loki's thunderous expression, I run my finger down *Little Loki*, who instantly perks up; he'll be disappointed. "…him."

"Damn you, Infernal," Loki hisses. "But you know, it'd be an honor if Kit even wrote…"

He breaks off. Pink stains the high points of his cheeks.

Unexpectedly, the roots writhe in agitation.

"What is this?" Loki snarls. "Lady TOF, haven't you torn enough from me? I beg you, no more."

"It's not TOF's fault." I can't help defending TOF. She's controlling, quirky, and a pain in my ass. But she's also the protector of every realm and my friend. "The Time Cave is created by roots, which are soaked in the waters of a magical well. They're like leeches, sucking you dry of the most toxic memories that are poisoning you. Why couldn't Ecstasy have tried to change my mind over a candlelit dinner or movie night? Her idea of a date sucks."

"This is a *date*?" Loki growls.

Instantly, I'm dragged away from Loki, falling into past memories again. My mouth is dry; my mind is hazy.

Then I'm shoved to my knees, which bruise against the cold, stone floor. My pulse is thrashing in my ears, but I can still make out the crash of the ocean (which soaks the air in a salty tang). It's dark, and I'm shivering.

Smoke drifts from bonfires, stinging my eyes.

I stare down at my knees. I'm naked, and I have an adult-sized dick.

Loki's dick.

Even though it's his memory, however, I know where I am.

Sweet Hecate, I can't see this. I don't want to know this secret. *I take it back. I take it back. I take it back.*

Wailing…whoops…drumming.

I'm in the secret caves for the male initiates at the Bacchanalia a thousand years ago. If I witness this, then I can't pretend that I'm the innocent anymore or that the Bacchants are. Perhaps, I've always known that.

My mind becomes woozy, and I clutch my head.

Why am I on my knees? It's too dangerous to kneel around those as steeped in frenzy as the Bacchants.

How dare they insult me? Treat me like I'm invisible? Valhalla! They pretend to worship chaos and then spit in the face of the *god of chaos*.

Soft fingers caress my temple as if in concern, and I fight not to flinch.

Did he notice my panic? A god does not feel fear.

I refuse to raise my head to look at him. Bacchus adores to be admired. I won't give him the satisfaction.

"There, there, I'm here," Bacchus says with such fake concern that I roll my eyes. Bacchus notices (*giants and dwarfs, I've forgotten my lessons about masking my emotions and that's dangerous*). His fingers claw tightly around my chin instead, forcing my gaze to lift to meet his. There's no longer any pretend concern in his calculating gaze. "After your initiation, you'll belong to me and the Bacchants forever as a sacrifice to pleasure."

I stiffen at the way that he draws out the word *pleasure* like dripping honey.

Hide. Mask. Survive.

I clench my trembling hands on my knees, and my nails bite into my skin to ground me.

I can do this.

Perhaps, the bastard won't even whip me?

He's not Odin. He's not Odin. He's not…

I wish that there'd been another way. After Prince was captured, however, I had no choice. I knew about these caves, and the terrible things that happened to the male mages, if they didn't go along with the Bacchants (although, I'd heard that Ecstasy led the initiations).

Why did she leave me here alone with Bacchus? But then, what cult is kind? What god good?

In the name of the World Tree, I'll save my friend. Prince isn't a half-breed. He doesn't deserve to be sacrificed.

He's not me.

My stomach is twisted in knots, and my breath too shallow. I force myself, however, to blank my expression.

"Do you give such personal attention to all the offerings?" I ask.

"Only you." Bacchus strokes down my cheek; my skin crawls. "You're special."

"Even if I tell you to go fuck yourself and then drown yourself in the ocean?"

The boot to my balls is not unexpected but it is agonizing. Involuntary tears spring to my eyes.

Idiot. Idiot. Idiot.

Next time, I'll bite my tongue, instead.

Hide. Mask. Survive.

I grunt and double over. Bacchus grips me by the neck, forcing my head even lower, until I'm prostrate in front of him. Now I feel sick.

"Such a pretty silver-tongue," Bacchus coos.

"Don't call me that," I rasp.

Only one person has ever called me Silver-tongue, and that's an Omega werewolf called Prince, who right now, is caged and waiting to be murdered by this son of a troll. Not literally a son of a troll, although that'd explain why Bacchus is such a murdering bastard who demands the blood of shifters and the bodies of vessels to possess.

When I save Prince, he can choose where we travel next. He's been nagging me about wanting to see the Light Elves. Omens and runes, after this, he can choose to adopt a Light Elf if he wants. I don't care. He's my wildly adventurous companion, who's braver than I shall ever be.

With him, I'm neither alone nor invisible.

I close my eyes, forcing myself not to also obsess over the beautiful Bacchant and her delicious chaos magic, who's lined up to be hollowed out and possessed as the next vessel.

I warned her. *I tried.*

"*Pretty* or *Silver-tongue*?" Bacchus violently rams his knee into my back, slamming me to my stomach.

I hiss, as my dick's crushed against the jagged stones, which litter the floor of the cave. I can't stop my panted breaths. No warrior can let himself be this vulnerable: naked and on his stomach.

For Prince, for Prince, for Prince…

Bacchus straddles me; his weight presses against me, hot and oppressive. His warm, honey presence scents the air, and I choke on it.

"It's time for you to repay the debt that you owe, half-breed." Bacchus wraps my hair around his fingers and wrenches back my head harshly. "I helped free you from the All-Father. How have you found your hard-fought for freedom?"

"Lonely and difficult."

"Then why didn't you stay with me, where you belonged?" Bacchus' expression darkens. "Without me, you wouldn't have been able to hide within Yggdrasil's branches. We're alike, you and me. We're both rebels amongst the gods — wild and chaotic. You promised that you understood my need for pleasure. But then, you disappeared on me, jotunn bitch."

He punches me between the shoulder blades with his free fist.

I snarl, lost in the pain. Then I shake my head, forcing myself to remember where I am.

I'm not back in Odin's Hall. I'll survive this.

I'm with Bacchus, god of ecstasy, frenzy, ritual madness, wine, and fertility.

Knowledge is power.

"Not alike," I rasp.

Bacchus yanks on my hair. "True because even though we're both beautiful, you're the one who entices others," his voice is sugary and cruel. "If you hadn't run from me, we could've been powerful together, inciting madness in others. But now, you'll simply be *mine,* and it's your fault for bewitching me. No god could resist."

Lies.

I twist my neck to look at him. His eyes gleam. *He knows.*

He's using my Frost Giant heritage to blame me for what happens next. On fear of the Valkyries, I won't let him.

"Interesting theory." I'm struggling. I can't stop, even as he smacks my hip like a stallion who needs taming. "But every other god has controlled themselves. Odin's cock, you're nothing but a predator. You use vessels and shifters, stealing their magic and blood. And now you want to steal my…"

"Behave." Bacchus slams my head against the ground so hard that white lights, like dancing moths, flutter across my vision. I'm sinking down and down and I don't want to ever come back up again. "I have a right to steal…"

All of a sudden, I'm dragged fully into unconsciousness. When my eyes open again, my cheeks are wet, even though Loki's are dry. He wraps his arms around my waist, as if I'm the one who needs comforting. Except, it's true…I do.

I felt like it happened to me, just then. What Loki went through was real to me. I shake, confused. I can't get rid of the sensation that it was *me* in that cave with Bacchus.

How could the god who spoke so sweetly to me with honeyed words, only minutes before have been so brutal and insulting to Loki?

It was all a lie.

Shifters were murdered as blood offerings, initiates were violated, and Bacchus never loved me, Ecstasy, or the other Bacchants.

He's merely using us all.

The werewolf in the cage was Loki's friend, and Loki suffered to free him. Where's Prince now? It twists me inside that after a thousand years, he must be dead. I'm lucky to love gods and spirits, but how many lovers and friends has Loki lost?

Did Loki break me that night or did Bacchus?

Wait, has Loki ever shared what happened to him with anyone?

When I meet his gaze, I know that he hasn't.

He huddles closer to me. He's sweating. His curls are damp, and strands stick to his forehead.

Loki's eyes flutter closed. "I can't afford to allow myself to love others because when I get close, look what happens." *Is he attempting to convince me or himself?* "I'm bad, but at least I know it. How much worse is a god who wreathes himself in false golden goodness? Maybe the Soul Bond will work because I'm connected to Bacchus. I don't know. But by the runes, here's a sharp shard of a secret: At the Bacchanalia, I was never meant as an offering for you. I was a special gift for Bacchus. Do you think the asshole cares about returning your magic? You saw what he did, and that was before I defied him and broke free. *This is a blood-feud.* What will his revenge be this time?"

CHAPTER FOURTEEN

Petal's Garden

How did this happen? I'm caught in a war between two ancient — *bad* — gods, Bacchus and Loki. Their scheming blood-feud has played out across the realms for millennia.

For the first time since I was a kid, I feel young and small.

The Bacchants are Bacchus' army or his pawns. But not me. Not anymore.

Sweet Hecate, I'm not blessed with the skill of prophecy. All I know is that this change will lead to beautiful mayhem.

Let. It. Come.

It's as if I'm only just awakening from the poisonous frenzy of the thyrsus. It took the god of lies to show me the truth.

And now, I'm Soul Bonding with him.

I stand in the garden under the moonlight and bright stars. TOF's branches sway above my head, dancing in celebration. My crimson dress is woven out of dyed leaves, which are threaded together. The train sweeps along the ground, rustling in the light breeze. Petal's roses circle me, and tiny suns that are lit with Ra's power (fragile in the dark), burn around the garden like fallen stars.

Ecstasy thinks that she's forcing this on me for my own good like the foul-smelling potion she made me drink every night before bed as a teenager. It dampened my magic while I was sleeping, after a too sexy dream of Bacchus brought one of his statues to life. He was beautiful, confused, and nothing like the real Bacchus. I was heartbroken when Ecstasy insisted that gods weren't pets and transformed him back into stone.

Yet ironically, she also thinks that she's forcing me into a Soul-bond to please the god she loves, who's just as fake as my statue Bacchus.

Yet she isn't.

Loki and I are choosing to walk this path. We're playing this trick together. We're both taking back the control.

Crimson candles hover in the air around the tree;

their flames flicker ghostly. I wrinkle my nose at their intoxicating scent of rose.

My lovers surround me in a protective circle. Petal rides on Bard's head; he rests in his ear like it's the best seat in the house. They're each dressed in gorgeous classic black suits with pale pink shirts, which match the roses pinned in their lapels that Petal has provided. Kit wanted the shirts to be black as well like a funeral because the Soul Bond with Loki was the *death of his hopes and dreams*. Then he sniffled for dramatic effect.

Loki took Kit's hands between his. "Aren't I more like a nightmare?"

When Kit squeaked in outrage, and Ra fought hard to hide his smile, I knew that the Guardians were going to be all right.

I wanted Caesar to be with me. After all, I created him when I was only a kid. He was my bear, and I loved his growly, cuddly ass. Yet just like at the night of the Bacchanalia, Ecstasy insisted that Caesar remain shut away in the cave in my bedroom.

Bubbling cauldrons, I didn't expect to be plotting a toy revolution, but I'm adding Caesar to my Rebel Against Bacchus List.

He already has a taste for chasing Bacchants.

Ra's wings looked stunning, when he insisted on flying me in his arms to the spot for the ceremony, as my current Soul Bond. Just for a moment, I didn't want to let go of the circle of his arms and the warmth of his chest.

I knew this. It was safe.

Then Ra carefully stepped back, stroking my cheek. "You can do this. The rest of us aren't going anywhere. *My life.*"

"*My Soul,*" I breathed.

Now, I focus on the whispering of the breeze through the branches of the tree. My heart pounds.

At last, I raise my gaze to look at my groom.

Loki's suit is black to match my other lovers', but his shirt is a slash of scarlet: a blood offering. His face is hidden in shadow, but his emerald eyes gleam brighter than they ever have. He's studying me, open and loving. He doesn't try and hide it, as our gazes meet.

My breath catches.

Sweet Hecate, this god will be my Soul Bond...

"Let's get this sham over and done with, darlings." Ecstasy rests against TOF, stroking Pocus' head, who lazes on a low branch. Pocus watches Loki with narrowed eyes. "This is ancient binding magic and restitution, and not a marriage. Why did you bother with all this romantic nonsense? If you wanted that, I could've arranged for a matching with a pretty little thing from any of the best covens. Hey, I know, there's a virgin called Lucian, who has the most cutie pie ass.

Well, we can talk about that soon. We can make an excellent alliance."

She looks so pleased with herself.

From the scrabbling behind me, I'm guessing that Ra is holding back Kit.

Loki shoots me a concerned glance almost like he expects me to take up the offer of a *pretty little virgin called Lucian* on the night of our Soul Bond.

"How about you force one lover on me at a time?" *Please, let Loki know that it's an act.* When Loki's lips twitch at one side, I know that he does. "All I want is to get this done and then reap the Shadow Traitor."

Ecstasy rolls her eyes. "All work and no play, makes Autumn a *frustrated* witch. Don't forget the First Night."

Trust the Cock Charmer to prioritize that over saving the forest.

But…*witching heavens*…I can't hide my shiver at the thought. Ecstasy catches it. *Of course she does.*

She smirks. "Don't worry. When haven't I been a good older sister?" I bite the inside of my cheek hard. *Don't answer that.* "I won't let you forget who you are or your needs. You're a witch born into the House of Ecstasy. We're created for pleasure, and men are created to give it to us." My skin crawls. Loki's expression has become a shuttered mask again. Does she truly believe that? Ecstasy's eyes swirl to amber, and her magic prickles across my skin. "I banish shadows and bad spirits," her voice booms across the garden, as she lifts her hands towards the night-time sky.

"That's you told, Kit," Bard mutters.

Kit growls.

"Tree of Life, bless the bonding of these two Souls." Ecstasy snatches my right hand.

How many times has my sister held my hand? Held it through nightmares? Led me as a kid through the walled garden? Danced with me and caught me when I stumbled?

On the night of the Bacchanalia?

And now, she repeats the same ritual that she did when she Soul Bonded me to Ra, taking my hand and passing it into Loki's right hand.

One moment, I'm clutching my sister's familiar hand, safe in the memories and the next, I'm in Loki's cold, firm hold.

His fingers tighten around mine like he expects me to pull away.

This is new and dangerous, but it's what I've chosen.

Hecate above, this is happening.

I swallow hard, and the back of my neck is damp with sweat. But then, Loki squeezes my hand, and I know that I'm not alone. I calm, and a joy that I didn't expect, floods me. *An excitement.*

"Wherever you go," I vow, "there also go I, your Soul Bond."

Loki steps closer, until our joined hands are pressed between us; his smile is secret, dancing in his eyes for me alone. "Wherever you go, there also I go, your Soul Bond."

"*Now that's beautiful, see, just how a bond should be*," Petal says, sounding like he's about to cry.

Bard simply *whoops*, as Ra and Kit break into applause.

Ecstasy pulls a face, but she still drags Pocus off his branch, hugging him to her chest. He purrs, rubbing his ears against her.

Does she at least love him?

I gasp, as a second Leaf Tattoo burns ice-cold onto my arm, underneath the one that connects me to Ra. Is it frozen because Loki is half Frost Giant?

I stagger at the same time as Loki, but we both hold the other up.

It's too much...*overwhelming*... I can feel him...*everything*...all at once.

Loki's magic coils through me — *chaos*. I can taste it. I'm alive with magic again, even if it's through the bond. My pupils dilate, as I stare at Loki. The whole world is more vibrant again. His hair is fiery red, his eyes are glistening emeralds, and his shirt is blood.

The light glistens off the blazing suns, and every rustle of the wind is a storm.

I'm reborn through Loki.

Is it as intense for Loki to feel me in the bond? By the tremors wracking him, I think that it must be.

He's inside me.

"You're astounding," he whispers. "I knew that you would be."

His cool lips press to mine in a kiss that burns with hot passion. He tastes of strawberries and magic. I bite his lip and suck on it, as he moans; his blood offering is for me alone. I claim it. His darkness is mine. I feel it now moving inside like a desire so terrible that it could bring realms to their knees.

All of a sudden, an alternative rock song with gritty, raspy vocals like a wicked seduction winds over the garden: Royal Deluxe's "Bad."

I draw back from the kiss with a huff. "Your choice?"

Loki inclines his head.

"Witches above, you're one..."

Loki arches his brow. "Badass god?"

"God with serious balls."

Loki smirks. "I can't disagree."

"*Yay, dance time!*" Petal slides down Bard's hair and into the pocket of his suit. "*Congratulations; you make a lush sight together. But what about your pretty best friend? I'm calling it. I get the next marriage, bitches.*"

"Language," I call.

"Less talking, more dancing." Bard holds out his arms to Ra, who snatches him around the waist with his wings and dances in a way that's definitely dancing like you're fucking.

All right, that's hot.

When Kit's shoulders slump, Ra glances back at him. "Come on, nine-tails. Don't you want to be bad with us?"

I grin, as Kit bounces to Ra without even trying to hide his haste. He wraps his arms around Ra's neck from behind, at the same time as twining his tails around his middle. Then the three of them dance in a way that I have to persuade them to try out in bed.

When Loki chuckles, I know that he can tell what I'm thinking. I flush.

Loki pulls me by the hand further onto the lawn that's strewn with rose petals. "Let's try the humans' tradition of the first dance."

He slides his arm around my waist, and I curl my arm around his neck. Then he pulls me tight to his body with my head to his chest. I can feel the fast thudding of his heart, and the hard outline of his dick through his pants. Then we dance to the crunchy guitars and deep grooves like two bad creatures in the dark who never want to see the light again.

He strokes the hollow of my back. "Isn't it delicious to pull off a trick beneath the nose of your sister and god?" I raise my head to glance at Ecstasy, who's swaying with Pocus, lost in her own version of frenzy. Loki's eyes glint with mischief. "She believes that she's playing you, but *you're* playing *her*. No one ever suspects the puppet can suddenly develop a mind of its own and bite back." His lips ghost mine. "*We will bite back.*"

My brow furrows. "We need to break the hex first."

I can feel the crimson chains binding Loki even more now and their wrongness. A Guardian shouldn't be bound by them. And a Soul Bond that's entered into willingly, should never also be wrapped in chains.

Suddenly, he sobers. "Do you trust me?"

I caress my fingers down his neck, and he shudders. "We're Soul Bonded. We have to trust each other."

His eyes widen. Then he pulls me into another kiss, but this time it's gentle and tender.

When he draws back, something crosses his expression that I haven't seen before — and it unsettles me. "Then remember that I always make the first move. You think that your sister has me wrapped in chains." His breath gusts against my ear, as he whispers, "If I'm in them, then I choose to be."

I startle but before I can reply, I'm snatched out of Loki's hold by Ra.

"My turn." Ra kisses me on my forehead.

I laugh, snuggling into his wings, before he passes me onto Bard. I stare into Bard's shining silver eyes, as he kisses me in turn.

"By my horns, you look beautiful," Bard murmurs.

Then Kit dives on Bard like he's stolen his candy, wrapping his tails around me.

Sweet Hecate, does he mean to squeeze the breath from me?

"Kit loves you." Kit rubs his fox ears against me, marking me, as if I don't believe him (like I haven't known it for centuries). "Love Kit?"

"I do. So much." I tilt up his chin, so that he'll look into my eyes. "Soul Bonding with Loki, doesn't mean that I love you less. Do you understand?"

Kit nods.

Candles and bells, let him believe it.

"As you have the bride, time for me to just have a cozy little chat with the groom." Ra's eyes blaze with fire, as he snatches Loki's arm and drags him away from me towards the boundary.

Uh-oh.

Why do I think there's not going to be anything cozy about it...? Although, gods and demons have weird definitions of cozy.

Loki isn't shaking Ra's hand off his arm. Didn't

Loki say that he isn't chained unless he chooses to be...?

I march after them but don't interrupt. I trust both of my lovers to deal with this.

Ra's wings are stretched out and he towers over Loki; I forget how tall Ra is.

"You won't hurt her." Ra's eyes narrow. "I can swallow your Soul."

I roll my eyes. Ra playing protective always comes across as freaky. Yet Ra's act doesn't scare Loki. Instead, Loki looks like a geeky kid on Christmas morning, unwrapping a science kit.

He peers at Ra. "Really? Fascinating."

Ra blinks and let's go of Loki. "Probably not. It'd be a fun power though."

Ra's wings droop, and he looks across at me as if for help. I hold back a laugh. I adore that even now Ra's looking out for me.

I stroll closer. "It'd make my life easier."

"Lazy reaper," Ra chides with a grin. Then he straightens Loki's pinned rose. "And Autumn told us...enough. You saved my life and protected me from the big, bad Autumn over there. I didn't need protecting, but it's the thought that counts. *She's* not the one who put me into a cage; she's the one who opened the door and set me free. I know that she'll do the same for you. We all will."

Loki tilts his head. "You still look caged to me."

Ra's eyes flash. "Not where it counts. But you're right, we're breaking free of the House of Ecstasy. On the eye of Horus, we're all rebels here, so let's get rebellious."

Before the ceremony, the Guardians accepted my whispered explanation about Bacchus hurting shifters and Loki. I didn't tell them details because it wasn't my story to tell. I shouldn't have been surprised how swiftly they turned against Bacchus, but it only struck me then how they'd been holding back for my sake.

When fireworks burst above our heads in the shape of golden foxes, I glance at Kit. *Why do I forget the power of his magic and illusions?*

Kit wraps his tails around himself. "Kit's gift."

"Your kitsune is special." Loki's eyes are bright with admiration.

"*Our* kistune," I reply.

"I take it that it's time for gifts…?" Ecstasy is smiling but there's something predatory about it. "Loki, I have a Soul Bond gift for you."

I perk up. Last time, she gave me the Box of Tricks as a Soul Bonding gift. What will it be tonight? An enchanted leaf-shaped dildo? Vibrating rose quartz butt plug to reveal your aura? A magical aphrodisiac of sweet orange and jasmine to turn you feral for ten hours straight?

Ecstasy places Pocus down on the floor with more gentleness than she's ever treated any of my lovers and then pulls something small out of her pocket. It gleams when the light falls on it. Its sharp, glinting like a chaos moment.

A shard of glass or...?

Loki draws in his breath. *He knows.*

"Take it," she holds it out temptingly to Loki. "It's yours. Don't you want to see your sons?"

"A magic mirror." Ra's expression is grim. "Silver-tongue, she only means to hurt you by..."

Loki darts to Ecstasy faster than I knew that he could move. He snatches the mirror from her like he thinks she'll retract the offer. Then he falls to his knees. He's shaking, as he stares at his sons, stroking the glass.

And he watches what he can't have. Who's missing from the night of our Soul Bond because they're being held hostage at my sister's mercy.

This is a threat.

He traces his thumb across the glass.

Despair. Loss. Terror.

The emotions crash through the Soul Bond. Next to me, Ra shudders as well; he must feel it too because all three of us are connected. And underlying all of it, a dad's love for his kids

"You didn't need to... I won't... You have me, so why would you...? If you hurt them, then the things that I shall do to you will make the stars weep." Loki grasps the shard so hard that it slices his hand. "Just, *please…*"

When Ecstasy pats Loki on the head and then leaves her hand there like she owns him through his kids, I storm to her and knock away her hand. She stares at me in shock.

"Don't touch him," I snarl.

"Possessive," she grins. "It always adds fire in the bedroom." Then she points at the mirror. "That's real time, darlings. You can watch your cutie-pie son, if you miss him. And if you're bad, little leaf can smash the glass."

Loki clutches the mirror to his chest like it's his sons and as if he can protect either of them from us.

"I'll never do that," I hiss.

After a single moment more, Loki forces his gaze away from his sons and slides the glass into his suit pocket. Then he pushes himself to his feet with an air of nonchalance like he hasn't just been kneeling at a witch's feet.

"Worlds have turned for longer than any of us have been alive and the stars have watched." Loki appears calm, but the look that he shoots my sister makes even me shiver. "Huh, I wonder just what it'd take to make them weep. I hope for your sake that you don't find out."

Ecstasy becomes ashen, before trembling with

fury. She takes a step toward Loki, who meets her glare defiantly.

At that moment, however, a blackness like tendrils of writhing tar seep across the garden.

I freeze in terrified shock.

Not now. Not here.

Loki's eyes widen, and Ra cries out in warning.

Magic sparks across Ecstasy in panicked waves. "It's impossible. How are the Shadow Demons strong enough to break my wards…?"

The Shadow Demons stretch out, wrapping around my waist and dragging me into the forest.

And I scream.

CHAPTER FIFTEEN

Petal's Garden

The Shadow Demons' writhing hold pins my arms to my side. Tar-like tendrils creep over my face. Their touch shoots electric sparks through me, and I shudder in agony.

Their touch is worse than death. It's a nothingness. *Void.* It shouldn't exist in our realm, and it hungers to fill up my hollowed-out insides.

The Shadow Demons' crimson eyes burn on all sides of me. I'm surrounded and alone.

I need to hurl.

Sweet Hecate, don't let my lovers enter the forest after me. They can't fight this mass of Shadow Demons. They don't have the Infernal Scythe.

Ra can't leave the boundaries of TOF anyway,

except in spirit form. *He must be wrecked not to be able to save me.*

I bite my lip. At least I trust Ra to stop Kit and Bard killing themselves on a suicide mission.

How did the Shadow Demons break the wards? They've never been able to get this close to TOF before.

In the darkness of the forest, beneath the canopy of the branches, I struggle in terror. I'll be torn apart just like my parents.

The Shadow Demons have already murdered the trees, whose trunks are gnarled and withered. The floor is a sea of black leaves. I scrunch my nose against the bonfire smell of burning and ash.

Then my new Leaf Tattoo burns like ice is being pressed to it, and I scream again. Loki is reaching through the Bond. I push back hard.

Don't you dare.

Is the newest Guardian wild...arrogant...*reckless* enough to throw himself into a battle against Shadow Demons?

Crack my cauldron, *of course* he is.

A web of brilliant magic flashes through the Soul Bond, catching around my waist and over the shadows. Then Loki is dragged by the Bond underneath the trees and through the Shadow Demons like an avenging god.

He's formidable.

He battles through the black waves of shadows with a war cry. His chaos magic bursts from him like a tsunami. The shadows fall back just long enough for him to reach me.

"How…?" I ask in shock.

No one has ever survived the Shadow Demons, let alone tamed them.

Loki grasps my hands, assessing the way that I'm pinned. "I'll always hold onto you against the shadows." He narrows his eyes. "You shan't take her," he snarls like he thinks the Shadow Demons will obey him.

Why's he risking his life? Shadow Demons can kill a god.

My eyes widen at the giant Shadow Demon behind Loki that steps out of the mass of its brothers. Is he the Chief? He towers as tall as the trees, and his arms are black mists that wrap around Loki's neck, dragging him backward.

Loki's fingers slip out of mine.

"Lopter," I holler.

I grit my teeth, struggling harder. Loki's not my prisoner or servant. He's more than a Guardian. He's my Soul Bond and the man who I've been unable to forget for a thousand years. He's under my skin and in my heart. His magic flows through me; I'm in his head and he's in mine.

He can't die. This story isn't over.

I boot my shoes through the blackened leaves. The train of my dress rips, as I twist and turn. As if to punish me, the shadows tighten their hold. One of my ribs cracks like I've been punched in the gut, and I gasp.

The Chief Shadow Demon stares down at Loki with flaring red eyes and then lifts him like he weighs nothing.

"What are you waiting for?" Loki growls. "Either kiss me or put me down. Don't be a prick tease."

What in the witching heavens is he doing?

When the Chief Shadow Demon rears back, lifting Loki even further into the air, I realize that Loki is distracting attention onto himself.

It works.

The Chief Shadow Demon slams Loki into the nearest tree with a crack that sounds like he now has matching broken ribs to mine. I wince. Then like Loki's a ragdoll, the Chief Shadow Demon swings him between the trees, smashing him carelessly into them.

Smash — smash — smash.

I shudder, as Loki's pain shocks me through the bond. Yet I also feel Loki's defiance. He's taking the bruises for me.

The Chief Shadow Demon tightens its hold and squeezes.

It's going to kill Loki.

Blessed Hecate, I can't lose him, not like this.

"Stop it." I clench my jaw. Yet when will I have an opportunity to talk to a Shadow Demon again? They never communicate with other demons or gods. They're destruction. That's all I know about them. Perhaps, I can reach out with words as well as weapons. "Why in Hecate's name are you here? What do you want?"

To my surprise, the Chief Demon stops hurting Loki, dropping him in a heap amongst the writhing tendrils of his brothers. Then he turns his heavy gaze onto me. I wasn't truly expecting a response. Having his attention is terrifying.

Loki struggles to his feet, smoothing down his suit, which is torn. Loki straightens his shoulders, adjusting the withered rose on his lapel.

How is he so calm? I crave to reap every single Shadow Demon for killing the rose that I pinned on Loki myself.

Loki looks at me through his purpling eyes and sighs. "Attempting to play the chew toy distraction over here. You're not helping."

When the Chief Shadow Demon's legs melt to mists and he moves towards me in a lurching, hideous rush with a screech that raises the hair on the back of my neck, something shatters in Loki.

"I said you shan't take her," he howls.

He's the storm. The wild. *Chaos.*

It's in his eyes: their emerald glass fractures into a thousand, glinting chaos moments, and I can see every single moment.

I shake because he's more terrifying than the Shadow Demons. *Shouldn't I always have known that?*

Loki grins with a sharp savagery. In his possessive rage, he's transformed into a violent madness. He drags the shadows away from his neck like he's the monster they should fear. Now it's the Chief Shadow Demon who melts away into the forest, abandoning his brothers.

Loki stands in the middle of a whirlwind of pure, glowing *chaos*, while emerald magic burns in his palms. He rips apart the Shadow Demons, laughing in the midst of the destruction, as he breaks through a path to me.

I can't look away from him. Our connection is more powerful than anything I've ever felt before.

Eternity's in his gaze.

Then Loki snaps the shadows that bind me and catches me as I fall.

CHAPTER SIXTEEN

Tree of Life, Autumn's Bedroom

L oki and I fall through the entranceway into my bedroom, banging the door shut behind us. We tumble, slamming into the wall. It'd help us to balance, if we let go of each other for even a moment or stopped kissing. But his arms are locked around my waist, my body is pressed to his, and our lips are a tangle of bruising need, *want*, need.

We're alive.

When Loki tightens his hold, I wince at the stabbing pain from my ribs. Yet it only makes the pleasure more intense.

We could've died...almost died...but we're alive now.

It's our First Night together, and the shadows could've killed us.

Loki saved me.

I wrap my fingers around his curls and tell him with every caress what I can't in words.

We touched death tonight but we survived together. Is it strange that I've never felt so alive?

I moan into the kiss, as Loki twists me, pinning my hands above my head. The taste of Loki mingles with the room in a delicious mix like strawberries dipped in honey. The magical fire in the orb sizzles and flares but then dims. My eyelashes flutter, as I force myself to glance over Loki's shoulder at the four-poster bed. It's never looked so far away.

Hecate's tit, with the way that Loki's thumbs are stroking my wrists with just the right amount of pressure, and his thighs are nudging mine apart, I'll take a hard wall over satin sheets.

Loki's eyes twinkle, and he pulls me towards my desk.

Cursed frogs, he wouldn't...?

He's the god of Mischief, of course he would.

With a single swipe of his arm, Loki knocks my paperwork flying and hoists me onto the desk. He muffles my outraged cry with a searing kiss that flows magic through me like budding branches that burst with *life*.

I tingle from the top of my head to my curling toes and I melt like I've been massaged by Ra. My muscles relax, and I lie back on the desk. Loki follows me, caging me beneath him; his hard prick tents his pants and presses against my hip. He sucks on my lip, before pushing his tongue back into my mouth with passionate thrusts.

It's perfect. *How did I ever live without him?*

Who cares what happens to the Bacchants' business? Sorting paperwork isn't even in my Top Hundred Witchy Priority List right now.

There's nothing on my mind but Loki and his talented tongue. In the frantic way that our hands stroke over each other in frenzied desperation, our fear, excitement, and survivors' high spiral together.

I can't tear myself away from Loki and I don't want to. I press my fingers to a bruise on his cheek. His suit is torn and dirtied. He's been battered by the Shadow Demons but not broken.

Never broken.

I crave to press on every single injury, which he gained to save me.

Finally, I turn my head to the side, breaking the kiss. Loki raises his eyebrow at me, as I study the way that the mottled bruises and rough scratches continue down his neck and collarbone, beneath the line of his ripped shirt. *I want to see every mark.*

"Too many clothes," I say.

"Is that an order?"

"Do you want it to be?"

He pecks a soft kiss to my lips, before vanishing his clothes in a slow striptease. My breath catches as his pale, lean beauty is revealed, wreathed in purple shadows. Around his middle, the marks darken to black; he must have at least several broken ribs.

How long will he take to heal?

Concern washes through me. "Do we need to get ice for your ribs or…?"

Loki shakes his head, before glancing down at himself. He looks more uncertain, as if I'll reject him because of the marks. *Now that he's not perfect.*

"Hey, I have an inbuilt ice feature, remember? Anyway, this is nothing. I know how to take a beating." I wince. I hate that just like Ra, he can say things like that so casually. He bites his lip. "Sorry you got the damaged doll but you did choose the action figure."

Yet I can't drag my gaze away from him: he's gorgeous and he's mine.

"Sweet Hecate…" I murmur, appreciatively.

I was trapped with Loki in the Time Cave, and we were close. Yet it was different then. Now, we're Soul Bonded, and I can feel him moving inside me, as well as being pressed above me with his dick rubbing against my inner thigh.

Come on…just an inch to the right…you know the spot…so close…

My sister, the Cock Charmer would be able to call Little Loki where she wanted him.

Loki smirks, confidence restored. "*Hecate*? Have you forgotten my name already? Should I carve it into your skin?"

That should not make my Little Autumn (and I truly have never thought of naming my clit before, but why don't women?), get a lady boner.

Loki licks **LOPTER** — each letter teasingly slow — down from behind my ear to the bottom of my neck, marking me. I hold my breath, more aware of the skin that he touches than I ever have been. It prickles and tingles, branded with his tongue.

I reach out, tracing the bruises along his chest and arms, accepting them in turn like they're proof of…*what?*

Love?

When Loki raises his head, his gaze is intense. My heart clenches at the thought that he can see inside me, as much as I can feel him.

"Protection?" He asks. "I usually carry my own, but I've just vanished my clothes."

"We don't need it."

His gaze becomes icy. "Not happening."

I blink. "Bubbling cauldrons, I only mean that…" How do I explain that since that night a thousand years ago, I can't conceive? That Bacchus' immortality gave me an immunity to all diseases, even if it left me infected with his spark? "I forget that you haven't slept with a Bacchant before. Trust me that we don't need protection."

Hecate above, I forget just how much he's trusting me already. For a moment, his expression becomes open and raw like he's remembering it too.

But then, Loki's look turns sly. "One of us is ready to do their duty, but the other is seriously wearing too many clothes."

I grin, before kicking off my shoes.

"Too slow." Loki waves his hands, and my clothes vanish.

I stare down at my naked body in shock. "In the name of chaos, bring my dress back. I want to keep it." I blush. "It may have sentimental value."

"Really?" Loki tilts his head, and curls fall over his eyes. "*Hmm*, what will you give me in return? I like deals."

"You're holding my clothes hostage?"

His eyes light up. "I *am* bad."

I close my hand around his balls. "So am I. These are large and valuable, right? So, deal?"

Loki laughs, even if he's trying to hide how my touch is affecting him. "On fear of Ragnarök, you're a hard negotiator. Impressive. Okay, my large, precious balls for your clothes, which are safe in a shadow realm with *my* clothes. I'll retrieve them later. Right now, we have need of those balls, don't we?"

I loosen my hold and play with his balls; he fights for his legs not to buckle. "I witching hope so. You have quite the reputation as a legendary lover, after all."

"Hey, I don't disappoint." He bats away my teasing fingers. "Let's get more comfortable."

I squeak, as he slips his hands beneath me and pulls me up into his arms in a bridal carry. Then he sweeps me to the bed and throws me down into the center of the berry blankets. He crawls over me with predatory grace.

For the first time, it hits me with total clarity that my enemy is in bed with me, and yet it feels like he always should've been.

Yet I have to be certain.

"You don't need to do this," I offer. "It's your choice. You can do nothing, and we'll lie to Ecstasy that we—"

"*Do nothing?*" Loki circles my nipple maddeningly slowly, as if this is an answer. "I've long feared your cult but always desired you." *Wait, what...?* He lowers himself even closer, and his breath gusts against my cheek. "And I've a hundred wicked things planned for you, my shining chaos."

I tremble, wrapping my arms around him. My fingers claw into his back.

All of a sudden, Drake's soulful R & B "Find Your Love" bursts from the roof. Its Jamaican beat and bump-and-grind seductiveness winds around Loki and me.

Loki hesitates, leaning up on his elbows. "So, is this your Fuck the Guardians play list?"

I huff. *I need his dick...mouth...hands...something...* I should really have learned how to become the Cock Charmer.

"It's Oni's Fuck the Infernal Play List."

Loki strokes a strand of my hair back from my cheek. "I can't wait to meet this demon lover of yours."

"*Ex* and..." I narrow my eyes. "You're a god. Don't you think lots of prejudiced anti-demon things?"

Loki freezes. "Does Ra?"

I shake my head.

"Huh, interesting. Do you think that since I'm a *half-breed*, who's lived my life suffering at the hands of prejudiced assholes, I'd do the same to anyone? The world is coated with lies. Everyone is smothered in them: magical and non-magical. I don't judge anyone by the realm's lies. Everything is myth; we can make ourselves real. And that's what I see. Do you?"

I cup his cheek. I need him to know this — *feel it.*

"You woke me up," I whisper. "You make me see, when before I was blinded. Everything is changed now."

His breath catches, and his gaze is searching.

Does he believe me?

I'm here… I chose you like you chose me… This is our path… I'm here with you.

His hand curls into mine, and his grin becomes sharp. "Now, we had a deal. Prepare yourself for the best fuck in your long, long life."

I return his grin and it's equally as sharp. "Cocky."

"Confident."

I nip his lip in a challenge. "Prove it."

I want him wild…*need it*. I can't forget his towering strength in the Eternal Forest and the way that his eyes shattered into a thousand glinting chaos moments. I should be terrified but instead, I shiver with the thrill of danger.

Loki rolls his hips and hard dick against me. "By the Norns, I will."

His fingers tighten in my hair, and he wrenches back my head to give himself better access to my neck. He bites down on it with a new savagery. My eyes close, and I shudder at the sensations, as his other hand slides down my body, tweaking at my nipple and then circling my hip.

"I want you to fuck me, until the entire Eternal Forest knows that we're Soul Bonded." I wrap both my arms tightly around him again, digging my nails into his back.

"Harder," he breathes. "Let me feel you." He

gasps, as I hook my nails in *harder*, and he ruts against me with a feral wildness, even as his fingers gently circle my clit and then hook into my pussy. He hisses with pain, and I know that he's hurting his ribs. Except, he ignores it; his pain only spurs him on. I feel stretched too thin inside, coiling higher and higher. He smiles against my neck, nipping kisses alongside his earlier bites. "I love the way that your breath hitches when I do this…"

He curls his fingers in my pussy and…*witching heavens*…my breath hitches.

I slide my hand around to his dick and rub its head. Loki trembles, drawing in a shuddery breath.

"And I love the way that *your* breath hitches when I do that," I reply.

Who says sex isn't a contest?

Loki's pupils dilate. "Feisty little sex fiend, huh?" I pump down the shaft of his dick in retaliation, and he quickens the speed of his fingers. "A-ll you w-want me f-for is m-my b-body."

He pants on almost each word, barely getting it out. He's denying himself his own orgasm.

Respect.

Except, I'm a sweaty, wrecked mess. So, who's winning?

I'd say both of us.

"You've discovered my villainous plot." I drag him into a desperate kiss. "And I need you now."

When I release his dick, he slumps against me.

"Thank the Valkyries. I'm a god but even I have limits." He slides his fingers out of my pussy, before nudging his cock at its entrance instead. "Is this okay? Tell me when you're…"

"If you don't put your dick in me right now…"

"Demanding." Loki grins. "I knew that you had a thing about giving orders."

Then he thrusts into me, and I fall apart.

Yet Loki's arms are cradled around me; I'm safe in his hold. He snatches my hands, pinning them to the bed at either side of my head and entangling our fingers together. He catches my gaze; I'm lost in the emerald. His rhythmic thrusts build like waves inside me, along with the chaos magic: cycles of time. His magic surrounds us, sparking against the walls and pulsing across my skin.

It's beautiful and spellbinding.

"*Lopter*," I scream, arching in pleasure.

Loki thrusts more erratically and then he comes from hearing his name on my lips. He rests his forehead on mine. His breathing is rapid and ragged. He lies there like he doesn't want to pull away from me but could be joined with me forever.

On the other hand, he's heavy. So, finally I bat at him.

Loki grumbles, pecking my nose, before rolling onto his back. I turn to rest my head on his chest and curl my arm around his waist. He looks at me in shock like cuddling is more intimate than any of the things that we've just done together or like he hasn't just had his dick inside me.

"So, was that your best...?" He asks, casually.

Except, by the stiffness of his shoulders, it's not casual at all.

Witching heavens, save me from men and their Dick Egos.

I trace a pattern on his chest. "I never compare my lovers."

"Good to know."

He snatches my finger and strokes it. "Would you like to be the first woman to write on my skin?"

"*Ehm*, is this some kind of humiliation kink? Do you want me to write **SPANK ME** on your ass in marker pen?"

"Maybe another time." Loki chuckles. "I was thinking more along the lines of a rune and recording a magical message."

An infinity of yes.

My throat is tight; I struggle to speak. "Isn't that permanent?"

"You mean like a Soul Bond...?" He studies me closely. "You've seen inside me, and now I wish to carry your words inside as well." When his expression falls, before becoming shuttered, I regret it. "Hey, it was just an idea. Forget it."

I grip his chin. "I'd be honored."

He gives a curt nod, before he slides the pad of his thumb over the nail of my index finger. The nail hardens and sharpens.

He doesn't mean that I'll literally carve into his skin, right?

When he covers my hand with his, directing it to his chest, I realize that *he does*. I lick over my dry lips.

I can do this.

"Blood to seal the rune magic," Loki explains. "Odin is the master of this magic and he taught me. Let me guide your hand, while you say the words that you want recorded. Tell me when you're ready."

Magic hangs in the air between us: ancient and powerful.

I nod, and Loki pulls my nail to his pale skin over his heart, scratching until the blood bleeds a beautiful rune. He smiles at me, and I relax.

This time, he's choosing to bleed for me.

The rune glows, and I panic. What should I say? Why am I getting performance anxiety now?

At last, the right words trip off my tongue like they were always waiting there, "You are my chaos, and I am yours."

Loki's eyes gleam, as he shudders.

The rune glows brighter, before sealing and fading back into his chest. My nail shrinks to its normal length, and Loki curls his hand around mine.

"On the World Tree, I'll keep your voice safe inside my heart." He lets go of my hand to trace over where I scratched the rune. "I can hear your secrets now. They're my newest magpie treasures."

"Thief." I grin and then yank the blanket off him.

"Hey," he tries to pull it back, but I'm too quick.

I scramble off the bed, dragging the blanket around me, and Loki gives up. He sprawls on the satin sheets in godly glorious nakedness.

"There was someone left out of the celebration," I explain. "Caesar's been with me since I was a kid, but Ecstasy's never treated him fairly."

I walk to the wall, dropping to my knees beside the vines, which peel back to reveal the low cave. Caesar is curled with his bronze head on his paws, sleeping.

Loki pulls himself up and peers into the cave. His brow furrows. "I'm glad that you have your mechanical toy bear or whatever that creature is to you. I guess love is love but…"

I snort and then cover my mouth not to startle Caesar awake. "He's my friend like Petal. I'm his creator."

"Thank the Norns." Loki waves his elegant hand at Caesar. "Even I'm not into bear loving and I'm adventurous."

"That's a shame because I've bought you the furry outfit and everything." I ignore Loki's blush and glance at Caesar, stroking my hand over his ear. "Shall I wake him?"

"Not if it encourages you in the delusion that I'll dress as a furry." Loki sighs. "Hey, it strikes me that you should let sleeping bears lie."

I nod, standing and stepping back. The vines cover Caesar's cave again.

Loki gives me a considering look, before the magic mirror that my sister gave him as a cruel, taunting Soul Bond gift appears in his hand. "I called it from the shadow realm." He stares at it like he can't wrench away his gaze. "My sons are sleeping too. It's good to know that they're at least getting enough sleep. Sleipnir used to be a brat about going to bed every night, preferring to stay up to watch the stars and play guitar." His fingers tighten around the mirror. "Do you want to see?"

I know it's costing him to share this secret. But then, I've just shared Caesar.

"I'd love to." I shuffle to his side, holding up the blanket as it trails after me like a mockery of a wedding dress.

Loki darts a glance at me, before he turns the shard of glass, so that we can both see the sleeping face of the young god. Sleipnir's dressed in striped pink and black pajamas. He has cotton candy pink hair, which falls in gentle spikes. He reminds me of Loki: the same cheekbones and jawline.

"He's handsome," I say.

Because how many times has Loki been told that his sons were monsters?

Loki glances at me in surprise but then nods like he doesn't trust himself to speak. His eyes gleam in the light.

How can Loki bear to look at Sleipnir, knowing that he's a hostage in Rebel Academy? Asleep and vulnerable like this, I can imagine Sleipnir as a kid — held in Loki's arms.

"It hurts to look at my sons," Loki says quietly, "but it'd hurt more to look away. It's like when my sons were newborns, I was honestly terrified to watch them at night in case their chest would stop rising and falling but I was more scared that if I looked away, then it would. By Odin's beard, I was exhausted in those first weeks because I was so certain that something as special as them would be snatched away from me. My sons couldn't survive being mine." Loki's voice drops to a whisper, "What if they don't?"

"I'll find a solution to all of this." My eyes blaze, and my voice shakes. "I promise, we'll find a way to reunite you with your sons, right? I won't cage anyone either, but this can be a family for all of you, if you want it. But only if we're free. I'll tear down this world if I need to. Do you believe me?"

Loki's gaze is searching. "I believe that you'll try."

Well, it's a start.

It still slices me deep that I can't help Loki take Sleipnir back yet but I can help him keep the magical connection to him safe. I stride to the desk (and witches above, it's going to be hard to look at this desk and not remember the feel of my ass against it, as Loki grinds his dick against me), before beckoning Loki over.

"Sorry about the…" He gestures at the sea of crumpled paperwork on the floor, as he stalks to my side still clutching the mirror like the security blanket of a lost kid. "Although, I can't see much of a difference to your previous filing system. Do you call it the Chaos Method?"

The arrogant god won't look so smug, when he discovers that he'll be the one sorting out the paperwork for me.

I satisfy myself with a smile. "Pretty much."

When I pass my hand over a secret compartment underneath the desk, it pops open.

"Why, you have secrets of your own." Loki's eyes glint hungrily. "Show me."

I nudge him with my shoulder. "Magpie." He grins unashamedly. "This is about keeping *your* secrets safe. Only I can open it. If you put the magic mirror inside and then press your palm to the drawer as you close it, you'll be able to open it as well."

"Such trust," he whispers.

As if it's painful, he forces himself to place the mirror in the drawer and then close it with the palm of his hand.

"It's safe?"

"Safe," I promise.

It's not his sons, but it's as close as I can manage.

Unexpectedly, Loki draws back. His eyes become stormy, as his magic gathers in furious clouds around him.

"Do you hear that outside?" His voice is fierce. "Someone's spying on us."

Before I can stop Loki, he prowls to the door, wrenching it open.

CHAPTER SEVENTEEN

Tree of Life, Autumn's Bedroom

When Loki pulls open the door with chaos magic swirling around him like he's ready to dive into the Shadow Demons and tear them apart to rescue me once again, Kit tumbles through onto his front with a shocked squeak.

What an interesting spy.

In human form, Kit's ears flatten to his head. He pushes himself to his knees, attempting to ignore Loki and peer past him and into the bedroom at me like he thinks Loki may have *ravaged* me or something equally dramatic. Does he believe that I'm a damsel from the human romance novels that he hides and pretends that he doesn't read?

Loki blocks his view, however, resting his hands on his hips in the typical *pissed off dad move*.

Kit's cheeks bloom with pink because that would be the less usual *naked pissed off dad with a boner*.

"Stop waving around your godly dick," Kit wails. "Kit's blinded."

Loki snorts. "Kit's a voyeur." Then he glances over his shoulder at me. "Hey, why didn't you go with Godly Dick, rather than Little Loki?"

My lips quirk. "I have my reasons. Anyway, you're an exhibitionist, so you two are well-matched."

"I never said that we weren't." Loki arches his brow at Kit. "Are you staying down there because you've finally decided to get in that dick sucking practice we talked about? Don't worry, I'm a patient teacher."

Kit fluffs up in outrage, prowling to his feet. But he keeps his nine-tails swept in front of himself around his hips. I rest back on the desk, still clutching the blanket around my shoulders. Then I realize: Kit's hiding his tented pants with his tails.

The naughty fox-spirit was listening behind the door.

Is he ever going to stop being so possessive? Sweet Hecate, it's hot that he's turned on and wants…*both of us together?*

"Kit was guarding my Infernal," Kit lies. Then his eyes narrow. "If he's been a bad Loki, we can still throw him out to demons, *munch munch*. One little boot…"

I pull the blanket tighter around myself. "You're not convincing anyone, Voyeur Kitsune."

Loki chuckles, and the storm clouds are driven from his eyes. When Kit presses his fingers together anxiously, Loki tangles their hands together, instead.

Kit's shoulders start to relax, but then he yelps, as Loki sweeps him into a bridal carry, in the same way that earlier, he held me (although, I didn't kick my legs like Kit). It shows impressive strength, even if Kit is smaller than Loki.

Loki catches my eye; the gleam in them is wicked.

"Bad exhibitionist god," Kit growls. "Kit is no bride."

Loki arranges his expression into one of sombre seriousness. "By the Norns, you must be. After all, you're here on the First Night and you're in my arms."

"Don't you want to snuggle?" I coax, diving onto the bed and patting the place next to me.

In the name of chaos, I know my Guardians' weaknesses as well as their strengths, and Kit can never resist an excuse to wind around another's warmth or cuddle on a bed.

He was denied both by Hestia.

Kit attempts to hide his eagerness. Except, he can't hide the way that his tails perk up (revealing the sizable tenting in his suit pants).

"With my Infernal, always," Kit replies.

Loki lays Kit next to me in the bed far more gently than I threw myself onto it. Then he meets my gaze, and my heart clenches. His look is fond, loving, and witches above, *what did I ever do to deserve for him to look at me like that?*

Kit's scent of sweet apple blossoms winds around me, and I run my fingers down his long silky white hair that drapes across the bed.

Loki strokes Kit's cheek. "Of course, if he isn't the bride, then he's an imposter, who we'll have to punish with kisses."

I wince at Loki's misstep.

Take it back: quick, quick, quick.

Hecate above, why did he have to say *punish*?

"It's a joke," I rush to say. "He doesn't mean it."

Loki blinks at me in confusion. But it's too late. Kit's lost in the past and his own conditioned fear.

Kit scrambles to the bottom of the bed in a flurry of tails. His nails extend, shredding the sheets in his fear. His breath is ragged, and his eyes are wide. He's falling apart, and I can't stop it.

"P-punish Kit? Kit b-broke rules? Kit in t-trouble?" Kit whines.

Kit falls onto his stomach with his head lowered and his ears flat against his head. His tails curl underneath his body. Tremors wrack him.

My throat is tight. *I hate this.* Some things can't be

reaped or defeated. At least, not on the outside. The greatest fight is inside all of us.

Loki stares at Kit's trembling back in shock. Then he turns to me, touching my shoulder like he's begging for forgiveness. Yet I don't blame him. It took me centuries to know how to help Kit and what triggers to avoid.

I incline my head at Kit, and Loki crawls towards him, although he's careful not to touch him.

"May I take you hand?" Loki asks, carefully.

Kit hesitates but then, he shakes his head. "Not allowed. Punished."

Loki's expression hardens. "Honestly, I get it. Do you know how long I spent in a world where I couldn't move without breaking a rule and being punished for it? Do you know what it feels like to have your mouth sewn shut? I do." My guts churn. *Don't hurl, don't hurl, don't...* Bubbling cauldrons, how could someone do that? Perhaps, this universe isn't so different to the alternate one with the dripping snake venom (and I'm definitely not asking Loki about whether *that* ever happened here as well). I press my nails into my palms to keep still. Kit needs to hear this, and by the twitching of his ears, he is. "But I got out and so have you. We're survivors. I'll never cage anyone like that, and I've come to see that neither will Autumn. Words can't touch you. You're safe here in our bed, hearts, and lives. Yet we'll catch you if you fall or break. Take the time you need." He held out his palm towards Kit. "Would you like to take my hand?"

I hold my breath.

Let this work.

Kit's hand edges into Loki's; their fingers entwine. Loki doesn't pull back from the scratch of his sharp claws. Then Kit's ears rise, and he sits up. His cheeks are dry, but his eyes shimmer with tears.

"Thank you," Kit whispers. "Okay, won't boot you out to be *munched* by the demons."

Loki smiles. "You're a gracious host."

"Kit knows."

I settle against the headboard, opening my arms. Kit launches himself into my embrace, and Loki lets out a startled *oomph*, as he's also dragged in Kit's hold along with him. I end up with them both sprawled, straddling my lap.

Their lips are so close to each other that I can't help teasing, "Now how about a *reward* of kissing?"

Sweet Hecate, that'd be hot.

What I don't expect is for Kit's sly, "*You're* the voyeur. Kit will make you happy. How about my reward bad god?"

Loki's tongue darts out to wet his lips; his gaze flicks to me.

Warmth curls through me, and I nod my encouragement.

Loki leans forward. "Valhalla! I'm all for positive reinforcement."

Loki's plush lips press against Kit's. I wrap my fingers around Loki's curls and Kit's silky hair; apple blossoms mingle with strawberries.

I expect Loki to fight for dominance in the kiss with the same fire that he has when he kisses me. Yet with Kit he's different: soft and gentle.

When Loki draws back, he shoots me a calculating look. "Acceptable?"

Yet it's Kit who answers in a daze, "Acceptable."

"How about my reward?" I ask with pretend innocence.

"Kiss Kit?" Kit says with such hope that my heart breaks.

I know why I've fought so many centuries against taking Kit fully as a lover. I still feel that he needs to go slowly, since he's bound to me by a spell. Yet is it unfair to deny him love and intimacy because of something that neither of us control? He's my magical kitsune in the same way that Oni is bound to me as my magical bodyguard in the Eternal Forest. Should I give Oni a second chance as well?

My heart thuds in my chest. I can barely breathe with excitement. Everything's changing so quickly. It feels like new life and hope.

I pull Kit to me by his hair and kiss him with all the savage passion that's been bottled inside for hundreds of years. He moans into the kiss, allowing me to lead.

His lips are soft, delicious, and mine. Why does this feel so right that it's Loki and me who kiss him like a claiming?

Yet something's missing — *someone.*

All of a sudden, I'm desperate for Ra. I've loved him for centuries. I'm Soul Bonded, and through the Bond, so is Loki. Lying on this bed and surrounded on both sides by Loki and Kit with their hard bodies pressed against me, I can't bear not to also have Ra.

When I pull back from Kit, his eyes are glazed, and his cheeks are flushed. His expression is soft with happiness in a way that I've never seen it.

I'll be kissing him a lot more to get that look.

Loki glances down at me like he can sense my unease. "Problem?"

When I trace my fingers over Ra's Leaf Tattoo, Loki instinctively understands. He slips off my lap, as if he's making room for Ra.

Kit shoots him a confused glance. I know that there's no witching way Kit's giving up his place.

Yet I don't want Loki to think that just because he's the newest Guardian and Soul Bond that means he always needs to step aside. That's not how it works. Instead, I reach for his hand and pull it towards *his* Leaf Tattoo, which is beneath Ra's.

He tilts his head in confusion but then, hisses in

shock as his fingers touch the skin. I shiver in delight at his touch; I can feel it all the way deep inside.

"It's cold," Loki mutters.

"Like you." I smile.

When Loki snatches back his hand, my stomach drops. "Are you teasing me?"

"I'm loving you. All of you. And this…" I press my own fingers to the tattoo, "…is part of that. TOF chose the bond, which means that it's Fated. She never joins partners who aren't. It's what my sister doesn't understand because she's too up her own witchy ass to take the time to learn the ways of the Eternal Forest. I didn't know until the very last moment if this Bond would even take but it did. Don't you trust TOF? Do you think that she could get this wrong?"

"If Lady TOF herself has chosen, along with the Norns, to bind us together even by the wickedest frost part of me," Loki says (and I'll do whatever it takes to make him understand how loved his Frost Giant side can be), "then I'm honored."

"TOF is no longer friends with Kit," Kit pouts.

When the room pulses a warning purple, I narrow my eyes at Kit.

"Do you want to spend the rest of the night tied to the wall in Reflect? Don't insult TOF. You know that you're her favorite. I'd rather snuggle, than persuade TOF to let you down," I urge.

Kit pales. "Kit's sorry. But our love is Fated too!

TOF just needs to make another leaf appear *poof.* Then we're all Bonded."

My lips curl into a smile. "I love you, Kit, but spirits can't Soul Bond. We don't need it."

Kit ducks his head, but his eyes flash with danger. "Kit still wants it."

"I know."

When Loki presses his lips to the tattoo (and I know a distraction when it branches tingling through me), I gasp at the intense sensation. He smiles against my skin, before licking around the outline. Then he mouths against Ra's tattoo, and I get the point.

We both want Ra.

"I need you, my Sun-bird," I holler, projecting the call through the bond.

Loki rears back. "That's what the Bond feels like…? The tugging of threads or…? Omens and runes, it's…"

Panicked, I stare at him. "You can feel the pull as well? Tell me it doesn't feel like the hex's chains?"

My shoulders slump in relief, when Loki shakes his head. "It's like pure Fate woven by the Norns. It's as strong as spider's silk and as beautiful. We're caught, but seriously, I'd never want to escape its web. I can feel Ra too: his spirit. His power is like…"

Loki shoves himself to his feet, wrapping his arms around his middle. He looks like he's thinking hard. I've come to understand that calculating expression.

Ra wears a similar one himself, when he's working out a particularly dangerous potion in his workshop.

Why's Loki so troubled?

"The sun?" I venture.

Loki's brow furrows, but his voice is edged equally with awe and fear, "More like he could *put out the sun.*"

Cold floods through me.

Before I can reply (although, what the witching hell do I say to that?), my skin prickles with ancient magic.

Ra is here.

The Sun-bird swoops into the room in a brilliant *whoosh* of flames. His golden feathers and tails flare with flame. His body is dark with ash. When I taste the Sun-bird's power fizzing on my tongue, I know that Loki is right. Ra's never lied or tried to hide how dangerous he is. He can create worlds but he can also destroy them *or put out the sun.*

Before my Sun-bird lands, he transforms back into a man. He's changed into his armor. I glance at Loki, and I have a feeling that the same as Kit with his guarding of my bedroom door, this is for his benefit or possibly mine.

As if I could forget that I love Ra.

Ra is regal in his falcon helmet, which is crowned with a sun disk; the golden coils of a cobra hang down. Magic skitters across his skin. Loki studies Ra's feathered gold armor, as Ra prowls towards me.

A blush spreads up Loki's neck. "Impressive."

"You haven't seen anything yet." Ra walks Loki backwards, nudging him onto the bed, before crawling between my legs and running his hands up and down my thighs. "Looks like you're having a party, and everyone's invited." He casts a censorious glance at the scattered paperwork. "Phoenixes and pharaohs, it appears the night's already turned wild. Do you want me to tidy up?"

Now those are the words that I'll never grow tired of hearing. Ra offering to tidy up my messy room or paperwork at the end of a long day.

Loki's grin is sharp. "Hey, the warrior maid's turned up."

Ra cocks his head. "You made the mess, you're clearing it up with me, godly maid."

Kit giggles.

Loki leans towards Ra, until their foreheads are touching. "May I kiss you?"

Ra's breath hitches, and he blushes. "*Hmm, Autumn?*"

My grin is as sharp as Loki's. "All Guardians are free to kiss each other and, you know, other sexy things. Although, not Petal because there'd be a risk of swallowing him."

Petal would probably think that the risk was worth it.

Ra's Kohl smudged eyes become half-lidded; his lips part in invitation. I bite my own cheek to keep quiet, as Loki presses a chaste kiss to Ra's lips, before drawing back.

Am I imagining the flash of disappointment across Ra's face?

"So, what was that for?" Ra asks.

Loki waves his hand. "I already kissed the kitsune and Autumn, and you must always seal a deal with a kiss."

Ra's concerned gaze darts to mine. I shrug my shoulders.

"What deal?" Ra demands.

Loki pretends to be interested in non-existent fluff on the sheets. "Just because you don't know the details yet, doesn't mean that a deal hasn't been struck."

I nod at Ra, whose eyes flash like swirling suns. He twists over Loki, pushing him down. His wings burst out in a dominant display.

Kit snarls, turning as if to defend Loki, but I place a calming hand on his neck. Ra won't hurt Loki. I know him well enough to be sure of that.

"On the Eye of Horus, what do you mean?" Magical flames flare along Ra's wings; the fire is reflected in his glass phoenix collar.

"Careful, Sun-bird," Loki hisses, "would you trust in a wolf's tameness?"

"But you're not a wolf. You're a stallion. And they can be broken."

Loki stares up at Ra like he's only just seeing him. "Oh, you're good little bird with broken wings in your gilded cage. You play submission, but that's the mask." When he bares his teeth, he does look more like a wolf. "Hello, Atum-Ra, it's a pleasure to finally meet you. And if you imagine what you said is true, then you know nothing about ancient wild stallions or godly ones."

Ra's wings beat in agitation. He's not winning this battle. Why do Loki's words make something twist deep inside me?

I won't have my Soul Bonds ripping each other apart.

"Don't." I push my need for them both through the Bond. Ra pulls back from Loki, curling his wings around himself. Loki slowly sits up. "You're both wild and dangerous. Sweet Hecate, it's no secret. Yet you're also both Guardians, my Soul Bonds, and are you going to make me spell out the chemistry between you because that's an awkward moment we can do without." They both look away in silence. *It's still awkward.* "The true monsters are out there in the forest." Then my eyes widen. "Where's Bard?"

Ra's expression softens with concern. "Ecstasy

insisted that I wait until dawn to tell you. Strategically it makes sense because the Shadow Demons have less strength in the light and by my wings, we've already seen how strong they've become. Ecstasy's ordered that you try your connection with Loki's shifter spirit and hunt with him, rather than me."

What...? Well, that explains Ra's protective and possessive act.

"But Loki's never fought by my side in spirit form. As an Infernal, I've never hunted with him." I clench my hands into fists.

This can't be happening. A hunt on the First Night after Soul Bonding and after a Soul as powerful as the Shadow Traitor...?

I have no idea if I can control Loki or if we'll work well as a team. What will his spirit be like? I felt an overwhelming connection to his stallion on the night of the Bacchanalia. Yet what if he's wild like he says, and it destroys the hunt?

What it means Oni loses his horns?

Loki is still carefully not looking at me.

Ra's shoulders are stiff. "What a shame other Bacchants don't respect my opinion like you. After all, this She-Soul and her Shadow Demons are training level reaping. Wait, I mean *deadly Advanced* level reaping. Almost the same."

"Bard," I repeat. "You still haven't said where he is."

Ra's lips pinch. "He's already left to meet up with Oni and act as…"

"Bait," I gasp.

I pull away from Kit's hold and launch myself off the bed.

The safety, warmth, and love of this night in my bedroom was the lie. The danger out in the cold, shadows of the forest is the truth.

It's time to face the danger and become the Infernal with my scythe and Loki's stallion spirit to hunt the She-Soul. I'll have one chance to reap the Shadow Traitor or to protect my forest and Guardians from the Shadow Demons, I'll lose my immortal life and die.

CHAPTER EIGHTEEN

Eternal Forest

I once believed that gods either possess you or break you.

Yet even if the Norns weave our Fates, I can still sew my own third way: *gods can love you.*

And I can love them too.

I tip back my head and howl into the forest's dawn.

I am the wild.

This is my home amongst the savage creatures of the Eternal Forest. Dew glistens on the trunks like tears. I wrinkle my nose at the scent of damp moss. Yet it's too silent, as if the animals and birds are in hiding.

In the pale light of dawn, which filters like mist

through the thick canopy of the branches, the veils between all the worlds are at their thinnest. I can feel the magic of the Other World, the underworlds, and godly realms like a second skin, tingling over mine. It calls to me: a deadly temptation.

How many unwary travelers and humans have been called to their doom at these moments when the worlds come together?

My grip tightens around the ancient ash shaft of my Infernal Scythe. It's familiar in my hold like an extension of my arm, coiling magic through me, along with the need to catch the She-Soul, who escaped being devoured.

Live and seek savage death…

At the back of my mind, I can still feel the thread of fear for Oni and Bard, but the thrill of the hunt has taken me over.

I'm a hunter — *a predator*.

I shiver with delight because now I have the god who my cult hunted for a thousand years as my partner, and I know with startling certainty that he's a predator too.

Has *he* always been the hunter?

At a low *nicker* behind me, followed by a soft nudge through the Soul Bond, I glance behind me.

Sweet Hecate, Loki's spirit shifter is beautiful and powerful.

The black stallion raises his head, and his ears

twitch forward. He's even more stunning at my side than I ever hoped. Yet he's also deadlier. He's caught between the veils of life and death, as much as the Eternal Forest is at the dawn and twilight. I can see the cracks, and they flare with chaos. Emerald magic flames from his tail and hooves, and he can grow smaller in size, weaving between the trees and then returning to his normal size. He shakes his mane with such joy that I twirl in a circle, shaking my hair to mimic him. Loki's happiness in the freedom of the forest, after being trapped inside, blooms through the Bond. I can tell that he's electrified by the hunt as much as I am, and he's just as wild as me.

How is it possible to feel like we've been hunting side by side for centuries, rather than this being our first time?

The Infernal Scythe pulls out a spirit form of the shifter, which is bound through the Soul Bond. Ecstasy thinks that it turns them into a weapon, but it doesn't. They become an extension of your own spirit and the forest, which means that I guard them with the same fierceness. Loki is trapped in shifter form as well, until I release him. I won't forget that responsibility. Funny how Loki understood about responsibility before I did.

Loki's breath is cool against my shoulder.

Is he trying to tell me something? He can touch in spirit form but not talk. Merlin's cock, I thought that was a blessing, but he's not Ra who I can read like a feathery book in phoenix form. It may take me longer than a single day to work out horse body language.

Loki nuzzles my neck, before dancing to the side and twisting to disappear into the shadows of a glade towards the east.

I grin. Perhaps, all I need to know is Loki Body Language.

Is he playing? I never knew that hunting could be a game. Especially in the deathly chill of a morning, when our lives rest on catching the Shadow Traitor.

I can't help the way that my treacherous brain loves the element of fun. The god of mischief is a bad influence. Shocker.

I dart through the trees, listening out for the sound of Loki's hooves. So far, we haven't come across any Shadow Demons but I don't want to be too far from him for when we do. *Because I'm certain that we will.*

Yet it'll only take a thought to call Loki back, and he'll only need to call me through his emotions. He's much faster than me and can scout for the other Guardians.

All of a sudden, there's a *crack* of a twig snapping.

I freeze. My fingers tighten around the Infernal Scythe. My mouth becomes dry.

That wasn't from the direction Loki went. It's behind me.

Is it the Shadow Traitor?

Bring it on.

Slowly, I turn. Then I call for Loki through the Bond.

Loki, Loki, Loki.

I hear Loki's answering *whicker*, as he gallops back. Yet as I scan the thick undergrowth between the trees, there's no She-Soul or Shadow Demon.

I narrow my eyes. Something's behind the tree…*someone.*

I take a step forward, uncomfortable. Why does it feel like I'm being hunted?

I catch a glimpse of a man's face with burning, wine-red eyes. My breath catches in my throat. It's a god — *a Shifter God.* I can feel his dark magic from here; it winds like shadows.

The veils are thin. The gods often pass through my forest, and this is the time that the realms slip. Yet why is he watching me? I can't help how I'm drawn towards him, even as I'm shaking. His eyes are mesmerizing.

Then he moves, and the dawn light spears across his face. Instantly, I stumble back, clutching harder onto my scythe.

The light reveals a god, who's a mountain of muscles with midnight black hair, and velvet, ebony skin. He's brooding and spellbinding.

No, no, no…

I thought that Loki was a bad, rebel god but now my forest has the wickedest god of them all hunting it. *Hunting me.*

Hades: King of the Underworld.

The stories about the god of the dead are even more legendary than those about Loki. They're whispered at night: the savage king below in the Greek underworld. He's the nightmare that the other gods use to scare their kids into behaving with; if you're not good, Hades will come and whisk you away forever. Yet as long as I've lived, the terrifying god has only left his throne once.

Bacchus had just moved me into the Tree of Life and wanted to meet with Persephone (Ecstasy got on with her so well it was like she was a Bacchant). To my shock, she also brought Hades with her, although by the way he hung around in the garden in brooding silence, I wondered if he was guarding her. It was the last time that he left the underworld.

I let out a breath, as Loki thunders into the clearing. Emerald magic flares from his nostrils, and his whole body is tense. He charges in front of me, shielding me with his flanks. I can feel his protective magic washing over me. His tail swishes in agitation. But then, he turns to me, and I glance back at the trees.

Hades is gone.

Why do I get the feeling that this is winning a battle and not the war?

If Loki isn't keen on Norse Gods, then I already know that the Greek Gods are more brutal than any of the others (and the Egyptian Gods are terrifyingly self-obsessed with cycles of death and destruction).

Catching the interest of Hades, who is known to be the bad god of the Greeks, can't be good. Is he working with the Shadow Demons?

I meet Loki's eye. "Let's get this done, before he decides to come back. You're enough bad god for me."

Loki snorts his agreement. Then he swings his neck towards the direction, from which he thundered to help me.

My eyes widen. "You found them?" *Witches above, on his first hunt…?* My lips tug into a smile. "You beat Ra. Don't tell him unless you want one sad phoenix, and I tell you, no one can resist a phoenix's puppy dog eyes." *Is a horse able to look smug because I'm pretty certain that Loki manages it?* "Sweet Hecate, thank you. Sorry, why do I keep forgetting your name? You licked it onto my skin." I can feel the skin of my neck tingling. "Lopter, thank you."

He lowers his head, and his ears hang relaxed to the side, as he trots away, expecting me to follow. My smile widens. Even in horse form, Loki's dominant and arrogant. Since he's discovered where the She-Soul is, however, he's earned the right. And if I'm honest, it's one of the things that I love about him. I can admit it now.

Ra knows me better than anyone, apart from possibly Oni (and definitely better than my sister who thinks that I'm the same cloistered kid that she knew over a thousand years ago). His **CASE OF LOKI'S ASS** was embarrassing, but it wasn't wrong.

If Loki's obsessive love has shadowed me for all the time that we've been apart, then I've never forgotten him either. How can I untangle it from the pain that he's caused me? Perhaps, I never can. But he's the dark Chaos Mage to my light Chaos Witch.

We need each other; Fate knows it. The love coursing through me knows it too.

My thighs burn, as I sprint after Loki through the forest. I leap over fallen logs and duck low branches. This is my world. Yet as he leads me further, I shudder at the signs of the gradual death of the forest around me. It hurts deep inside to see the place that I love and guard destroyed like this. The trees become withered and blackened. Above my head, the branches grow increasingly twisted. I understand now how Loki found the She-Soul: he followed the path of destruction caused by Shadow Demons.

I catch a glimpse of Loki's flaring magic, as he

bursts into a glade up ahead, and dart after him. I stop on the edge in shock.

The glade looks like it's been blasted by fire. Everything is dead. It's still and silent. If any animals were caught in this, then they'd be as charred as the trees.

Please, Hecate, let them have escaped.

Except, a silver cage that's bound in ropes hangs from the branches of a yew tree that look so scorched that they could break at any moment. My breach catches, and my heart thuds.

What if it breaks? What if the Shadow Demons return, before I can free the cage's occupants? Because I knew that Oni and Bard were intending to be bait but not that they were going to dangle themselves on a hook.

"Aren't you taking the method acting a bit far?" I storm towards the cage. "How did you even put yourself in there?"

Oni raises his head in shock, and his curved horns *clang* against the bars. He attempts to hide the wince. His skin gleams like crushed sapphires, the same as his sweep of hair. He's naked, which isn't a surprise.

I can't resist reaching through and stroking his horn in reassurance because even if he has caged himself, I know how much he hates being trapped. He's too tall for the cage, of course, and his muscles are bunched uncomfortably, but he's still using his body to shield Bard, who's squashed in the steel hold of his arms.

Wait, if they put themselves into the cage, why's Bard's cheek bruised?

My eyes widen, and I twirl, scanning the glade.

Nothing.

"I have many skills like flirting, kissing, and wild, savage, fucking." Oni waggles his eyebrows. "But they don't include locking myself up, love. It's not a hidden kink of mine."

"So, are you going to claim that it was thirteen gods who overpowered you this time? Obviously, you could've easily crushed them with your hammer, if they only hadn't attacked you from behind."

Oni's chest puffs up. "Would you believe me?"

"Of course."

"Really?"

I snort. "No."

"Away with you, there's an injured satyr squished under here." Bard peers through the bars at me.

When he pushes his ear through the bars, I stroke along it in apology. Then I widen my eyes in shock. The fur's been ripped out in a clump like someone's twisted his ear or dragged him along by it.

The mouths on my scythe gape, desperate to devour in revenge. Whoever hurt Bard will feel the wrath of my Infernal rage.

I raise his ear to my lips, gently kissing it better.

Bard sighs, before drawing back. "Who knew war wounds meant kisses? I'll weave a grand tale out of this one day, about the brave satyr who sacrificed his ear for his love."

"I think the humans already did that one," I reply. "It's about a painter called Van Gogh."

Bard waves his hand, dismissively. "All the best stories steal from others anyway."

Oni curls a claw around a bar in the cage; the sudden seriousness of his expression fills me with dread. "Anwealda's in the forest."

I freeze. The Emperor rarely comes out of the underworld. This is bad.

"You said you broke a minor rule. *Minor*," I hiss.

Oni's eyes sparkle. "My demon pride doesn't know if it's hurt that you assume it's me or pleased that you think I could get the Emperor himself to come into the forest. By my claws, he's here for *you*. So, you little rebel, what have you done to piss off Anwealda? I tried to protect you, but I'll be honest, since we ended up in a cage, it didn't go how I'd hoped. Has Kit been writing rude limericks about demons again because sending them to the Emperor may not have been the best idea?"

Despite myself, I laugh.

"Sweet Hecate, I wish this was about limericks." I glance at Loki.

Why would the Emperor be here for Loki? Yet I

haven't done anything else to anger him. I still have time to catch the She-Soul. I've already stopped one of the murderers of his sons. So, why is the Demon Emperor ambushing me, in the same way that I'm ambushing the Shadow Traitor?

If the underworld has become involved, this has become even deadlier. The only thing that's changed in the balance of this forest is Loki.

Was I too quick to forget that Loki always takes the first move in chess?

Oni clears his throat. "On my horns, am I going to be the one to raise the elephant...I mean, the horse... in the room? Why do you have your own My Little Radioactive Pony at your shoulder?" At Loki's death glare and stamping hooves, Oni stares back, unimpressed. "Make him stop that. It's freaky."

Loki has met his match.

I glance at Loki, who's turned his back now on Oni in an attempt at quiet dignity, and is instead, patrolling the glade, which remains as quiet as before. "He's the *stallion* who found you. He's a shifter spirit and—"

"He's Soul Bonded?" Oni growls.

I bite my lip. "You know, it was a crisis and..."

"*Whoops*," Bard mutters. "Here's the thing of it, there wasn't time to explain, what with the whole trying not to die."

"You can Soul Bond with as many men as you

like; I don't own you." Yet the anguish that shakes through Oni, shakes through me as well. "It makes me happy that your needs are met. I just want you to know that my love is real too. I'm yours with every beat that my heart will ever take. And just as much as some freaky pony."

"He has a name."

"I prefer freaky pony."

"He's Loki," I venture, before holding my breath. *Three, two, one…*

"Loki?" Oni snarls, rattling the bars of the cage. This is the first time that I've ever been glad that he's locked in. Loki raises his head in defiance, pawing at the ground. *Not helping.* "The god who broke you and led to you losing your magic? Who I spent centuries helping you recover from in this very forest? Shouldn't he be a prisoner or here's an idea, *reaped?* All of us Guardians know that you have a thing for him, love, but if you want to ride me around like a horse to get it out of your system, then go ahead. Isn't that better than…?"

I stop his words with a kiss.

Cinnamon scented dark magic sizzles from his soft lips to mine. I shiver, and my Soul aches.

A demon's kiss is always a deal of some sort, and I know Oni understands. This time he's not stealing anything from me, I'm granting it.

Surely, we can have a second chance?

Our love is complicated, but I no longer care. Ex-lover…lover…when the Shadow Traitor is caught, and I have a *long* conversation with the Emperor about how he's treating my Guardian, I'll then have one with Oni. He'll always have his own life outside in the forest, and I'll always have mine inside TOF. But I can't deny his love. After all, I can't deny Loki's.

Is it fair to deny a demon's, if I accept a god's?

When I pull back, Oni's eyes are glazed, and his breathing is ragged.

"You'll break me if you don't mean this," Oni says.

He won't meet my eye.

"I mean that we'll talk about it, and we'll try again," I reply.

If I can't break Loki, then I'll never break Oni.

Oni glances at Loki. "And him?"

"He's a Guardian. And he's part of the deal."

Oni nods. "Then sign me up."

All of a sudden, the light in the glade darkens. Day becomes night. When Bard whines, Oni shifts to hook his arm around him more securely. I glare at the Shadow Demons that have swarmed the glade, covering it like writhing tar and casting it into darkness: we're surrounded.

I spin to the cage, smashing the Infernal Scythe against the lock to free Oni and Bard.

The lock doesn't break. It must've been strengthened by the Emperor himself.

Oni cusses, and I stare at the lock in shock. My lovers are helpless, swinging in the cage. Yet Shadow Demons have never swarmed in such numbers like this (not until the Shadow Traitor). How are they learning so many tricks?

I try to raise my scythe again, but it's too late. A ghastly screech fills the glade. The She-Soul is here. Just like last time, she's hunted me, even though I believed that I was hunting her. She's smart and sly. A scheming Soul who once attempted to destroy her own world.

Yet she isn't surrounded by those who she loves in a forest that she swore to protect, and I am.

I am the Infernal, and I'm stopping her now.

My fingers tighten until my knuckles are white around the shaft of the scythe, which calls to me.

Devour...devour...devour...

This time, I equally thirst to reap the Soul.

The Shadow Traitor rushes into the glade in a hideous tangle of arms and legs, which bulge in and out of the orb. Horns stick from the top. I clench my jaw not to drop my gaze from the malicious black eyes.

The orb has grown. It's swollen like *it's* devoured all the living creatures that it's killed, pulling in their life force, and now it wants to devour me.

The Infernal Scythe howls, heating in my palms in fury at the outrage.

The orb suddenly brightens. The fire demon is about to blast flames at me again, but before it can, Loki lowers his head and charges.

"Stop," I holler. "Don't touch the flames."

Loki's hide begins to smolder. His magic rises from him like mist. Fire from an orb is death to any living creature, and I don't know what it'll do to a shifter spirit like Loki who straddles both life and death.

Don't let me lose him, not like this.

I drag on Loki through the Bond and the ties of the Infernal. Yet there's no fear in his emotions, only pride and a dark delight.

Confused, I throw myself after Loki. To my shock, however, the fire blast never comes. Instead, it's the She-Soul who lets out a ghostly wail and rears back. Then she rises up towards the canopy of shadow wreathed branches, almost like Loki is the cavalry that she's been waiting for.

My eyes widen, before my fingers slacken on the scythe's shaft.

When Loki shakes his mane, pacing around the glade, hot and cold wash over me. Sweet Hecate, he couldn't have led me into this ambush, right? Been tricking me? Was this his plan all along?

I can't believe it. I won't.

Distracted, it's only Oni's warning holler, which makes me look up.

The She-Soul drops down on me from above. Her warped face pushes out of the orb. Her sharp teeth snap at me. A single, thin arm reaches out, grasping to snatch hold of my neck and wrench me to my death.

I duck, rolling to the side. All at once, I'm calm and focused.

I tighten my hold on the Infernal Scythe; its magic burns through me. I'm connected to every Infernal who held it before me, and what I am now, is death.

I stand up, straightening my shoulders, before swinging the scythe over my head with a *swoosh*. When the orb darts towards the cage, I can't move quickly enough to intercept. Yet Loki does, snorting out flames and blocking the orb, which sends the She-Soul tumbling back towards me.

This is it.

I leap into the air. My heart is thumping at the thrill of the battle and reaping because that's how this will end. It must. I bring the scythe down in an aerial attack, and it slashes right through the fat head of the orb all the way to its swollen belly.

Light spills out, even as the Shadow Demon shrieks. I can't return the Emperor's murdered son, but reaping the demons who killed him feels like justice.

The gaping mouths of the Infernal Scythe open

and devour the orb. I shake with the stinging dark magic. This time, however, I welcome the sense that the realms are shaking around me in triumph or terrible, tearing *change*.

I howl in victory at the same time as Oni, whose hand is grasped in Bard's. I've saved Oni's horns from being ripped from his head, and the forest from the tyranny of the Shadow Demons, at least for one more day.

Witching heavens, I'll take the win.

The Emperor is here, and there's brooding gods of death hunting me. The Shadow Demons are still a threat. Yet I've protected the Eternal Forest from the Shadow Traitors, which was my Infernal Mission.

Plus, Loki helped, didn't he?

When I glance at Loki, I throw as much of my savage joy as I can through the Bond, and his own joy is reflected back. He roars, and my spine tingles. He glistens with dangerous magic, as he trots towards me. Then his nostrils flare, and his ears become pinned back, as he stares into the forest behind me.

I spin around.

Hades prowls into the clearing. He's even taller than I realized; his shoulders are broader. He's devastatingly handsome, but there's something wrong with his wine-red eyes. They're dazed like he's not truly seeing me, and he's panting. He looks confused but more dangerous because of it like he's working out who he should attack first.

Hecate save me from feral gods.

My scythe warms in my hands, and I raise it. "Why are you here?"

"By the Graces, madam," his voice is a low rumble with a deep Scottish lilt (which does something to my insides, which should be illegal), "I wish I knew."

It's the truth. He's lost, drowning. *What's happened to him?*

He shakes his head, slamming his hands against his temples, as if in agonizing pain or maybe to clear his fogged confusion. Then in a spray of obsidian sparkles that curl like shadows, Hades transforms into a savage hellhound with glistening black fur and crimson eyes.

Loki rears up, pawing his hooves through the air like a war horse. He's going to attack; I can sense it through the Bond. He wasn't scared of the She-Soul or the Shadow Demons, but I can feel his fear of Hades.

Hecate above, how monstrous is Hades to make Loki of all the gods fear him?

Despite that, Loki's still at my side, facing the threat like a true Guardian. I won't let my own nerves show, especially as Oni's wildly shaking the cage in desperation to face this threat with me. He's been my bodyguard for so long that it hurts him worse to be forced to watch without protecting me.

I can reap gods, but it's not the same as reaping a god or demon who've already died. Can I cross that final line? I don't know, even for one who sings with death like Hades…such impossibly *beautiful* death.

Is this the day in my long life that I finally die?

Hades in hellhound form is huge. He could crush me with a single paw or slash me open with his silver claws. He's growling in the same feral way, as when he was in his godly form.

Hades' eyes narrow. It's the only warning that I get, before he lunges for my neck.

The End…For Now

Continue Autumn and her Guardians' adventures in the Eternal Forest in BAD HADES NOW
https://rosemaryajohns.com

Thanks for reading Bad Loki! If you enjoyed reading this book, **please consider leaving a review on Amazon.** Your support is really important to us authors. Plus, I love hearing from my readers!
Thanks, you're awesome!
Rosemary A Johns
X
Sign up to Rosemary A Johns' Rebel Newsletter for

FREE novellas. Also, these special perks: promotions, discounts, and news of hot releases before anyone else.

Become a Rebel here today by joining Rosemary's Rebels Group on Facebook!

WHAT TO READ NEXT: BAD HADES!

When the gods turn bad…

…shifters come out to play.

I'm Autumn, an Infernal reaper, and I'm bound to my rebel gods by their shifter spirits. Hades is a scorching hot hell hound: *Cerberus*. Yet each of my gods — Loki, Ra, and Hades — hide dangerous secrets about their pasts. My demon lover, Oni, may be hiding the biggest secret of them all that could tear me apart.

When a deadly threat that should've stayed buried in the underworld comes back to haunt Hades, can we survive the coming shadows?

When the gods are rebels, the demons are wicked, and the shifters are savage, it's lucky that I love bad boys...

READ BAD HADES NOW!

WHAT TO READ NEXT: COMPLETE SERIES
REBEL ACADEMY
Meet Loki's sons!

How had I ever doubted that a monster could love? Yet why had I craved to feel this *agony*, which was like my heart was being crushed in my chest?

I hunched on the bed in our room in the West Wing with my knees tucked close beneath me. Feverish, I shivered with chills, despite the pink fires that blazed in the braziers. An aroma like bonfires sparking with rich magic wrapped around me.

I'd stripped down to my pants, and my chest was slicked with sweat. My hair hung into my face; it transformed in a rainbow display from aquamarine, to pink, and then red, as my brothers fought to the surface, and I wasn't able to balance the cycle of my emotions. Shimmering sea serpent tattoos coiled around the werewolf tattoos on my arms in a desperate embrace.

It was only in times of extreme distress that my brothers could see and hug each other, which was seriously messed up. *I wouldn't lose control of my monster.*

I bit my lip, until I tasted copper blood. Then I bit harder again.

By the Norns, Magenta had been gone too long. What if she'd been stolen away?

Magenta, hear the son of Loki, I trust you. The veils parted and Fate joined us.

I'd always wished for a friend who'd believe in me. Couldn't I be that friend for Magenta?

I reached for my guitar, which rested next to the bed, hugging its body like I could clasp Magenta. I ran my thumb down its neck, before strumming across the strings, breathing out. My heartbeat slowed. My music had soothed me for centuries.

Hunted by witches? A guitar ballad. Terrified in a wood? A classical solo. Trapped in caves? Acoustic rock.

Perhaps, in a past life I'd been a bard…?

I grimaced. Omens and runes, I hoped not. *Bards were dicks.*

As if in agreement, Mist raised his head and snorted. His mane was red, his fur was aquamarine, but his tail was candyfloss pink, which reflected my own instability. He trembled, curled on the headboard. When he turned his head away from me it was like a kick in the balls.

I strummed Billy Eilish's epic "No Time to Die", which wept from my guitar with the lightest of touches; its grief and longing fed my own.

I closed my eyes, softly singing the verse with an added rock twist. I let the song take me over, losing myself in the lyrics.

In the music, there was no struggle between my brothers. When I sang, I was simply…*me*.

I clutched my guitar more tightly.

Let the real world just fall away…build the song like cresting waves…drown in this utter peace, until the music stops.

Why does the music always have to stop?

I howled, tossing the guitar to the end of the bed, then I hurled myself across the room, sweeping our schoolbooks off the desks and kicking over the neat piles. The blaziers exploded in furious bursts.

Why should I control the monster? There were enough other monsters roaming this academy…

READ AND DISCOVER WHAT HAPPENS TO LOKI'S SONS AND THE WITCHES IN REBEL ACADEMY!

WHAT TO READ NEXT: COMPLETE SERIES
REBEL WEREWOLVES

The werewolf's lips brushed across mine, and I jolted. "May I caress you…here?"

I nodded, shuddering. He drew circles over my skin, and I heated like he was touching me inside, coiling the pleasure higher.

Lower…please, touch me lower…

When I squirmed to encourage his fingers below the fabric of my ball gown, he chuckled but only continued his maddeningly slow teasing.

"Kiss her neck, prince," the god ordered; his voice was like winding silk.

My crimson magic burst out, while I experienced each of the men's pulsing, panting pleasure.

"Hold the witch's hands above her head," the god commanded. "She won't be able to stay still for what comes next…"

Escape into the world of bad, bad wolves and wicked witches in REBEL WEREWOLVES. Discover the war between witches and wolves and why Loki is fighting for Omega werewolves like Prince...

APPENDIX ONE: GUARDIANS

Autumn, Immortal witch of the House of Ecstasy, Bacchant and Infernal, ex-Chaos Witch
  Oni, demon
  Ra, Egyptian Sun God, Sun-bird
  Kit, kitsune fox-spirit
  Bard, Bacchus' satyr
  Petal, pixie
  Loki/Lopter, half Aesir god of mischief and half jotunn, Chaos Mage

Gods

Mut, Egyptian goddess, Lady of the Heavens, Ra's ex-wife

Ra, Egyptian Sun God and Sun-bird

Bacchus, Roman god of ecstasy, worshiped by Bacchant cult

Hades, Greek god, Shifter God, King of the Underworld

Persephone, Queen of the Underworld, Hades' wife

Loki/Lopter, half Aesir god of mischief and half jotunn, Shifter God, Chaos Mage

Sleipnir/Jormungand/Fenrir, Shifter Gods, Loki's sons

Lady Laufrey, Aesir god, Loki's mother

Odin, the All-father, Aesir god, King of Asgard

Prince Baldr, favorite of the Aesir gods, Odin's son

Prince Thor, Aesir god of thunder, Odin's son

Prince Hod, blind Aesir god, Odin's son

Heimdall, the Watchman of the Aesir gods

Demons

Oni, demon, Guardian

Prince Sol, fire demon

Demon Emperor, Anwealda, ruler of the demon underworld

Shadow Demons

Chief Shadow Demon

Shadow Traitors, fire demons

APPRENDIX THREE: WITCHES & SUPERNATURALS

Witches

Bacchants, cult of frenzy and pleasure, worshipers of Bacchus

Autumn, House of Ecstasy, Infernal and born Chaos Witch

Ecstasy, House of Ecstasy, leader of Bacchants, Autumn's sister

Hestia, witch who first bound Kit

Supernaturals

Farbauti, jotunn, Loki's father

Frost Giants/jotunns from the realm of Jotunheim

Tree of Life/TOF/Yggdrasil/the World Tree

Caesar, mechanical bear, created by Autumn

Infernal Scythe, magical scythe used by Infernal, Autumn

ABOUT THE AUTHOR

ROSEMARY A JOHNS is a USA Today bestselling and award-winning romance and fantasy author, music fanatic, and paranormal anti-hero addict. She writes sexy shifters and immortals, swoonworthy book boyfriends, and epic battles.

Winner of the Silver Award in the National Wishing Shelf Book Awards. Finalist in the IAN Book of the Year Awards. Runner-up in the Best Fantasy Book of the Year, Reality Bites Book Awards. Honorable Mention in the Readers' Favorite Book Awards.

Shortlisted in the International Rubery Book Awards.

Rosemary is also a traditionally published short story writer. She studied history at Oxford University and ran her own theater company. She's always been a rebel…

Thanks for leaving a review. You're awesome!

Want to read more and stay up to date on Rosemary's newest releases? **Sign up for her *VIP* Rebel Newsletter and get FREE novellas!**

Have you read all the series in the Rebel Verse by Rosemary A Johns?
Rebel Academy
Rebel Werewolves
Rebel: House of Fae
Rebel Angels
Rebel Gods
Rebel Vampires
Rebel Legends

Read More from Rosemary A Johns
Website
Bookbub
Facebook
Instagram
Twitter: @RosemaryAJohns
Become a Rebel here today by joining Rosemary's Rebels Group on Facebook!

CPSIA information can be obtained
at www.ICGtesting.com
Printed in the USA
BVHW031125110721
611670BV00007B/449